THE
EMMALEE
AFFAIRS

A novel by
MICHAEL LINDLEY
Sage River Press

Novels by
MICHAEL LINDLEY

THE *EMMALEE* AFFAIRS

Amazon Five Star reviews for
THE EMMALEE AFFAIRS

"Engaging, captivating, beautiful writing."

"Wonderful! Loved every minute of every page!"

"From the first word to the last, I was hooked!"

"A sweet reminder of loves lost and new beginnings."

"You won't be able to put it down!"

"Beautifully merges storylines of then and now."

"I wish I could give this book ten stars!"

* * * * *

A Sage River Press Novel

Chapter One

Our small town rests on a strip of land between the lakes now known as Michigan and Charlevoix. The lakes are connected by a narrow channel, running only about a mile, which has carved a natural access through this land for thousands of years. This cut in the land became known as the Pine River when the white men began arriving in the 1700's. Tall pines high on the sand bluffs at the mouth of the channel on Lake Michigan were a beacon to traders and missionaries and the many Indians who first made this land their home.

In the middle of the channel, halfway between the lakes, the Pine River swelled into a small inland harbor and it became known as Round Lake. The water here was protected and deep enough to allow safe harbor for traveling vessels. It also became the center of commerce around which the first settlement of Charlevoix began.

The town grew slowly at first, fueled by the determination of the early founders to battle the harsh and cold terrain. Fishing and logging brought more opportunity to the area. Small companies grew from these industries and jobs attracted more men and families to move to the North Country.

In the late 1800's, the true promise of the area was discovered by a few wealthy families and religious leaders from the cities to the south. The summers in Northern Michigan were wonderfully mild and appealing compared to the heat *and hustle of activity in cities like Detroit and Chicago. The beauty of the land and the water was breathtaking. Summer homes were built along the waterfronts and families moved north to spend time relaxing on the water and to socialize with others from their class. Resident associations were formed to bring a sense of elite membership and status.*

Resort towns like Charlevoix, Petoskey and Harbor Springs flourished with the wealth that poured in each summer. Railroads were built and cruise lines formed to make travel more convenient from the south. Businesses were established to serve the summer residents and jobs were created to make their lives easier. Great hotels were built to house their guests and other visitors.

And now, the EmmaLee is coming home. She brings with her an incredible history. As she cruised into the channel today, it was like stepping back in time for many of us. Her early days in Charlevoix saw our little town at perhaps its finest hour and, at times, its worst. The memories of those days linger for those of us old enough to remember, or those who have heard the stories. Many of our families and friends were here during those years before and after the Second World War and lived through the turbulent and often unfortunate circumstances of those times. The EmmaLee shared an important place in that saga, as did the many people who loved her.

I often think back to the summers of my youth in this little town of Charlevoix. My name is George Hansen. It was the summer of 1941, when my friend Jonathan McKendry first met Emily Compton.

He walked along the old gray docks at the edge of the water. The leather of his worn boot soles echoed among the sounds of the waterfront coming to life. The first waking light of early morning tried to force its way through the heavy fog that had settled in the night before. A damp mist closed in around him and he could feel the dewy moisture hang on his face. The boats loomed above him in soft focus and the smell of fish and diesel fumes lay heavy on each breath.

He made his way with purpose. Men in their boats took notice of him and a few greeted him as he passed. They knew the boy and his father well. It was a family that drew respect from working men.

He was a boy of just 17 years of age. His name was Jonathan McKendry. He was tall for his age and strongly built from work on his father's boats. He kept his long brown hair tucked under a gray and faded canvas cap. His clothes were simple and made for work and his face showed more age than time would suggest. His past years in the sun and extreme weather had begun to take their toll on his skin like sanded varnish on a weathered hull.

He continued along the docks, a small paper sack in his arms. A soft breath of wind chilled his face and he looked up to see the foggy clouds moving in different directions, breaking apart. Overhead, gulls squawked at each other as they hovered and searched for their next meal. Deck hands conversed in loud, rough voices, shouting orders and exchanging stories. Occasionally, a foghorn would blow as boats made their way in through the channel from Lake Michigan. Riggings from the boats clanged and slapped, setting a steady rhythm for the work to be done.

The town was awakening to another day of labor. Fisherman prepared their nets and boats and shopkeepers up on the hill along Bridge Street swept in front of their stores and prepared for the day's trade. Traffic along the narrow street was sparse. Only a few cars were making their way through town. Several trucks were parked along the main road delivering supplies and a few people made their way on bicycles. Along the waterfront the boatyards were coming to life to prepare the boats for the summer people.

Jonathan was on his way back to his father's boatyard on the south side of Round Lake. He had made his morning trip to the grocery store up on Bridge Street to get fresh bread and fruit for his family's breakfast. McKendry's Boatworks had been founded by his grandfather many years before. He lived there in a small apartment behind the main storage building with his mother, father and older brother.

He was approaching the pier that was the summer dock for the cruising yacht, *EmmaLee*. It was the most beautiful boat on the water in Jonathan's eye and he always stopped to admire it when he passed. It was a magnificent private yacht owned by the Stewart Compton family. At more than 180 feet in length, its hull and upper cabins were painted a gleaming white. Shining and richly stained teak wood accented the ship's lines. The stern was all teak with *EmmaLee* painted in black and gold in an elegant script.

Jonathan had been told the ship had a full-time crew of eight men including a chef, and that she had been built out east in Newport. The Compton family had the *EmmaLee* brought up from Palm Beach, Florida each summer. They had a home up on the hill above the lake. Mrs. Compton and her children spent each summer in Charlevoix. Mr. Compton would come up on the train from Detroit on weekends. It was said he was in the automobile business.

Jonathan had seen the family out on the deck of the *EmmaLee* as she made her way out of the small harbor of Round Lake, out through the channel to Lake Michigan to the west or to Lake Charlevoix to the east. The family would be dressed all in white, servants and crew scurrying around them. Emily Compton, for whom the ship had been named, was the only daughter in the family and the youngest of three children. The two boys, Ernest and James Jr., were in their later teens. Jonathan thought Emily looked to be near his age. He had seen her only from a distance on the ship and had been struck by her

4

looks, even from afar. He found himself thinking about her more than he would ever admit. Even under a large brimmed sunhat he had been able to see a remarkably beautiful face framed by wavy long brown hair. She seemed quite tall, even next to her older brothers and she held herself confidently on the ship's deck, clearly enjoying her time on the big ship.

As Jonathan approached the *EmmaLee* on this quiet morning, there was no crew in sight. He had never seen the family out on the boat at such an early hour either. He came alongside the immense hull and stopped to look her over again for the countless time. He knew boats well. His father and grandfather had worked on boats on this lake for many years and he had been helping them since he was a small boy. They had never worked on a ship of this magnitude, but mostly on small commercial boats for the fishing fleet and smaller runabouts for the summer people. The McKendry's Boatworks was a fixture on the Round Lake waterfront.

He reached out and ran his hand along the smooth painted surface of the boat. He could smell the paint and stain and feel her power, even at rest. He moved back a few steps to look up over the rail to the upper cabin. There were no lights on, but he could see into the captain's bridge sitting above the main cabin. He saw the large wheel in the bridge and some of the controls. The inner walls were darkly stained wood.

He imagined himself at the helm of the *EmmaLee*, his hands firmly holding the big wheel, steering her out through the channel. He saw Emily Compton at his side, holding his arm and laughing with the joy of the trip. He had dreamed of someday designing and building such a boat, but he was also a practical boy and tried to not let his dreams and imaginings overwhelm him. As he patted the hull with affection and began walking away, he was startled by a voice from up on the ship that carried a heavy accent.

"Hey, boy! Keep your bloody hands away from the ship, lad. We don't want you falling in and cracking your head and gettin' blood all over our *EmmaLee* now."

Jonathan looked up to see it was one of the deckhands.

The crewman had a white sailor's uniform and cap. He held a bucket and before Jonathan realized what was happening, the man threw the water from the bucket out over the rail. He couldn't move fast enough to avoid the drenching. It knocked his cap off and left him drenched in the early morning chill.

As he reached down to get his cap, he heard another crew member join in the laughter. He glared up at them and felt a burning anger well up within him. He looked at the stairs up to the deck of the ship. The two crew members continued to heckle him. He dropped his sack of groceries on the dock and ran to the stairs. By the time he reached the rail, the two men were there to confront him.

"What is it, lad?" the man who had thrown the water said. "It looks like you have a problem."

The other man laughed.

"My problem is about to get his ass kicked," said Jonathan in a low and steady voice.

From behind the crew members, a voice yelled out, "What have we got here?"

Jonathan looked beyond the men at an older bearded man in what appeared to be an officer's uniform.

"Nothing we can't handle, Captain," the crewman said. "Just a young pup looking for trouble."

The captain stepped between Jonathan and the two men. "Would you care to explain yourself, young man?" he asked.

"I just need a few minutes alone with your fellows here," Jonathan said. "We had a little disagreement we need to work out."

The captain turned to his men. "You both go below. I'll be down to deal with you in a moment." They both left without

6

protest. "Son, it looks like you've been tossed in the lake once already this morning. I'd say that should be enough. Now, I suggest you get off this ship immediately, or I will personally toss you back in again and feel damned pleased with myself with the chance to do so."

Jonathan's anger was settling with the departure of the two crewmen and he certainly had no fight with this man, particularly since he was the captain of the *EmmaLee*. Common sense told him to back away and not make any more fuss. He saw little to be gained now from a scuffle, other than the wrath of the summer people who supported the town and his family.

"Just be on your way and I advise you to keep away from my men and this ship," the captain said. "I'll be giving them the same advice about you."

As Jonathan walked down the stairs, he saw another face looking out at him from a window along the main cabin. Even in the dim light, he could see it was her. When he made eye contact with Emily Compton, she quickly pulled a curtain closed. *Well, that wasn't the kind of introduction I had hoped for*, he thought.

The family's boatyard was another several hundred paces down the docks. He turned up toward the large main building where boats were built, stored and repaired. There was a large double door that was pulled open to each side. Above the door was a slightly faded sign that was painted with "McKendry's Boatworks". He walked through the boathouse to the rear. There was no one working yet and several boats sat in the silence on weathered wood cradles. He walked through a door into the large yard that stored other boats. Up a short hill sat another smaller building that held an office, a storage area for equipment and tools, and the family's apartment.

He walked inside and kicked off his wet boots. He placed his cap on a hook next to the door and made his way back along a dark hall toward the kitchen. The small house smelled stale and hung on him like a shirt worn too many days.

His mother was working at the sink. He could smell coffee brewing and bacon cooking on the stove. He placed the wet bag of fruit and bread on the counter and started off to his room to change his wet clothes. His mother stopped him when she noticed he was dripping wet.

"Did you fall in the lake, son?" she asked softly. He turned to face her as his father walked in from the back.

"What in God's name happened to you, Johnny?" he asked.

He considered making up a tale of some sort to avoid retelling his earlier encounter, but thought better of it. He had been raised to be forthright and honest in all dealings. He spoke slowly, "I had a bit of a run-in with the crew of the *EmmaLee*. They thought it would be good fun to dump their swab bucket on me."

His father sat at the kitchen table and pulled out another chair for him to join him. "You need to stay away from that boat and those people. Those are summer people and we need to give them their way up here."

"They're just damned boat crew... "

"Don't speak that way in front of your mother and keep away from those people," his father said, sternly. "We'll paint their boats and take their money and put up with them for a few months each year, but they're different and we can't be mixing with them. Do you understand me?" His father took a cup of coffee from his wife.

Jonathan nodded with his head down.

"And I don't want you and your boys out looking for those men in town either. That will lead to nothin' but trouble. Is that clear?" he said with emphasis.

"Yes, sir."

"Now get changed and get back here for some food so we can get to work," his father said. "And roust your brother out of bed. I'll not have him sleeping any more of the morning away."

Jonathan walked back to the small bedroom he shared with his brother, Luke. He was snoring loudly and tangled in his sheets and blanket. He saw his brother's shriveled left leg sticking out from the covers. He had been born with the deformity and walked with a noticeable limp.

Jonathan also saw a half-empty pint bottle of whiskey sitting on the nightstand with the top off. He found the top and placed it back on the bottle, then slid it under his brother's bed. He didn't want his father finding it. There was enough trouble between those two.

He sat down on his own bed and scratched his wet hair. He thought of the eyes of Emily Compton looking down at him from the boat's cabin. He looked out the window of his bedroom at the coming light of morning. The fog was breaking up and he could see patches of blue sky starting to break through the gray clouds. He unbuttoned his wet shirt and threw it in a pile in the corner.

Chapter Two

Present Day

It was a glorious morning with waves running in slow climbing swells. The wind was quartering gently out of the southwest. The weather radar was clear all the way across Lake Michigan to Wisconsin and the sun, just making its way above the hills onshore, warmed the coming day.

Ben Clark stood on the bridge of the *EmmaLee* with his crew captain and twelve-year-old daughter, Megan. They left Mackinaw Island earlier in the morning for the last leg of their journey to Charlevoix, Michigan. Now, just out from the southern point of Little Traverse Bay, they could see the lighthouse on the end of the channel pier leading into the harbor at Charlevoix not more than a mile off in the distance.

He was dressed comfortably in tan slacks with a white golf shirt all the crew wore. The name of his boat, *EmmaLee*, was printed on the front. The early traces of gray touched at his brown hair. His skin was darkly tanned from the past few weeks on the boat. His eyes were a soft green, almost the color of the lake in the early morning light. It was a face that had graced many magazine covers and news stories over the years as his business continued to grow.

To the east, the coastline was framed with tall sand dunes spilling down into the deep blue and green water of Lake

Michigan. The dunes were crested with scattered pines and cottonwoods set off against the sky and the roofs of a few homes could be seen tucked back in the clearings. Looking out to the west, Ben watched the endless series of white-capped waves rolling relentlessly towards them across a hundred miles of open water.

Within the past hour a steady procession of boats of all shapes and sizes had come out to greet the *Emmalee* and accompany them into Charlevoix. They were surrounded now by dozens of boats to each side and to the stern. They could already see a huge crowd milling about up ahead on the piers on both sides of the channel. A flare pistol was fired from the end of the pier and it startled Megan. She grabbed her father's hand and gripped it firmly. She wore a navy-blue sweatshirt with the name *EmmaLee* printed on the front in bold white letters. The flare was followed by several minutes of fireworks coming from a barge anchored just offshore from the channel.

Ben looked down at his daughter and smiled. "I guess we're in the right place." He squeezed her hand and thought of her mother and how he wished she could be with them. Megan had so many traits from her mother. Her eyes and dark hair were a match and so many other similar features and mannerisms continued to amaze him.

His wife had been gone nearly three years now. Cancer had taken her from them. It was a time he remembered now as dark and full of overwhelming fear and despair. In the last months of her life, he put all matters of business aside as he and Megan watched her slowly fade away from them. He forced the thoughts back deep within, as he had to do so often, and looked back down.

"Megan, let's go up on the bow." He led her out through the bridge cabin door and along the deck up to the massive bow of the ship. "This is *EmmaLee's* old home, honey. She spent her early days here."

11

"I think she's happy to be back, Daddy."

They stood at the rail at the point of the bow and watched the huge wake push out from the ship's hull. The accompanying boats started to blow their horns when they saw Ben and Megan moving forward on the ship's deck and both waved back enthusiastically.

"Will the real Emily be here today to welcome us?" the little girl asked.

"No dear, Emily Compton died many years ago."

"Is she in heaven with Mommy?"

"Oh, I'm sure she is."

At the end of the south pier at the base of the tall red lighthouse, George Hansen stood in front of a huge crowd that stretched all the way back along the pier to the drawbridge at Bridge Street in town. He wore a blue sport coat with a Venetian Festival badge on the breast pocket. Wisps of his gray hair blew in the light breeze. Across the channel, a similar crowd had gathered on the north break wall. He fired the flare gun out over the lake to signal the start of the welcoming ceremony and the fireworks exploded up from a barge anchored out in the lake. Even in the bright morning light, they were spectacular against the deep blue sky. The deafening sound of the bursts above was mixed with boat horns and cheering people.

George could see the *EmmaLee* clearly now off to the north of the channel. She was slowing to make her final approach. Even among the many other boats surrounding her, she stood apart not only in size, but also in sheer beauty, her magnificent lines cutting through the green Lake Michigan swells. He felt a chill surge within. *What a marvelous day!*

He was joined by family and friends, and thousands of other local residents and visitors who had come out this morning for the special event. There would be other ceremonies and banquets later for the *EmmaLee* and for the Venetian Festival week, but these first moments of her return were the most anticipated. The ship had last been seen in these waters in the fall of 1952. She was returning now nearly seventy years later, restored to her original splendor.

George was anxious to get the ship into the dock in Round Lake and to go aboard and meet her new owner in person. Old memories of the ship came back to him and he thought about the effect it had on so many people he knew and loved.

Standing at his side was another special guest for the day. He looked at the woman now and saw tears in her eyes. He reached out and took her hand. She turned and smiled at him and whispered, "Thank you."

A few minutes later, the captain of the *EmmaLee* brought her about to the east to guide her into the channel. The many boats alongside her slowly dropped back to follow. As the large white ship first entered the channel, George Hansen saw Ben Clark and his daughter out on the bow, and he saluted them in *welcome*. Onboard, they saw him and waved back with broad smiles.

"She's more beautiful than I ever remembered," George said, more to himself than to those around him. The cheering from the crowd continued to grow and everyone was waving back to the people on the deck of the *EmmaLee*. The great ship, nearly two hundred feet at the waterline, made her way slowly down the channel toward town. The rest of the ship's crew stood on the rear deck dressed in their official gear, enjoying the morning's events and waving to the crowds.

George motioned to those around him, "Let's go, we need to get down to the docks."

The Captain sounded the *EmmaLee* ship's horn to signal the bridge keeper to raise the drawbridge up ahead at the entrance into Round Lake. George saw the massive blue sections of the bridge slowly lift to make way for the ship's entrance into the harbor. The entire crowd slowly made their way back along the pier trying to keep up with the *EmmaLee*.

A special mooring had been reserved for the *EmmaLee* along the docks where the Coast Guard Cutter Acacia had rested for so many years. A large decorated gangplank stood poised to be lowered to the deck of the ship as it came alongside the dock. Banners hung from each side reading *Welcome Home EmmaLee*. Lines were thrown to men on the dock and the ship slid gracefully into place along the wooden pier. The lines were secured and the gangplank lowered into place.

George Hansen and his welcoming party came down through the dense and cheering crowds. They walked up the gangplank to greet Ben Clark who was standing at the ship's rail with his daughter.

George reached out his hand, "Welcome to Charlevoix, Mr. Clark, and welcome to you, young lady. You must be Megan? I'm George Hansen and I have the privilege of being the chairman of the Venetian Festival." He shook both their hands. "And welcome home to you, *Miss EmmaLee*," he said, looking down the long expanse of the ship's deck.

The Charlevoix High School marching band began playing *America, the Beautiful*, their music barely heard above the welcoming roar and applause from the crowd.

Ben returned the handshake, "Thank you, Mr. Hansen. This welcome is overwhelming. I can't thank you enough for inviting us to bring the *EmmaLee* back to Charlevoix. Your town is beautiful and all these people, it's just unbelievable. Come aboard!"

George came on deck with five other members of the Festival committee who he introduced to the town's new guests. Then he motioned for one other to join him at the front of the group. A tall and striking woman came up and stood beside him, dressed simply in a blue cotton dress cut just above the knees and sleeveless, exposing long tanned arms and firm shoulders. Her blonde hair was gathered in the back with a ribbon and a few loose strands fluttered around her face in the wind.

"Ben Clark and Megan, I would like you to meet Emily Compton's daughter, Sally Thomason," George Hansen said in introduction.

Ben Clark reached out his hand in greeting. Her grip was firm, and he found himself a bit off balance. He hesitated a moment, not anticipating meeting any of the past owners' family. When he had gathered himself, he said, "Sally, it's nice to meet you. I'm so glad you could come for this homecoming."

Sally released her grip and smiled, "I wouldn't have missed this for the world, Ben. My mother told me so many stories about this ship and her love for the *EmmaLee*."

"Did you come far for the Festival?" he asked.

"No," she said, smiling. "Just a few blocks actually. I live up on the big lake just north of the channel."

"Well, I'm sure you would like to see what we've done with the 'Old Lady'. Did you ever have an opportunity to see her before?"

"No, I wasn't born when the *EmmaLee* left Charlevoix. I knew she was being kept out East, but I just didn't want to see her in that condition. I was thrilled to hear you were working on restoring her. She looks magnificent. My parents and my grandparents would be very pleased at all you've done."

She reached down and greeted young Megan, taking her hand. "My mother would have been about your age when she used to cruise on the *EmmaLee*."

"I'm sorry she's dead and can't be here today," the little girl said with stern sincerity. "My daddy says she's in heaven with my mother."

Ben was embarrassed and began to say something, but Sally answered quickly, "Oh dear, I'm sorry your mother is gone, too. They both would have loved this day, I'm sure."

Ben smiled at his daughter, then back at Sally. "We have a cocktail reception onboard planned for later this afternoon. I'm sure George has invited all of you to attend, but can I take you on a quick tour right now?"

George spoke first, "Absolutely!"

Ben led the group up onto the foredeck, speaking as he walked along the rail. "I happened upon the *EmmaLee* one day when I was down at the boatyard in Newport for the first time. I had moved my sailboat over from another location and was wandering around to get familiar with the place. The *EmmaLee* was tied up at an old pier hidden by a dozen old boats up on cradles. I have to say she was in pretty bad shape. Sitting out in the elements for all those years had taken quite a toll on her."

He turned to face his guests as they assembled at the front of the ship. Megan stood by his side, holding his hand. "I immediately fell in love with her even though she looked like an abandoned shipwreck. In a way, I guess she was. It took a while, but I finally managed to pull all the strings to buy her and arrange for her reconditioning. It was one of the most amazing projects I've ever been involved with. We did our best to restore her to her original condition. We saved as much of the wood surfaces and planking as we could, but a lot of dry rot had to be replaced. The interior was a bit easier. The engines were far beyond hope and we've given her a new power plant. You'll notice the instrumentation is also much more advanced than what she had back in the early days. She's really rigged now to cruise overseas. I'm planning a trip to the Mediterranean with her next year."

George Hansen spoke up, "Why did the past owners leave her abandoned for so long?"

"I'm told they ran into financial difficulties. The ship needed quite a bit of work at the time and they couldn't find a buyer willing to take her off their hands and pay for the extensive repairs that were needed. She really should have been scuttled long ago, but fortunately, no one wanted to spend the money to dispose of her."

Ben continued to lead the tour throughout the ship, pointing out the special work that had been done in many areas. They finished back at the side rail looking out over the large crowds still milling about the docks admiring the ship.

"The *EmmaLee* will be open for tours tomorrow leading up to the boat parade," Ben said as they reached the gangplank. "I hope you can all come back for our reception this afternoon. George helped me put an invitation list together of about 100 people."

"We wouldn't miss it," George said.

"And Ms. Thomason...?"

"It's Sally."

"Sally, will you be able to make it? Is there any other family who would like to come?"

"No, they're all gone now," she said.

"I'm sorry."

"I have some wonderful old photo albums you might want to see with a lot of pictures of the *EmmaLee* and my family," she said. "There are really too many to bring over to the boat. We'll have to plan a time when you and Megan can come up to the house. How long are you planning to be in town?"

"We'll be here in Charlevoix for a week," Ben said, "so I'm sure we can find some time. I would really enjoy that."

Everyone said their thanks and goodbyes. As the welcome party left the ship, Megan asked her father, "Will Sally have more pictures of Emily when she was a little girl?"

"I think she will," he said, picking her up to look out over the crowds below. "Let's take a little walk around town. What do you say?"

He turned to watch Sally Thomason walking away through the crowds. He remembered the chill he felt when they were introduced. Since he first saw the pictures of the *EmmaLee* that

George Hansen had sent along, he had begun to feel a bond with the old Compton family who first sailed this ship on these waters. He remembered one picture in particular. It was a picture of young Emily Compton on the deck of the *EmmaLee* laughing at whoever was behind the camera. The eyes of the young girl were hauntingly beautiful. He felt as if he had just looked into them again this afternoon over half a century later.

Chapter Three

Sally sat out on the rear porch of her house in a wicker chair with large soft cushions. She looked out over the expanse of lawn and the vista of Lake Michigan beyond. The clear sky reflected down onto the lake leaving it a brilliant blue. White-capped waves continued onshore with a crashing rhythm. It was mid-afternoon, and the sun was just falling below the porch roof. She could feel the warmth coming through the windows. The summer flowers around her porch waved gently in the breeze and a hummingbird made its rounds, darting away quickly at the slightest threat.

She sat with an old leather-bound photo album on her lap. It was open to a page that had a large black and white photograph taped to it. The album paper had yellowed, and a few words had been written in below the picture in pencil. In an elegant cursive hand, the caption read, *Emily, age 17, on the EmmaLee – Charlevoix, Mi. 1941.* The picture had been taken of her mother leaning on the rail of the ship, smiling widely at the camera. She was dressed in a knee-length white skirt and white buttoned blouse. On her head, she wore a large-brimmed straw sunhat that shaded her face. Behind her were the main cabin of the ship and a glimpse of the Charlevoix docks and buildings along Bridge Street.

Sally stared down at the picture. She was always struck by how much she resembled her mother. Her hair was a different color, but their facial features were so similar. Her mother and father had been gone now for many years. This had been their house and Sally had grown up here. They left it to her in their will and she had never moved away.

Turning the pages of the album slowly, she had seen all of the photos many times before, but today's events on the *EmmaLee* gave the images a new and special feeling. She came to a photo of her grandparents and their three children on the front porch of their old home over on the hill above Round Lake. The picture was taken from the street, showing the entire façade of the house. It was a large Victorian style home with a porch that wrapped around both sides. Its trim was ornately decorated in the style from that time. The house was painted all in white with dark shutters that Sally had been told were green in those years. There were two spruce trees planted on both sides of the front walk that made its way up the front lawn to the center of the porch.

Her mother stood on a step with her two brothers on each side and her parents stood behind them. A caption read, *Going to church – August 1939.* Her two uncles were still alive; one was out in Los Angeles, retired from the real estate business. The other was in New York. Neither had returned to Charlevoix in over twenty years. They had sold her grandparent's house soon after Sally's mother had passed away. One of her uncles had spoken to her before they put the home on the market. She was quite comfortable here in this house and had told them she had no interest in buying the family's old place or having it stay in the family. She had received a check for a third of the selling price a few months later.

On the next page there were several smaller photos. One was of her mother with her Irish Setter, Blaze, on the beach down on Lake Charlevoix. Another showed her mother beside a long Packard convertible with the top down and a young man at her side. She remembered her mother telling her about the car and her first romance with a boy from Chicago named Connor.

Sally closed the album and placed it on the small table beside her. Reaching for a glass of cold tea, she sat back and looked out over the lake. Thinking back on her own time in this small town, it had always given her all she wanted from life. She had good friends during her childhood and through high school. She kept very active with school activities and an occasional boyfriend, and also found time for her painting which turned out to be her true passion.

She had left to attend college for four years out East and studied art. The first summer she was back after graduation, her parents helped her open her gallery down on Bridge Street. She had been in the business ever since, selling her own work and that of other area artists.

Then, she had met Matthew Thomason. He was from Chicago and came to Charlevoix each summer to stay at his parent's place down on the lake in Oyster Bay. They had met at a dance held down at the old Casino at the Belvedere Club. A summer romance continued for a couple of years until he was out of college. They continued to see each other and she occasionally went down to Chicago to see him at his parents' house in Lake Forest.

When she was twenty-four, he asked her to marry him on Christmas Day. She said *yes,* and he agreed to move his investment business up to Charlevoix. He could continue to cultivate clients back in Chicago and from the wealthier residents "Up North."

The marriage worked well for the first few years. They had a beautiful daughter that fourth year before Matthew was away in Chicago more often. Before she knew it, they had been married seven years. The relationship had continued to grow more distant and less loving. They weren't the type that fought often or had ugly scenes. Their love and the relationship just seemed to slowly fade.

She remembered the night Matthew had called from his apartment in Chicago. They spoke most evenings at around nine if he was out of town. She always shuddered when she remembered hearing another voice in the background. It was a woman laughing. Matthew had tried to cover it up by saying it was his assistant from down at the office dropping some papers off. She asked him about it again that weekend when he had come up to Charlevoix. He finally admitted he had been seeing another woman in the city for nearly three years.

He left town that night and never returned. Their divorce was final about a year later. She hadn't wanted anything from him. She kept her parent's house and her own money. When it was over, she continued on with her daughter and friends, the business with her partner Gwen and her painting.

She had set up a painting studio on the second floor of the house with several large windows looking out across the lake. While she painted, she easily slipped away to other places in her mind. She liked to paint scenes from around the North Country, lakes and rivers, the homes and boats, and occasionally the people. There was a large painting of her mother in the front entry of the house. Several more pieces of her work were displayed in other rooms.

As she sat there, it occurred to her she now had an opportunity to paint the *EmmaLee*. She would have to remember to take her camera with her to the party. She had already taken many pictures as the ship had come into Charlevoix this morning. *I should have more than enough reference*, she thought.

She got up, remembering she had to get ready to go down to the Clark's party on the boat. She took her glass and the album inside and set them on the kitchen table. Walking through the old house, she thought how much the place felt like a comfortable old bath robe. She had redecorated most of the rooms after her parents were gone. It wasn't that they weren't tastefully done before, but she wanted to make the house truly hers.

She went upstairs to her bedroom and pulled another dress from the closet. It was a print dress she had planned to wear for the evening's event. Walking into the bathroom, she held it up to her shoulders in front of the mirror. She shook her head. It just didn't feel right, so she hung it back in her closet and looked through the racks of clothes, not finding exactly what she was looking for.

"What difference does it make?" she said aloud to herself in frustration.

She took off her blue dress and hung it on a rack, then went back to the mirror and let her hair down to assess the face and body staring back at her. In the soft afternoon light, her face still looked young and firm. Her blonde hair was cut evenly just below her shoulders and it hung across the side of her face. She pulled it back behind her ear and felt some sense of satisfaction that her body was still trim for the most part in her middle years. She touched up her makeup and went back to the closet and grabbed the original print dress.

Ben and Megan Clark had finished their walk through the small shopping district of Charlevoix. The streets were jammed with visitors in town for the festival. There was a carnival set up on one of the back streets and Megan rode a small Ferris wheel and a carousel. They shopped for sweatshirts that read "Charlevoix" as a souvenir of their trip and Megan couldn't resist as they walked by a fudge shop. They came out a few minutes later with four different flavors.

Walking back down to the docks across a large park that fronted Round Lake, they stopped to listen to one of the many bands playing this week in the quaint stone band shell that had been built years ago. As they listened, Ben marveled at the beauty of the little town. Out on Round Lake beyond the docks there must have been over 100 boats moored or cruising around. The small lake was ringed with magnificent homes, condominiums, boathouses and docks. He tried to imagine what it must have looked like back when the *EmmaLee* had first sailed here. George Hansen had sent a few photos and he remembered he had to make time to get over to the city library and the Historical Society while they were in town.

He found himself looking forward to visiting Sally Thomason and seeing some of her old family albums. He was intrigued by the history of the ship and the stories Hansen had related. He definitely wanted to learn more about Sally and her family.

"We need to get back to the ship and make sure everything is ready for our guests, Megan."

"I'll let them have some of my fudge," she said as they walked down the grass lawn to the docks.

"If any of that fudge is left by dinner time, I'll be amazed," he said and laughed as he held her hand, walking down the hill.

Guests began arriving promptly at four. Everyone seemed most anxious to get a closer look at the *EmmaLee* and to meet the famed Mr. Clark. Sally Thomason arrived about a half-hour later. She had seen Ben Clark briefly when she arrived, and she was now standing on the rear deck with several friends from town including the Mayor, Martin Holloway. He was a loosely kept man in his sixties with clothes coming out at all angles around his portly frame. He had been mayor for many years and he also owned the restaurant and bar next to Sally's gallery. He sipped on a Bloody Mary as Sally reached over to straighten his tie.

"Look Martin, you've got tomato juice on your shirt here. You're such a mess," she said with a grin.

"Wait 'til I get through the hors d'oeuvres table, then you'll see me fully decorated."

"This is definitely a *'who's who'* gathering for our little town, isn't it?" she said, taking a sip from her glass of wine and looking out over the crowd.

The Mayor finished his drink looking for a waiter. "Yes, we seem to be well represented," he answered. "What do you think of the billionaire guy?"

"He certainly seems like a normal person and his little daughter is a doll," Sally said. She saw Ben and Megan standing across the deck speaking with George Hansen and his wife Elizabeth.

"I wonder if he wants to buy a restaurant," the Mayor said. "I'm ready to retire and head to Naples." He held his glass up to a passing waiter who was carrying a tray of drinks. He helped himself to another Bloody Mary. "I'd give him a good price."

"You're like me, Martin. You'll never leave this place. You get two miles out of town and you run out of anchor chain and get pulled back," Sally said and smiled at her friend.

"God, I hope you're wrong. Here comes our host. I wonder if he has his checkbook on him."

Sally elbowed him in his ample middle. She watched Ben Clark approaching. He looked different in some way from the photos she had seen of him. She couldn't quite figure what it was. Maybe it was the tan and his hair seemed to be longer. She pushed her thoughts aside.

"Hello Sally, thanks for coming," Ben said, taking her hand.

Introductions were made. The Mayor pulled in his stomach and in his most dignified voice, welcomed the visitor, "Let me officially welcome you to our town of Charlevoix. On behalf of my constituents, let me say you have brought a true treasure back to us." He raised his glass in a toast and the group joined him touching glasses. "You also make damn good Bloody Mary's!"

From across the deck, Sally noticed the approach of another town resident.

"Oh, this should be interesting," whispered the Mayor under his breath as he also noticed the approach of Mary Alice Gregory. Mary Alice was the daughter of the Gregory's from Grosse Pointe. They summered here each year and were leading benefactors in the community. Their daughter had been through two husbands in her brief thirty years and she had been clearly working all summer on finding number three. She was a stunning woman with a "Palm Beach" look and requisite dark tan. Her clothing and jewelry were immaculate, and her jet-black hair was pulled back tight, seeming to almost stretch her face.

The Mayor made room for Ms. Gregory. "Ben, this is one of our town's fairest flowers, Ms. Mary Alice Gregory."

The usual pleasantries were exchanged. Sally watched as Mary Alice slid in close to Ben Clark. She had known Mary Alice for many years, although they didn't run in the same circles. She stopped by the gallery occasionally looking for another piece for their summer home. Sally had always wondered about how friendly she had been to her ex-husband Matthew before the divorce. The woman often gave less than subtle hints that perhaps she knew Sally's former husband just a little more intimately than people might otherwise think.

Mary Alice was oozing with charm. Either Ben was being extremely gracious, or he was actually falling for it.

Sally watched her monopolize the conversation for several moments before she quietly interrupted, "Excuse me for a moment, I need to say hello to the Hansen's."

The Mayor gave her a knowing look and Ben wasn't able to say anything before Mary Alice started in with him again.

Sally walked across the deck, saying hello to a few acquaintances as she passed. She stopped at the far rail, looking out across Round Lake toward the east channel into Lake

Charlevoix. It was a scene worth painting. The Coast Guard Cutter Acacia was now at dock down at the Coast Guard station along the channel. There was some talk she was going to be decommissioned. *It would be sad to have her leave after all these years*, Sally thought.

Down to her right on the south side of the harbor was the old boathouse that had been owned by her grandparents. The docks there had been the summer home for the *EmmaLee*. The big building had been transformed into several condominium units.

In her mind, she could see the old photos with the *EmmaLee* tied up in front of the boathouse. There were always several other large motor yachts and sailboats moored in the harbor in those pictures. She could also see the giant Great Lakes cruise ships that used to come into port here, transporting passengers to different resort cities up and down the coast. It had been many years since those cruise lines had been shut down. Automobile travel and private planes became much too convenient. Even the railroad no longer ran through town. An old draw bridge used to cross the channel down by the Coast Guard station with tracks running north to the depot. The train depot was still there, recently refurbished by the Historical Society. The massive Inn at Lake Charlevoix had once sat on the hill above the depot with a grand view of Lake Charlevoix.

Sally felt a touch on her shoulder and turned to see George and Elizabeth Hansen.

"Lost in thought?" he asked.

"Just thinking back to what this scene must have looked like sixty years ago," she answered. "Hello Liz. It's nice to see you."

"Hello, dear."

"It was a much different time and place, as you can imagine," George said. "I wish your mother and father were with us here today. I don't mean to upset you, but your mother was such a lovely woman. I feel like she's standing here with us just the same."

"I know how you're feeling. You've told me so much about those times over the years... great memories."

"Yes, they are. She was one helluva lady, if I may say so. Your father was a lucky man," George said.

Chapter Four

I was seventeen years old that summer of 1941. My father was trying to convince me to learn the carpentry trade. I was more interested in fishing and girls. I had one more year to go in high school and I was just beginning to think about college and maybe even law school. On days when I wasn't working on a job with my father, I would spend time with my friend down on Horton Creek. We would either ride our bikes out to the lake road or take a boat if Jonathan could borrow one from his dad's boatworks.

There were still a lot of trout in the creek back then. They say Hemingway used to fish there. I've seen pictures of him taken down at Horton Bay where the creek runs into Lake Charlevoix. He's holding some damn nice trout. His first wedding was held there in the little village, the first of many for him, I guess. Hemingway was long gone from these parts by the time Jonathan and I found the creek.

"Can I be excused now? George and I want to get out to the creek tonight to fish?" Jonathan pleaded, as his family finished with their dinner.

His father finished his coffee, sitting at the head of the table in the small kitchen. "You'll want to take the old *Higgins* I suppose? That boat still has a hitch in the engine. Listen to it and let me know what you think."

The boy turned to his brother, "Luke, do you want to come along?"

The eldest brother, Luke McKendry, was twenty-two years old, still living at home and working in the boatyard with his father. He sat slumped at the table, pushing what was left of his dinner around his plate. His face was an older version of Jonathan's and they could have easily been twins if they were closer in age. Luke had let his beard grow in the past months and it made him look even older now. Gray circles under his eyes stood out against pale skin that rarely saw the sun.

"I don't have time for any damn fishin'." He pushed his chair back.

"Luke, that's enough of that kind of talk!" his father answered back in frustration.

"I got to be somewhere." He started walking out of the room.

Samuel McKendry got up quickly and followed him out the back door. The rest of the family could hear heated words as they disappeared around the corner.

Jonathan got up and helped his mother clear the table. "Really, can I go now?" he pleaded.

His mother nodded. He was out the door before anyone could change their mind or come up with a chore for him. He ran down to the door to the storage shed. Inside he found the bamboo fly rod his grandfather had made for him before he died. It was one of Jonathan's most prized possessions. He also grabbed an old vest that held a box of flies and a few other assorted pieces of gear. He hurried down the hill to the docks. The *Higgins* was floating smoothly on the calm waters of Round Lake. George was already sitting in the boat with his own fly rod propped in the back.

"Where the hell have you been, McKendry?"

"Just help me with these lines and let's get outta here."

"Catherine wanted to come along. I told her there wasn't any damn room for a sister on Horton Creek." Catherine Hansen was George's younger sister by a year.

Jonathan was thinking it might have been nice for her to come along tonight. He thought about his first kiss with Catherine earlier this summer.

"Come on, McKendry. Get this tug started."

Jonathan lifted the engine cover to air out the gas fumes and then after a few moments, turned the key to start the old wooden runabout. It had been partially restored by him and his father, but the engine was still running a bit rough. They gave it a few minutes to warm up before they pushed away from the docks. There were a few other boats on the water and the *Higgins* rocked gently in their wake as they made their way slowly out away from the pier.

Jonathan heard some commotion off to his left. He looked over his shoulder and saw there was a large crowd of people milling around on the rear deck of the *EmmaLee*. It looked like a party of some sort. Everyone was holding drinks and talking in small groups. The old *Higgins* seemed to steer by itself back toward the big ship.

"Where you goin'?" George asked.

Jonathan didn't answer.

"Come on. We need to get down to the creek," his friend pleaded. "I'm gettin' worried about you and this thing you've got for that boat. You're damn crazy if you think you got a chance to ever get on a boat like that."

"It'll just take a minute."

They cruised slowly back along the docks toward the big ship. It dwarfed his small runabout. The sun was beginning to ride low over the town and he squinted looking into the sun, trying to make out who was up on the deck. They came alongside about twenty yards out and kept moving slowly past.

Then, Jonathan saw Emily Compton at the front of the boat. She was talking to a boy who looked about the same age in a dark blue jacket and tie. She was dressed in something peach colored.

He watched them smile and talk comfortably. The boy reached over and touched her arm as they laughed together at something he'd said. The small boat was alongside the young couple now. The noise from the engine caught their attention and they both looked down at Jonathan and his friend passing in the old wood boat. The boy in the suit quickly looked back to Emily Compton, not much interested in two locals in an old wreck of a boat.

Emily held her glance a little longer. Their eyes met again, as they had a few mornings ago when he had been drenched by her ship's crew. There didn't seem to be any sense of recognition in her eyes, Jonathan thought. *Maybe it was so dark that morning, she didn't see me getting soaked.*

He finally realized he was staring and quickly looked away. He glanced back over his shoulder a moment later and saw the couple had returned to their conversation as if nothing eventful had happened.

He slowly turned the boat back to the center of the harbor.

"Let's go find some trout."

Emily Compton knew she should be more interested in the conversation. She was trying to be pleasant. Connor Harris had been a good friend for many summers now. They had shared their summer months with other families vacationing in Charlevoix since they were both in grade school. She and Connor had always had a special bond.

This summer had been different. They had both turned eighteen earlier this year. It was clear he saw her now as a desirable young woman, no longer as a childhood friend. At times, she found the new, more amorous Connor to be attractive and charming and fun to be around. As the summer had progressed though, she found his advances to be clumsy. She realized she didn't have those kind of feelings for him.

Emily had graduated from high school in Grosse Pointe in June. She was planning to start college in the fall at the university in Ann Arbor. She had known for many years she wanted to be a doctor. She was volunteering this summer at the hospital in Charlevoix and she found tremendous satisfaction in helping people in this way. Her parents were supportive of her ambitions. Connor and some of her other friends were less tolerant. They couldn't understand why she was spending so much of her summer vacation down at the hospital with sick people.

Her interest in medicine dated back to the time she spent in the hospital as a small child. She had become quite ill one evening with an extreme temperature and severe pain in her neck. Her father rushed her to the hospital that night and the doctors quickly diagnosed a dangerous case of spinal meningitis. Fortunately, they had caught the illness quite early, and though she had spent two weeks in the hospital, she had recovered completely. She often remembered the doctors and nurses who worked with her and made her feel so loved and comforted. Since that time, she had always hoped she could learn to help people in a similar way.

Connor Harris hadn't determined his calling. When he and Emily had spoken about it, he was uncertain and evasive. He was clearly not ready to deal with what the future might hold for him.

He was the son of Warren Harris, one of the more successful real estate developers in Chicago. His father's company had been involved in the construction of some of Chicago's most noteworthy buildings. At times, he had admitted he would likely join his father in the business. Other times he wasn't sure.

He had decided to attend Northwestern University near his home in Lake Forest in September. Beyond that, he said he wasn't particularly interested in worrying about the future.

Emily stood and listened to Connor continue on about the previous night's adventure when he and some of his friends had taken his car over to Boyne City on the other end of the lake. Connor and his parents had been invited to the party on the *EmmaLee* tonight. Her parents had been friends of the Harris family for many years.

"We pulled up in front of the movie house last night over in Boyne," Connor said. "There wasn't much of a crowd, just a few people going in. We were trying to decide if we wanted to see this Cary Grant picture when this old pick-up truck pulled in behind us making the most god-awful noises...sounded like the whole engine was going to fall out. So, this farm boy gets out with his girlfriend. As they're walking by, one of our guys makes a smart aleck comment about the truck. Well, the kid gets all in a lather, like we've insulted his mother, or something. A few words are exchanged. The next thing you know we're all out on the lake road heading out to Advance, lined up side-by-side to race this old farm wreck against my Packard." Connor paused to take a sip from his lemonade.

"We bet him five bucks we could beat him out to the market at Advance. He had to show us he had the money. His girlfriend was really angry at the whole thing, but she stayed in the truck with him. We started in front of the smelly old leather tannery. It was just before dark. You know how twisty that road is out there along the lake. We couldn't stay two abreast around some of those turns because you couldn't see if anyone was coming. That damn truck had some engine in it. He was keeping up with us, even passed us a couple of times."

"You're lucky you didn't kill each other," Emily said with true concern.

Connor laughed and continued. "We were about a quarter mile from Advance when he decides to pass us again. There's a sharp turn coming to the left and this crazy idiot tries to pass again. I guess he really didn't want to lose his five bucks. He manages to get by me again, then I see him swerve hard to the right. He almost takes us into the lake trying to avoid this car coming the other way around the bend. I slammed on my brakes and watched his pickup head off the road into the gravel. He tried to save it and hit the brakes hard, but he lost it in the gravel. It looked like he almost had it under control when the bank fell away into the lake and he slid down out of sight as we passed. When I stopped and backed up it was the funniest thing you've ever seen. This guy's standing on the hood of his truck. The truck's sitting in two feet of water, steam coming out of the hot engine like an old steamship. The girl is yelling at him from inside and we're laughing so hard it hurts. We called down to him to keep his five bucks and turned around and went back into town. It was a pretty good picture by the way, Cary Grant, I mean. I'll take you if you'd like."

"Connor, I can't believe you left them out there," Emily said. "Were they hurt?"

"No, they were fine. I'm sure they had some explaining to do when they got hauled out of the lake, but at least he still had his five bucks to pay for the tow," Connor said, smiling wickedly.

Emily just shook her head. She noticed a small boat coming up alongside. There were two boys onboard. It was an old wooden inboard that looked like it needed a little more work. They were cruising slowly past the *EmmaLee* like so many boats do, trying to get a closer look.

Connor turned when he saw the boat. "That engine sounds like the farm boy's truck last night," he said, shaking his head.

Emily continued to watch as it passed. She saw two fishing poles in the back of the boat, then noticed that the boy driving the boat was looking up at her. It wasn't a face she recognized, but she was struck by his gaze. She looked back to Connor as he continued on about the race last night. She heard the old inboard heading away but didn't think much more of it.

Luke McKendry sat on a worn stool at the bar. Glenn Miller was playing on the juke box. A few others sat down from him, but *The Helm* was fairly empty this early in the evening. It was one of a few bars along Bridge Street, this one appealing more to the locals. He held a cigarette in his left hand and watched the smoke rise slowly to join the haze above him. A shot of whiskey and a mug of beer sat in front of him, both half empty.

The place smelled of stale beer and the sweat of working men. The bartender, Bud, was down at the end of the bar talking to a couple of other patrons. Luke knew them from the waterfront but wasn't much interested in conversation tonight. He took another sip from the shot glass and followed that with a long drink from the cold beer. He felt the heat from the whiskey and chill from the beer merge together as it made its way down into his belly. He shook his head and grimaced at the shock to his body, then took another pull on his smoke.

His father's words from their argument were still ringing in his ears. It was getting to be a regular occurrence. *I have to get out of this damned town,* he thought.

"Jesus!" he said under his breath, thinking about the latest skirmish.

His father had tried to stop him from leaving and going into town again tonight. He knew Luke was coming down to *The Helm*. He told him there was no room for a drunk in the McKendry home, or in the business either. Luke had told him to *go to hell*. They had almost come to blows before Luke pulled himself away and stormed up the hill to Belvedere Avenue to walk into town.

He looked down at this left leg hanging limply alongside the stool. He felt the old anger burn inside. From his earliest days, he could remember the shame that leg had caused him. He found himself talking to it like it was some foreign object, unattached, but always lingering nearby. He looked up into the mirror behind the bar in disgust. The face looking back at him in the dim light was almost unrecognizable. His face was drawn and gaunt and the circles under his eyes had grown as dark as his newly grown beard. He shook his head and looked away out into the street through the open front door.

Flies were buzzing around his drinks and he waved them away with his hand, taking another drink. He finished both glasses and held the beer mug up to Bud to signal for a refill. Bud eventually came down and poured another shot and beer. He slid them across the bar in front of Luke.

"So, it's going to be another night like that is it, McKendry?" said the old bartender.

"Go to hell!"

The two boys in the *Higgins* had just made their way clear of the channel and out into Lake Charlevoix. The wind was calm, and the lake was rolling gently with swells from boat wakes earlier in the day. The sun was almost down below the trees behind them.

Jonathan pushed the throttle forward and felt the engine catch hold. The low rumble from the engine rose to a loud roar as they powered up into the lake. Slowly, the boat planed out and they could see the vast lake out ahead of them as the bow settled down at cruising speed, cutting into the chop. It was near fifteen miles down to the end of the lake at Boyne City. Horton Bay was a little over halfway, tucked into the north shore of the lake. There were only a few other boats out. Jonathan turned the running lights on and settled in for the run down to the bay.

Off to their right and fading away behind them was the beach along the Belvedere Club with its small beach cabanas lined up side-by-side, each painted in different pastel colors.

Closer to the channel was the Casino, sitting down on the waterfront below the big hotel. The Casino was painted a soft pea soup green and Jonathan saw several cars parked along the road in front. He had never been inside, but he had walked by on Saturday nights and had seen the crowds of rich summer members going in. The only locals on the premises were the waiters and the musicians in the band. He had caught a glimpse of the people dancing inside, hearing the band playing the latest dance tunes.

He always wondered why they called it the *Casino*. He had asked his dad about it, but his father didn't know either. The only gambling up this way was out on a couple of boats that cruised the lake in the summers, taking people out for a night of dinner, drinking and illegal gambling. An old lumber barge had been refitted and sailed the lake most weekends with a large party of gamblers and their women who came from far away to enjoy a night of poker and whiskey. Somehow the Feds never seemed to go after the old ship. Jonathan's father had explained that the owner knew which *palms to grease*, whatever the hell that meant.

The run down to Horton Bay was invigorating and the two friends rode without talking, enjoying the night out and the freedom of the trip. The few clouds in the sky glowed a bright red from the fading sun. Two gulls swept maniacally above, chasing at each other.

As they approached the point at the bay, Jonathan slowed the engine. They came around the point and glided on the smooth water, the engine sputtering at low idle. There were just a few old cabins in the bay, spread far apart and mostly hidden up in the heavy cedars. There was a brown painted boathouse and a few boats tied at a dock along the south shore. The bay was well-protected from the wind and the water was almost glass calm. The boys saw fish rising already down to their left at the mouth of the creek.

Jonathan steered away just to the north of the creek. In about two feet of water, just offshore, he cut the engine and let it ease to a slow stop. George was upfront and threw an anchor over the bow and tied the rope off. They both grabbed their rods and gear and jumped over the side into the cool shock of the lake. In bare feet and wet pants, they waded up to the shore, the loose sand squished under them.

Walking along the shore, they approached the small creek that emptied down into the bay. Tall grasses grew alongside on both banks. They walked down into the shallow water and felt the chill of the colder water from the stream current hit their legs.

A few mosquitoes buzzed at their heads, but they ignored them. They were more interested in the big lake mayflies the fish were feeding on. Jonathan looked up into the sky that was rapidly fading to a dull blue gray. He saw the big bugs hovering all around them. As they fell to the water, the trout quickly made a meal of them. Quiet slurps could be heard emerging from the rings of water spreading out from each rising fish. A large pod of fish was working about thirty paces out into the lake. George and Jonathan spread out to cast to the fish from opposite sides.

Jonathan waded out until he was up to his waist in the cool water. He reached down and pulled the big feather fly loose from the cork handle of his rod. It was a big mayfly imitation his father had taught him to tie. He pulled some greasy floatant from a container in his vest and rubbed it into the fly. Pulling line out, he enjoyed the sound of the click drag as the reel spun in his hands. The worn green fly line lay in circles on the surface in front of him and he began to cast the rod rhythmically, forward and back to throw more line out.

He had his eye on a soft circle fading on the quiet bay's surface where a trout had risen just a few moments before. He felt the pull of the heavy line with each false cast. When he knew he had enough line out, he let go with a long smooth cast toward where the fish had last come up. The line rolled out, placing the fly down lightly on the water. It sat there riding high on the surface. Jonathan waited without moving, almost without breathing. He felt a soft drumming in his ears as the anticipation of a strike grew. The fly still sat there unbothered. He pulled sharply on the fly line two times and sent the fly skittering a few inches across the surface.

The water erupted in a startling splash that Jonathan answered with an instinctive strike of the rod. He felt the hook of the fly set solidly in the big trout's mouth. The fish dove hard and away and Jonathan yelped, "Good fish! Good fish!"

George yelled back in encouragement.

The fly reel screamed in protest as the fish ripped off line trying to escape. Jonathan felt the line slow, knowing the fish would jump. Then he saw it explode up from the calm surface sending water in all directions as it twisted and bucked, trying to free the hook from its mouth. He saw the bright red side of the rainbow trout gleam in the last light of the evening. It fell back into the lake with a thunderous splash and went deep again to the bottom of the bay.

He began working the fish hard, pulling back to the side, then reeling fast to gain line. The boy and the fish went back and forth at each other. The trout would gain a bit, then fall back under the steady pull of the bamboo rod.

This is a good fish, he thought. His hands trembled, and he felt sweat dripping down his nose, even in the cool of the coming night.

"You need some help over there?" his friend yelled.

"I don't need you comin' over here and breakin' this fish off, if that's what you mean," Jonathan answered with a big smile on his face.

He saw the fish clearly now, its silvery sides gleaming in the clear water and the bright shock of red down its side. The trout came alongside him, and he reached down and eased his hand under its belly. He lifted gently, and the fish abandoned hope and sagged in his hand. He felt the satisfying weight and looked down into the eye of the fish. Its mouth opened and closed slowly.

He held it up for his friend to see across on the other side of the creek mouth. George whistled in admiration. He took a last look at the fish and reached behind and slipped it into a large pocket on the back of his vest. It felt heavy there and he felt it squirm a few times. Then it was still.

On the way home that night on the dark lake, Jonathan thought of the fish and the evening he had spent with his friend. It had been a good night, unless you were a fish.

He also thought again about the girl he had seen earlier up on the deck on the grand *EmmaLee. Damn!*

Chapter Five

It was a typical Saturday morning for Sally as she walked to work down Bridge Street, stopping in for coffee at her friend Ingrid's coffee shop. She had seen a few friends and chatted briefly. Her shop and the rest of the town were full of visitors in for the Venetian Festival. She had come down through the crowds of people on the sidewalk to her gallery at the end of the street. Her partner, Gwen Roberts, had already arrived and opened for business. A few people were milling around inside looking at the work she had on display. She nodded to Gwen with a smile and then went back into her studio and office.

There were a few phone messages from the previous day and a stack of mail that looked much too daunting this early in the morning. She sipped her coffee and looked through the messages. Sensing movement behind her, she turned and saw that Ben Clark was standing in the doorway.

"Good morning Sally, didn't mean to startle you."

"No...no, good morning."

Ben walked into the office. "May I?" he said, pointing to a chair next to her desk.

"Sure, would you like some coffee, or..."

He held up a cup from Ingrid's coffee shop.

"I see you've found the best coffee in town," Sally said. "Did you meet my friend, Ingrid?"

"She was so busy, I don't think she has time to meet anyone this morning," he said with a smile, taking a sip from his coffee. "You have a wonderful gallery here. I was just looking at some of the work. I assume that the *S. Thomason* signed on some of the paintings would be you?"

Sally took a deep breath and smiled, "Why yes, it is. What do you think?"

"I think they're incredible."

"Well, thank you. That's very nice of you. Which is your favorite?"

"The scene of Round Lake and the sailboats moored is wonderful. Have you done any with the *EmmaLee*?"

"No, I've never painted the *EmmaLee*. I have terrific old photos from my mother, but I just haven't gotten around to it. Actually, I was thinking of it yesterday and was able to take some great photos for more reference as you were bringing her into town."

Ben looked directly at her for a few moments, seeming to take in what she had said. Sally returned his gaze, a little uncomfortable looking him straight in the eye. She noticed for the first time that his eyes were a deep green, like the lake she thought. He was dressed in worn jeans, a plain white golf shirt and boat deck shoes that had obviously been worn for more than a few seasons.

He nodded slowly and said, "Would you have the time to paint her this summer?"

"The *EmmaLee*?"

"Yes, there is a perfect space at the head of the table in the ship's dining cabin. Your work would look absolutely terrific there."

"I have two other commissions I'm trying to finish," she said, hesitating. "I'm sure I can find some time."

"Well, take all you need."

"Do you have any thoughts on how you'd like to see the ship, in what setting?" she asked.

Ben thought for a moment. "I'm fascinated with the period when she was first here, back in the 30's and 40's. I understand she had her own boathouse around on the south side of the harbor. I would love to see you recreate that time and place."

"Let me give it some thought and perhaps do a few sketches before we decide. Would that be okay?"

Ben stood up. "That would be great. Whenever you have time. I really don't want to impose."

"I'll let you know as soon as I can," she promised.

He took another quick sip from his coffee. "I was taking a walking tour around the town when I happened to notice your shop. Again, I hate to impose, but do you have some time this morning to join me and show some of the sites only the locals know?"

Sally hesitated for a moment. She hated to leave Gwen alone on such a busy morning but then justified to herself that a short walk couldn't hurt.

"Sure, I can get away for a bit," she said. "Is there anything in particular you would like to see?"

"You decide. Are you sure it's not a bother?"

"No, not at all. Let me check in with Gwen out front and then we can go."

She was surprised how easy she felt with Ben Clark. Having heard a lot about him before his visit from George Hansen, she wasn't sure exactly what she had expected, probably a computer geek with an attitude. She hadn't been ready for how normal he seemed, despite of his wealth and success. She usually wasn't all that comfortable talking with men she didn't know particularly well, but for some reason she had felt at ease with Ben from their first meeting yesterday. Maybe it was their common connection to the *EmmaLee,* she thought.

She introduced him to Gwen on the way out. "Ben, this is my partner, Gwen Roberts."

"Hello, Ben. It's very nice to meet you," Gwen said, shaking his hand. "I love your boat!"

"Good morning and thank you," he said. "Would you mind if I borrowed Sally for a quick tour of your town?"

"No, of course not," Gwen answered. "Enjoy this beautiful morning."

Sally gave Gwen a quick hug and then led Ben out of the store and turned left up the main street of town. Out across the street the city park spread out before them with a wide green lawn that sloped down to the boat docks. They could see the *EmmaLee* tied up at the far end. They made their way through the crowds with Sally pointing out some of the shops and restaurants along the way. It was another warm summer morning with just a little breeze.

Sally took him on a wide circle through town, up Park Street showing him some of the older homes along the channel and talking about some of their history. They turned south on State Street and walked slowly by the old Congregational Church and the Harsha House, explaining that it now held the Historical Society. She encouraged him to come back in the afternoon when they were open to see their file on the *EmmaLee*, explaining that it held a lot of old photos and information about the ship.

They headed back down along Bridge Street and she turned them east down Belvedere along the south shore of Round Lake. She wanted to show him her grandparents' old home. They walked slowly down the quiet street. The large hardwood trees shaded the sidewalk and old homes. They came to a corner with a large grass lawn.

"This is where the Belvedere Hotel stood for many years," she said. "It was really quite grand back in its day. You'll have to see some of the pictures I have of my family here. And that's the

Casino down on the beach. They still use it for dinners and receptions. I'm told there used to be some lively parties there back in my mother's day."

She turned and looked at him. "I hope I'm not boring you."

"Absolutely not," Ben said. This is a wonderful little town."

"I'd like to show you my grandparent's house. My uncles sold it years ago after my mother died."

"Lead the way. I'd love to see it."

They walked back up the sidewalk toward town and a few blocks down, turned on a street going up a steep hill. They turned right at the next corner and she stopped in front of a big white Victorian house.

"They lived here for many years in the summer," Sally explained. "My mother, Emily Compton, grew up here and loved the place. I can remember coming over to visit my grandparents when I was a little girl and how big this house seemed to me then. I guess it still is pretty big," she said, looking over at him.

Ben was taking in the scene. "You've painted this home, haven't you? I saw it down at the gallery."

"Yes, it's one of my favorite pieces."

"You really captured it beautifully."

Sally looked at her watch. "I really need to get back to give Gwen some help. Would you mind if we headed back?"

"No, not at all. Thank you for taking so much of your time."

Ben walked with her back to town and to the door of the gallery. "I'd like to take you up on that offer to look through your family's photo albums. Let me know when a good time would be."

"Of course," she said, but before she could fully answer, he broke in.

"I've also invited a number of people to join us tonight on the EmmaLee for the festival boat parade. Do you think you could join us?"

Sally thought for a moment. She had been invited to go with the Hansen's on their sailboat tonight, but she was sure George would understand. "That sounds great. What time are you heading out?"

"Well, we're planning to start around six with a little dinner onboard. It's going to be very casual. I'm sure you'll know most of the people. Maybe Gwen would like to come along. George can't make it. He has a long history of sailing his own boat in the parade, I hear."

"Yes, this is his favorite weekend of the year," Sally said. "I'm sure you could see how excited he was yesterday when you got here."

He reached out for her hand. "Six o'clock then?"

She took his hand and felt the firm warmth of it. "I'll be there, thank you for the invitation. Maybe tomorrow or Monday we can make some time to look through those old albums."

"We can talk about it tonight," Ben said. "Remind me to show you the dining cabin where I'd like to hang your painting of the *EmmaLee*."

"That sounds fine. I'll look forward to it." She watched him smile and then turn and walk away through the crowds.

At a little after three that afternoon, Sally was in the gallery talking with some customers when she heard a loud commotion coming through the front door. Looking over, she saw Mary Alice Gregory walking in with two other women. Mary Alice was making wild gestures with her arms trying to give emphasis to whatever point she was making with her friends. Her voice seemed to carry, even over the loud street noise, and as usual, she was dressed immaculately. She spotted Sally at the back of the gallery and headed that way. Her friends fanned out to look at some of the work displayed.

Sally excused herself for a moment from her customers. "Mary Alice, how are you today?"

"Oh Sally, I'm fine, but I'm in a bit of a rush and maybe you can help. I'm going out on the *EmmaLee* with Ben tonight for the boat parade," she said with obvious delight and thinly veiled arrogance.

Sally didn't show any emotion, but inside she was struggling to keep calm. *I have no reason to be jealous of this woman.*

"What could I possibly do to help you," Sally finally answered.

"I'm looking for a welcome gift for Ben and I'd like something he could keep on the boat. Do you have any ideas?"

Sally swallowed hard and gathered herself, "Don't you think a nice bottle of wine would suffice?"

"Oh, come on, Sally. He probably has a wine cellar onboard with a thousand selections. I'd like a special piece he wouldn't be able to find anywhere else." Mary Alice noticed a collection of bronze sculptures of sailboats against the far wall. "Who are these by?" she asked, walking over to the work.

"I've just brought them in," Sally said, walking along behind. "A young artist from Petoskey. Her name is Williams."

Mary Alice picked one up and examined it quickly. Without bothering to ask the price, she said, "This will be perfect. Can you wrap it?"

Sally reached for the piece. "Of course, I'm sure Mr. Clark will appreciate your thoughtfulness," she said with a not-so-subtle tone of sarcasm.

Mary Alice didn't seem to notice the comment. She was already walking to the counter, pulling a credit card from her purse. When the transaction was completed and the wrapped package ready to go, Sally brought it out and set it on the counter. Mary Alice walked over to take her present.

"Well, it should be a beautiful evening for the parade," she said. "Ben is having a little party for a few of us before the parade."

"Oh, how nice," Sally answered. She didn't think it was worth the time to explain she would be there as well.

"Thank you, Sally," Mary Alice said. "I can always count on you when I'm in a pinch." She gathered up her friends and headed out into the street.

Sally stood watching, shaking her head in disbelief. This should be quite an evening.

There was a small band playing on the rear deck when Sally and Gwen arrived at the *EmmaLee* that evening. The little gathering Mary Alice had alluded to looked more like half the town onboard. Sally smiled, thinking how disappointed Ms. Gregory would be in having to share Ben with such a huge crowd. They came up on deck and were greeted immediately by waiters with glasses of wine and trays of food. They both took drinks and walked through the milling crowd toward the rear of the ship. Sally knew most of the guests and stopped to say hello several times along the way.

She and Gwen found some room along the rail, looking out over Round Lake and the dozens of large sailboats and motor yachts that were assembling for the festival parade. The boats were decorated with lights and banners. The parade would start just after dark and the illuminated and decorated boats were always a spectacular scene sailing out through the channel into Lake Charlevoix, then back again. Fireworks would accompany their journey and light up the sky as well.

Sally looked over the crowd seeing who else was in attendance.

Gwen touched her arm. "How does a guy throw together a bash like this with such short notice? And he's already had the boat decorated with what looks like ten million lights."

"It's amazing what you can do when you have a few extra zeros at the end of your bank statement," Sally said with a grin. She hadn't seen Ben, or Mary Alice.

"So how was your little walk around town with the man of the hour?" Gwen asked, taking a long sip from her wine.

"I don't think I bored him, too much. He seems genuinely interested in the town and the people. I'm sure he travels a lot, but I think the charms of sleepy little Charlevoix may have gotten to him."

"Or maybe the charms of Mary Alice Gregory," said Gwen, gesturing to the arrival of the woman coming toward them hanging on Ben Clark's arm. "She is a slick little package, isn't she?"

"I'm not sure if *slick* does her justice," Sally said. "*Sly* might be more appropriate."

They both laughed and saluted each other in a mock toast with their glasses. They watched the couple walk across the deck to the other side of the boat, stopping to talk to a small group of people. A waiter came by again and they traded their glasses for refills.

Although the wine was helping to dull the irritation Sally was trying to suppress, she couldn't help thinking about her suspicions of Mary Alice with her ex-husband. The ache from that relationship had never really left her, not so much because she still had feelings for the man, but because she had been so blindly trusting, then betrayed. She suddenly thought how unexpected it had been for Ben to invite Gwen along this evening. She wondered if he had heard about their relationship.

About two years after her divorce was final, she had met Gwen Roberts one morning when she had walked into the gallery. Gwen was in town from New York and staying with some friends out on the lake for a week. She was very impressed with Sally's paintings and explained she worked at a gallery back in Manhattan. They spent the morning sharing stories of the business and finally decided to have lunch.

Sally remembered the bond she felt with Gwen Roberts that first day. They saw each other again later in the week for drinks and stayed in touch over the next several months. Gwen had invited her to come out to New York for a visit. They had a wonderful time in the city.

A year later, Gwen came back to Charlevoix in June and never left. They became lovers later that summer and Sally found a new sense of fulfillment and trust with her. Gwen had moved into her house that fall and they had been together for the past ten years.

She had been surprised by her feelings for a woman. It had never happened to her in the past, but it had felt so natural and comfortable from the outset. There had been a few difficult times when Gwen grew frustrated with the small town and being away from the city, but they had settled in fairly well over the past few years.

She reached out now and took her hand. There was no secret about their relationship, but they tried to be discreet, not wanting others in this small town to be uncomfortable around them. Gwen was several years younger than Sally, just past forty. She was as tall as Sally but more athletic and rail thin from regular morning runs. Her brown hair was cut at shoulder length and hung straight. Her eyes were a soft hazel and Sally found herself looking deeply into them now. What a blessing, she thought, that she had found someone like Gwen when everything in her life had grown so dark.

"Thank you for coming with me tonight," she said. "You're being awfully tolerant of all this old family business."

"I just wish I had met your parents before the accident."

Sally looked away.

"I'm sorry," said Gwen. "I should know better."

Sally looked back out over the harbor and the boats. The light was growing dim in the late evening and the boat owners had turned on the multi-colored strings of lights that adorned their vessels. The scene was a jumbled mass of boats and people and horns blaring. Some of the boat crews had large slingshot water balloon launchers and were firing them at nearby boats.

"Let me show you the rest of the ship." Sally pulled Gwen by the arm and they started to make their way back to the main cabin door on this side of the ship. Ben Clark nearly bumped into them, coming from the other way.

"Well, hello ladies," he said. "You both look beautiful tonight. Thank you for coming."

Gwen spoke first, "We were just going below. I haven't had a chance to take a tour."

"I wish I could go with you," he said. "I owe you one, don't I Sally, but I've got some people up forward I'm supposed to say hello to. I'll try to catch up with you. Make yourselves at home." He smiled and walked away.

"God, he's good looking," Gwen said.

"Don't start," Sally responded. "Come on, let's go see where Ben wants to hang my painting in the dining area."

At the bottom of the steps they met young Megan who was coming out of her cabin. She was dressed in a summer print dress and white sandals.

"Hi, Megan. Do you remember me?"

"Sure, Sally," said the little girl.

"This is my friend, Gwen. Gwen, this is Ben's beautiful daughter, Megan."

The girl shook hands politely with Gwen and said, "Sally, do you have our painting of the *EmmaLee* done yet?"

The two women both laughed. Sally leaned down to eye level with Megan. "Honey, it takes a long time to finish a painting. It could be a couple of months at least."

"But, we'll be gone by then," she said with real concern.

"Oh, I'm sure we'll find a way to get it safely delivered to you." Sally stood up and took the girl's hand. "We were just taking a quick tour. Can you show us where the dining cabin is and where your father wants to hang the painting?"

"Sure, come on," she said excitedly.

Megan showed them all of her favorite places on the ship, including the big galley kitchen. At the dining cabin, they saw the wall Ben had indicated for the painting. The empty space sat above a built-in mahogany bar at the end of the room. Sally made a mental note of the colors of the room and the furniture.

Eventually they came back up to the deck and found the party to be in full swing. The band was playing a livelier tune now and many people were dancing in a group in the middle of the crowd.

Megan pulled on Sally's arm. "Sally, would you dance with me?"

Sally hesitated for a moment, then saw the genuine excitement in the little girl's eyes. "You bet!"

She turned and looked back at Gwen with a funny look as she made her way into the dancing crowd. The song was an old disco tune from the 80's, and the crowd was bouncing around wildly. Megan joined in and Sally found some sense of rhythm from the past and started dancing with her new little friend. It had been a long time since she had been on a dance floor and it felt great. She looked over and saw Ben dancing with Mary Alice. He smiled back at her, seemingly pleased that Sally was entertaining his daughter.

The song came to an end and everyone applauded the band. They started up again quickly with a Rolling Stones number and the crowd began dancing again on cue. Sally declined another dance offer from Megan, and they walked through the crowd back over to Gwen.

"You're a great dancer, Sally," said the youngest Clark.

"Yeah, you can really shake it, lady," said Gwen with a devilish smile.

Sally frowned at her friend, then thanked Megan for the compliment. "Were there any kids your age invited to the party tonight?" she asked.

"Yes, Mary Alice brought her nephew, Steven. He's going into seventh grade. He's kind of a nerd."

Sally and Gwen laughed. "Maybe he'd like to dance? What do you think?" Sally asked.

"I think I'm too young to dance with boys, don't you?"

"I think you're just the right age," Sally replied. "Why don't you go find him? I'll bet he'd really like to dance with you."

"Do you think so?" Megan asked.

"You'd better hurry before someone else asks him," Sally said.

She gave Sally a quick hug around the middle and then ran off.

"Well, she certainly is a cutie," said Gwen.

"Yes, she is. Hey, let's go up and get a good spot at the front of the boat for the parade. And let's find a waiter. I think I feel the need for more wine."

As the sun set beyond the hills of town, darkness eased in over the lake and the boats shined more brightly. The time had come for the boats to begin assembling and the crew of the *EmmaLee* worked to free her lines and get the ship underway. Sally had always thought it remarkable during Venetian Festival each year that there weren't more collisions with the heavy traffic of boats and the heavy volumes of alcohol being consumed onboard.

After a while, the boats had formed into a procession heading around the small circumference of Round Lake. It had been arranged for the *EmmaLee* to lead. It was a beautifully clear night and the spectacle of the boat parade was exhilarating. Sally stood with Gwen and got lost in the excitement of the moment. She was startled by a loud explosion and the start of the fireworks display overhead. She squeezed her friend's hand and thought back on whether her mother had stood in this same spot during the parade those many years ago.

Chapter Six

My friend Jonathan and I had our share of trouble back in those days. There was the time we were both out deer hunting over east of Boyne Falls. It was November of our junior year in high school. When would that have been? 1940, I guess. We had scouted out a piece of state land over the previous month, or so. There was a high ridge along a tree line. It gave us a great view of a long meadow that sloped away into a cedar swamp. We had seen some big bucks come out of the swamp just before dark on some of our scouting trips.

Early morning on opening day we were positioned about twenty-five yards apart up on the ridge with our backs against big oak trees, looking down over the meadow. Our rifles lay resting across our legs. We had arrived two hours earlier to hike in and get in position.

As the light started to show out to the east, the scene before us began to take shape. From the darkness, I could see the faint image of the far cedar swamp line, a darker shadow against the low grass of the meadow. Then, I saw several shadows move just the slightest bit and I could tell they were deer. I remember looking over toward Jonathan, but it was still too dark to make him out clearly and I didn't dare try to talk to him for fear of spooking the herd. I figured he was seeing what I was seeing.

I quietly brought my rifle up under my right arm and pressed the safety release. Several minutes that seemed like forever passed and the light continued to bring shape and form to the deer down below us. Now, I saw there were two bucks, both with nice racks, one on each end of a herd of about a dozen does and smaller fawns. It was light enough now, and I could see Jonathan was getting into position to shoot.

I thought to myself we needed to figure a way to time our shots together, so we could take both bucks and not spook the other away. My hands were shaking, and my breath felt like my chest would explode. Jonathan motioned to get my attention. He held up five fingers and began counting down one finger at a time.

I lifted my rifle and took aim on the buck nearest to me on the left side of the herd. Counting down silently to myself, I tried to steady my arms and take good aim just behind the shoulder of the big deer. "Three, two..." then explosions rang out down below us to the right. It sounded like twenty rifles, but it was just three, we were soon to find. I watched my deer jump suddenly and fall over motionless. Jonathan's deer startled and ran a few steps, then stumbled and fell. The rest of the herd ran off in scattered directions toward the swamp. Then, there were more shots and one of the does fell in a heap.

I looked over at Jonathan in absolute shock. What in the hell had happened? I looked back down across the meadow and saw three men walking out of the woods from where the rifles had erupted. I threw my own rifle down to the ground next to me in disgust. I felt a mindless anger building up in me. I jumped up and ran down the hill toward the men and the fallen deer. I heard Jonathan yell something to me, but I couldn't make it out.

I yelled out in anger, "You shot my goddamned deer, you sonsofbitches!"

I kept running down the hill. I was within a few dozen steps of the men who were just squatting down by the first deer, when I yelled again. "Get the hell outta there!"

The three of them stood and turned to confront me. They held their rifles pointing down at the grass in front of them. I pulled up, breathing so hard I could barely speak. I was only a few steps away now and I could smell the whiskey on them even from where I stood. I didn't recognize any of them. They were all grown men, probably in their 40's.

One had a gray beard and spoke first. "Who the hell are you?" he said in a deep slow voice, slurred from the whiskey.

I couldn't catch my breath and just stood there staring at them. Then I heard Jonathan walk slowly up behind me. He stopped by my right shoulder and I saw his rifle barrel pointing out to the ground in front of us.

The gray beard spoke again. "You two boys better get the hell outta here now!" he spat.

I about fainted then when he cocked his rifle and put another shell in the chamber. Jonathan spoke with a voice so calm that to this day, it still amazes me. "Those are two nice bucks you boys shot there. Seems to me like we were just a little too late, weren't we, George?"

I still couldn't find words. My anger burned through my cheeks and I was shaking, standing there next to my friend.

I heard Jonathan speak again. "Nice shootin', boys. Come on George, let's get moving."

He grabbed me by the sleeve of my jacket and started pulling me back up towards the hill.

"You better get your buddy the hell outta here son," the older man said again, taking a pint bottle out his jacket and taking a long drink.

I watched the three men laugh at us and pass the bottle around as we backed our way up the hill.

It wasn't the first time Jonathan's cooler head kept me from getting in way over my own head. Years later, we would laugh about that morning and I would get mad again at Jonathan for not holding up just three fingers.

Jonathan looked forward to Sundays like little children looked forward to Christmas Eve. His life was hard, no harder than most others in this small town, but he worked hard at the boatyard. During the school year, he studied late most nights. School didn't come easy to him, but he kept his grades up. Even during the school year there was work to be done at home, household chores and work on the boats. There was so little time left and he was usually so tired he would fall into bed at the end of the day.

The McKendry family did take a break for Sundays though. Of Scottish blood and from a long line of Presbyterians, they rarely missed Sunday service with Pastor Reynolds at the Congregational church. Only Luke had broken away lately and had stopped joining them for the walk to church on Sunday mornings.

He sat with his parents and listened to them sing the hymns and recite the prayers. Listening to the pastor and his lesson, he said his own prayers for his family, particularly for his brother and he prayed for guidance in his own life.

When the choir sang the final hymn and led the congregation out of the sanctuary, Jonathan was the first to break and head for home, running far ahead of his family. Sunday afternoons were his time and he rarely wasted a moment.

Today, he was meeting Catherine Hansen out at the beach at North Point. She was bringing a picnic lunch and they would swim, look for Petoskey stones and lay in the sun together. She had been his girl for the past two years. He was thinking of Catherine now as he ran back to the house to change his clothes... her blonde hair... her new black bathing suit... her tanned legs.

"Thank God for Sundays!" he yelled as he ran along with thoughts of Catherine's new bathing suit anxious on his mind.

Twenty minutes later, he was riding his bike through town on his way to the beach. There was a lot of traffic along Bridge Street with people returning home from church and summer people with places to be. Jonathan rode quickly through the traffic, swerving to miss pedestrians trying to cross the street. A black convertible pulled out suddenly from a side street in front of him. He didn't have time to turn or stop. He instinctively skidded the bike sideways and slid to the pavement with the bike tumbling out in front of him. Both he and the bike ended in a pile next to the car that had also stopped when the driver saw the boy on the bike.

Jonathan was trying to get up and check the condition of his bike and his body at the same time. He heard voices above him in the car. A face peered over the driver's door and looked down at him. It was a younger man, his hair neatly combed back. Jonathan recognized him as the one on the boat standing with the Compton girl the other night.

"Are you blind? You need to watch where you're going, son," the driver scolded in a harsh tone.

Jonathan heard laughter from other people in the car.

"It's a damn good thing you didn't scratch this car, son, or I'd have to kick your ass all the way down Bridge Street," the young man said.

Jonathan got to his feet. He could now see that there were three other boys in the car. His legs and hands were burning from the scrapes and cuts from the pavement. They were still laughing at him.

Jonathan swallowed hard to gain his composure, but his anger got the best of him. "That looks like a stop sign there. You have trouble reading?" he said, looking directly into the eyes of the driver.

The passengers in the car grew silent and waited for their friend to respond. He sat for a moment, then reached down and pulled the door latch and opened his door slowly. He got out and stepped within a few inches of Jonathan's face.

"I'm not sure I heard you correctly. You want to repeat that?" the driver said, his eyes seething with a threatening glare. A crowd had gathered now, watching the confrontation.

Jonathan felt a fire burning up within. He was telling himself to back down, but he just couldn't. He looked beyond the driver and saw the three other boys were getting out of the car, too. *This will not turn out well*, he thought as he tried to quickly gauge the danger.

"I asked you a question, son," the driver said now. "Are you deaf *and* blind?" he said with more calm in his voice now, knowing his friends were behind him.

Jonathan looked him square in the eyes. "If you and I have a problem here, then why don't we walk alone down behind the store there and see if we can't settle this." He spoke slowly and with as much menace as he could muster.

Someone grabbed him from behind. It was the Sheriff, Willy Potts. He had been Sheriff of Charlevoix County as long as anyone could remember. He filled his uniform to full capacity with a girth that spread generously out over his gun belt.

"What's going on here, gentlemen?" the portly old police officer asked.

No one answered. Jonathan kept staring into the eyes of the driver.

"Are you okay, Jonathan?" Potts asked.

"I've been better."

"Why don't you boys get back in your car there and clear the street for me. You understand?"

Connor Harris ignored the request and continued to face down Jonathan. The sheriff edged his way between the two boys and stood facing Connor. "I said get out of here, and I mean now!" The sheriff pushed his big belly up against Connor's. "Now!"

Connor slowly backed away toward his car. He motioned for his friends to get back in the automobile. He pointed at Jonathan. "I'll be seeing you down the road, son." He turned away. "Come on fellas." He gave Jonathan one more dark look, then got in the car and pulled out into traffic.

Potts turned to Jonathan. "You sure you're okay? You got some nasty road burns there."

"I'll be fine."

"You stay away from those types. We don't need that kind of trouble around here."

"Yeah, right," Jonathan said.

The sheriff walked away.

Jonathan looked down at his bike and the people milling around him. Most looked away sheepishly and started moving on. George Hansen came running up, out of breath with a wild look in his eye.

"I just heard you were gettin' into a scrape down here. I was having a soda and Billy ran in and told me you were staring down a bunch of summer boys," George said, trying to catch his breath.

"I'm okay." Jonathan reached down and picked up his bike. It seemed to be in working order. "Look, I'm meeting Catherine out at the beach. I gotta go."

"You know, I shouldn't be letting you run around with my sister," George said.

"Aw, shut up." Jonathan pushed his friend back and got on his bike. "It's a little late to start playing big brother."

"You behave now, and you let me know if those summer boys start givin' you a hard time again," George said. "You and me can take those candy asses. You know that."

"Yeah right, George. Thanks for backing me up. I'll see ya. You want to go fishin' tonight?"

"When and where? I'll be there."

"I'll stop by your house after dinner... around seven." Jonathan pushed away and started up the hill across the bridge over the channel.

"You behave yourself now, McKendry," he heard his friend calling out as he rode away.

A few minutes later, he parked his bike in a small shaded pull-off in the woods leading up to the sand dunes and the beach. He started up the narrow path toward the lake. Shadows from the heavy tree cover dappled the sand path and low brush scratched at his legs. The burning and pain from his crash had subsided and he was thinking now of Catherine, the confrontation pushed to the back of his mind.

Catherine was really the first girl he had ever fallen for. They had played together occasionally as younger children when he had been over at George's house. It had been just a couple of years ago he had started seeing her in a new way. She had been the first to start taking more interest in him. First, they went to a few movies together and then a dance at school. Soon, it was a steady thing.

Jonathan wasn't sure what love was supposed to feel like, but he knew this felt pretty intense. He found himself thinking about Catherine often at night when he was lying awake in bed, fantasies of youth spinning through his head. They had begun to get more intimate with each other lately and Catherine was always playful and eager when they kissed or lay together on the beach.

At times, he found himself thinking about being with Catherine forever, as his wife and having children and a life together with her. It wasn't an unpleasant feeling. She was sixteen, a year younger than he and her brother George. She was a bright girl and Jonathan often asked her to help with his school work. She had the Hansen complexion, smooth skin that tanned quickly and freckles under her eyes and across the bridge of her sunburned nose. Her blonde hair was long, almost halfway down her back. She had an easy way with people and had a lot of friends.

The past few days though, thoughts about the Compton girl kept creeping into his mind. He would quickly try to push those thoughts aside and chastise himself. He would tell himself there couldn't be any harm in just thinking about the girl, what it would be like to be with her and to be part of the life she led.

The path widened as he reached the low dunes. The sun was hot, and the sand burned at his bare feet. He walked more quickly. There were large cumulus clouds drifting overhead, bright masses moving slowly with the breeze across the summer sky. He heard the shore waves crashing up ahead. He reached the top of the dunes and saw the vast panorama of Lake Michigan spread out before him. Well down to his left were the pier and the channel into Round Lake. Off to his right was the slow curve of North Point with large rocks breaking the water well out into the lake.

Catherine was sitting on a towel down by the water with her back to him, looking out over the water. A small picnic basket sat beside her. She had her new black swimming suit on, he noticed.

He walked up quietly behind her, taking his shirt off as he approached. When he got within range, he threw his shirt and caught her in the back with it.

She turned and gave him a disapproving scowl, then jumped up and ran over to him. She jumped into his arms and hugged him close to her. He felt her warm body ease into him and then she pulled back and looked into his eyes and kissed him.

He closed his eyes and savored the feel of her lips and the closeness of her body. He could feel the press of her breasts against him. He felt himself getting a bit too excited and he pushed her away gently in embarrassment and took her by the hand over to the towel and they sat down together.

She noticed his wounds. "What in the world have you done to yourself now?" she asked.

"I'm fine. I dumped my bike on the way over. Got scraped up a little. I'll be fine."

She touched the wound on his left knee. He thought again about the run-in with the summer boy. He knew it was just a matter of time until he would face him again.

Emily Compton sat on the front veranda of their house in a white wicker chair. Next to her sat her friend, Louise Kelly. Louise and the Kelly family were from Chicago and in the summer, they lived across the channel, over on the other side of Round Lake. Emily and Louise had become friends as little girls and spent most of their free time together. They had just attended church with the rest of the Compton family. When they came back to the house, they asked the cook, Ellie, for some lemonade. They sat now on the veranda, enjoying the cool beverage and sharing stories.

"You and Connor were getting quite friendly the other night at the party on the *EmmaLee*," Louise said, trying to get her friend to divulge more about her relationship with the handsome Mr. Harris.

Emily blushed with embarrassment and took a sip of the cool lemonade to think about her reply. She swallowed and looked at her friend. "What do you really think of Connor?" she asked. "He can be so nice and charming, then the next minute this dark cloud will come over him."

"He's got a little of a wild side, I hear," Louise answered. "I think that makes him all the more intriguing."

"Oh, he is definitely intriguing," Emily said.

"Has he tried to kiss you?" Louise asked.

Emily laughed and said, "Now if I tell you, I'll be reading about it in the Charlevoix paper next week."

"Oh, come on," Louise pleaded. "We always share."

"Connor took me for a ride last week in his new car. We went out to the turnaround at North Point and watched the sunset." She paused.

"Go on. What did he try?" Louise asked with growing excitement.

Emily looked over her shoulder to see if anyone was close enough to hear their conversation.

"It was a beautiful sunset," she teased.

"Are you going to tell me or not?"

"Well, by the time we got our clothes back on..."

Louise jumped out her chair. "Emily, what did you do?"

"I'm kidding, Louise. Nothing happened. He put his arm around me. We watched the sun go down."

"What about when he dropped you off?"

"He walked me up here on the porch and..."

"He kissed you, *goodnight,* " Louise said, finishing her friend's sentence.

"Yes, he kissed me *goodnight.*"

Louise was obviously enjoying all these revelations. "I'll bet he can really kiss?"

"He's not bad at it," Emily said with a giggle.

She saw her father coming out of the front door. She pushed Louise back down into her chair.

Stewart Compton was just past sixty years old. His hair had gone mostly gray and he had been putting on weight steadily for the past twenty years. Still dressed in his suit from church, he moved with the calm confidence of a man of accomplishment and high status.

"What are you girls up to?" he asked.

Louise tried to hide a nervous laugh. Emily answered, "Just discussing the pastor's message, Daddy."

The elder Compton laughed. "Oh, I'm sure that's the case. Hey, I'm having the crew get the *EmmaLee* ready for a cruise this afternoon. How would you two like to come along? We're going to head out to Beaver Island, do a little fishing, go swimming and have some dinner."

"Absolutely," said Emily. "Can you go?" she asked her friend.

"Let me call my mother."

Emily's father headed back into the house, then turned and said, "Get some clothes together and a bathing suit. We'll be leaving right after lunch. Why don't you two come in and we'll have Ellie throw a quick bite together before we go." He disappeared through the front door.

The girls got up to prepare for the trip. They grabbed their glasses and pushed the chairs back to their proper position.

"Has Connor let you know if he's going to school this fall in Ann Arbor with you, yet?" Louise asked.

"He's been accepted at Northwestern, but he's talking about taking a year off and traveling before he starts school."

"That's probably just as well," Louise answered. "I've heard there are some awfully nice boys down there in Ann Arbor."

Emily pulled her friend toward to the front door. "Do you ever think of anything else? Let's go call your mother."

Jonathan and Catherine were eating sandwiches and other food she had brought. It was spread out before them on towels along with two bottles of *Coca-Cola*. The breeze had picked up and was now blowing strongly in their face off the lake. The waves had grown and were crashing loudly on the shore.

66

Occasionally, one large wave would crash up high enough to touch their feet. It was close to 3 o'clock and the sun was falling lower off to the southwest.

Jonathan felt the sun burning his forehead and shoulders, but he didn't care. He rested back on his elbows and closed his eyes, savoring his Sunday and the time with Catherine. He reached over and laid an arm across her stomach. He moved closer so he could kiss her. She moved into him and they shared a long kiss and embrace.

He tried to move closer and knocked over his drink. They both sat up quickly trying to recover the spilled beverage and keep it from getting all over everything.

"Good timing, McKendry," she scolded.

Jonathan was helping to clean up the mess when he noticed a large ship coming out through the channel, well down the beach at the pier. He knew at once it was the *EmmaLee*. The main bridge cabin towered over the top of the pier. Its brilliant white color was set-off in stark contrast to the old gray Lifesaving Station and green tree-covered hills up behind the channel.

Catherine looked to see what had caught her boyfriend's attention. "Is that the Compton's boat?" she asked.

Jonathan nodded.

"I've heard Mr. Compton has more money than the Rockefellers," she said, taking Jonathan's hand in hers.

"I imagine they have enough to get by," Jonathan said.

The ship made its way out of the channel and they could now see the full length of the hull and its magnificent lines.

"They will never build another ship more beautiful," Jonathan said in a slow whisper-like voice.

"You are absolutely impossible! Here I am with you on the beach, lying in your arms and you're more fascinated by an old boat."

"I'll bet they're heading out to Beaver Island from the course they're taking."

"Jonathan!"

"What?"

"Forget the boat."

"Let's just watch her for a minute."

Catherine rolled over on her stomach, showing her disgust with her boyfriend's distraction.

"They say she has ten cabins."

"Ohmigod!" Catherine wailed. "I don't care how many cabins or anything else. Would you come over here?" She turned back over invitingly.

Jonathan looked away from the boat and down at her. She held her arms up for him. He responded finally and moved over, even though he was still thinking about the *EmmaLee*. He tried to imagine how many people were onboard and where they were headed. He thought about the captain up on the bridge guiding her through the heavy seas, cutting the big waves easily with the ship's sleek hull. He tried to keep his mind from drifting to thoughts of the Compton girl.

Yes, they were heading out to Beaver Island.

The captain and crew of the *EmmaLee* had pulled into Paradise Bay on the northeast side of the island. It was well protected from the heavy wind and waves on this summer afternoon and the big ship rested calmly in the quiet bay.

Beaver Island had been the home of James Jesse Strang who had declared himself King of Beaver Island. Traveling with a group of Mormons in the 1840's, he had explored the remote island up in the northern reaches of Lake Michigan. The island had seemed a perfect refuge for his band, sitting twenty miles offshore of what was then the early settlement of Charlevoix. He found it to his liking and settled there and soon attracted a large following from the Church of Latter-day Saints. Many Mormons were attracted to the area and lived a strained existence with the "gentiles" who were also trying to settle the land around Charlevoix at that time.

Strang's controversial reign was abruptly ended when he was assassinated under mysterious circumstances in 1856. The Mormon colony slowly dissolved after his passing and the island now supported a small population of hearty souls and crowds of visitors coming over by ferry and other boats during the summer months.

Emily and Louise stood at the opening in the rail along the starboard side of the boat. They had changed into swimming suits and were trying to muster the courage to jump down into the cool waters of the bay. Emily's two brothers were already in, splashing and yelling for the girls to join them.

Except for a few local boats tied up at the docks at the end of the inlet, the *EmmaLee* was the only boat moored out in the bay. She sat motionless in the calm waters with anchor lines securing her. Emily noticed movement and scanned the barren shore. A family of raccoons scampered along the shoreline, a mother and three babies. They paid no attention to the big ship, or the commotion coming from the lake. She watched them scurry over to a fish washed up on the sand. They settled in to make their meal. Overhead, a large brown hawk soared effortlessly, testing the currents and looking below for signs of its next prey.

Emily had always loved these adventures to remote islands on the big ship. She was glad Louise was able to come. Her father and mother came up behind them. They had put on swimming suits and were ready for a refreshing leap into the cool waters.

"Okay girls, let's not jam up the diving platform here," said Emily's father.

"Daddy, it's too cold. I know it's just too cold," said Emily, smiling at her friend.

Stuart Compton put his arm around his daughter's shoulder then picked her up suddenly under her legs. Emily squealed in surprise and the next thing she knew, she was flying through the air in her father's arms, the cold green surface of the lake coming rapidly up to greet them. The shock of the water's bracing chill and the huge explosion of water from her father's weight took her breath away. He released her and she felt herself being pulled back to the surface slowly from the air in her lungs.

The world was suddenly quiet and cold, and she watched her air bubbles floating to the surface beside her. She could see the sun above, a muted bright yellow ball of fire on the riffled surface. She burst through, gasping for air, just as her friend landed beside her, sending water in all directions. Her father came up as well and shook his head, spraying water on her from his hair.

"Daddy, I can't believe you did that! You're terrible!"

He laughed and swam over toward his sons. Emily noticed her mother was still up above them at the rail. Her skin was a pale white against the dark royal blue of her suit. She had a white bathing cap on to protect her hair.

"Come on mother, it's wonderful," Emily invited.

Her mother seemed to hesitate, then took two steps backward, out of sight from the girls down below. They heard a scream and watched as her mother ran and leaped out from the side of the boat. Her arms flapped wildly, and she continued to scream until she was swallowed up by the water. She came up moments later, gasping at the cold water, droplets twinkling around her pale blue eyes.

Emily swam over to her and gave her a hug. "That was the most beautiful dive, mother."

"A picture of grace, I'm sure."

A crew member threw boat cushions over the side for them to float on. Each of the women reached for one and propped themselves up comfortably, bobbing on the surface. Her father swam back over and pulled two cushions under his large frame.

"Emily, I was just telling the boys I think we need to get a new runabout for you. You're old enough now to have your own boat," the elder Compton said, slicking his sparse hair back with a free hand.

"What kind of boat, Daddy?" she asked with growing excitement.

"Oh, I think a nice inboard, twenty-five or so feet would be plenty of boat. We'll stop over at the boatyard tomorrow and see what they have."

Emily swam over and gave her father a kiss on the cheek.

Later, they had dressed and took a small launch over to a remote beach in the inlet. The staff had arrived earlier and had set up for dinner of fried whitefish over a big roaring beach fire. A table and chairs had been set up with linens and china. The chef poured wine for the adults and the children drank iced tea and helped with the fire.

The Compton family dined together with their guest, the young Miss Kelly, looking out over Paradise Bay and the beauty of Beaver Island and the *EmmaLee*, just offshore. Music was played just loudly enough on the ship that it provided a soothing backdrop for the meal on the beach. A full moon showed faintly on the horizon in the early evening light. The mosquitoes seemed more interested in the big fire than in the diners. Servants hovered nearby, filling glasses and serving more food.

Emily could hear conversation all around her, but she was lost in thought, thinking about her new boat.

Chapter Seven

Sally woke with a start. She had been dreaming and something unsettled her. She looked around the bedroom and saw it was a little past six o'clock on the alarm beside her bed. Daylight was just beginning to make its way through the house and the large bedroom that looked out on the back lawn and to the lake. There were sulking gray clouds moving quickly across the sky, tinged reddish orange from the rising sun. She saw Gwen was still asleep beside her.

She tried to remember her dream and, as with most dreams, she was having trouble connecting the random fragments of it. Parts of the dream would start to come back to her, then her mind would throw up a gray wall and the memory would slip away. Then, she remembered she had been on a beach and she was trying to catch up with someone.

Gwen stirred and made a soft, low moan. Sally pushed the covers away as gently as she could and walked quietly into her closet.

A half hour later, with a hot cup of coffee in her hand, she was walking down the narrow path on the face of the sand dune to the beach below. The clouds were breaking apart now and brilliant blue patches showed through, promising another beautiful summer day. She reached the flat expanse of sand below her house and walked down toward the water. There was a light offshore breeze just starting to build. Soft gusts blew by coming down from the dunes and chilled her. She watched the wind puffs chase out across the still morning waters like frightened schools of minnows scurrying across the surface.

Her feet were bare, and she rolled up the legs of her pants so she could walk along the shoreline. Her first step into the water delivered the expected cold shiver. Within a few steps she grew accustomed to the water's temperature and it felt soothing and fine. The brown sand along the waterline was soft beneath each step, and she left deep footprints as she made her way north along the beach. She saw nothing but empty beach and dunes all the way up to where the beach turned away around North Point.

Sally thought again of her dream. *Who was I trying to catch up with?*

She sensed someone coming up from behind and turned to see Gwen running toward her across the sand from the path. She had her running shorts on and a black sports bra. Sally always marveled at her friend's energy in the early morning. Gwen came up beside her and slowed to the pace she was making along the shore.

"Why don't you join me for a change this morning?" Gwen asked. "It's only two miles or so up to the Point and back. You'll be amazed how good you'll feel."

"Is that after I get out of traction and intensive care?" Sally responded.

"Okay, but I'm not going to give up on you. You know that, don't you?"

Sally smiled and kissed her on the cheek. "I guess I've always known that."

Gwen answered with a reassuring nod and turned to continue with her morning run. Sally watched her moving away, running with a smooth and graceful motion. She felt a tear welling up in her eye and wiped it away quickly. She took a long sip from her coffee and watched her friend grow steadily smaller down the beach.

She felt tired, even though she had walked just a short distance. She backed away from the water and sat down cross-legged on the sand. Some of her coffee splashed out of the cup and she watched the stain spread and seep into her jeans. She felt as if she could see all of the energy in her body drifting away on the morning breeze. She placed the coffee cup down in the sand and leaned back on her elbows.

Looking up, she saw the clouds drifting by and a few gulls soaring on the currents. She closed her eyes and tried to find the place within her that was suddenly so troubled. She hadn't seen it coming. There had been no warning. The dream had touched a nerve of doubt and anxiety somewhere deep within her. *What's the matter with me now?*

Was it something with Gwen, some missed signal about their relationship? Was it the recurring guilt she felt about her last days with her parents and the accident? Had her former husband's indiscretions come back to haunt her again in some new and perverse way? It was an overwhelming weight upon her soul that struck so suddenly she was frightened by its intensity. If she could only make the images focus in her brain. The pieces were still floating out there, trying to connect.

Looking down the beach, Sally saw Gwen was just a small spot, barely visible now in the distance. Maybe she had been taking Gwen for granted. She hadn't sensed any issues beyond the normal and trivial conflicts in their lives together. Earlier in their time as a couple, Sally had been forced to deal with feelings of doubt about a relationship with another woman and the normal fears of taking life in such a different direction. She also had to admit to herself she was concerned with what other people would think. Her parents were gone and her only close family was her two uncles. They had both come to love Gwen as much as she had.

With her friends in the community, the whole notion of the two of them together had just sort of slowly worked its way into the regular routine of things. After a while, she wasn't self-conscious or uncomfortable with her relationship with Gwen. But, it had taken time, she had to admit. It made her feel guilty to remember those times and those feelings, but they were real.

She reluctantly let her mind start to drift back to the night of the accident. She felt the familiar cold fear well up within her. She was practiced at allowing her inner defenses to come forward quickly to block the images and the memories. She stood and began running. She ran to the dunes and up to the house, leaving her coffee cup tipped on its side in the sand.

Ben called at half past ten and asked if it was still a good time to come over to look at her old albums. He wanted to bring Megan with him, as well. Sally had managed to collect herself. When Gwen had returned from her run, she didn't seem to sense anything was wrong. She had showered, grabbed a quick breakfast and headed down to the gallery, leaving Sally alone in the house. The ringing phone had startled her. She had been sitting in the living room staring out at the lake.

At first, she was tempted to say *no* to him. Today really isn't such a good day, she had wanted to say. But, the distraction of having someone else in the house seemed to be the type of escape she needed. She invited them to come over around noon for some lunch so she could spend a few hours down at the gallery.

After she hung up, it occurred to her there was little, if any food in the house. She showered quickly, then ran around to tidy up the house and then she drove up to the grocery store and picked up some food.

What do billionaires eat for lunch? What do little girls eat for lunch? She decided to keep things simple with a salad from the deli and some basic sandwich items. For Megan, she bought some peanut butter and jelly, just in case.

When she returned to the house, it was 11:45. She put the food away and walked into the living room. She looked at the photo albums on the bookshelf. There were three of them stacked together amid the other books, artwork and mementos on the shelves. She was starting to regret her invitation to the Clarks. Did she really want to go back again through all of these old memories, particularly after this morning's episode on the beach?

The doorbell rang. She took a deep breath, still looking at the albums. She forced herself to turn away and go to the door. She had put on a pair of khaki shorts and a simple white t-shirt. It was her home after all. Why worry about pretense?

She opened the door and saw Ben and Megan standing on the front porch. Ben was holding his daughter's hand. Sally forced a smile and tried to mask the ache she was feeling inside.

"Good morning," she managed.

"Hi, Sally. You have a great house!" Megan said, squirming with youthful excitement. "Daddy says you're right on the beach. Can I go look?"

"Sure, come on in." Sally led them toward the back of the house to the sun porch. She noticed Ben pausing along the way to look at some of her paintings on the walls.

"You have a wonderful view, Sally. How long have you had this house?" he asked as he joined them on the back porch.

"My parents bought this house back in the 50's. It was originally built twenty or so years before that. I grew up here and when my parents were gone, I just never saw fit to leave."

"Well I can understand why," he said. "It's a beautiful house and your paintings certainly help to bring it alive."

"Daddy, can I go down to the beach?"

Ben turned to Sally, "Is that okay?"

"Of course," Sally said. "Just be careful on the path. It's pretty steep in places. The water is very shallow, but don't go out past your knees, okay?"

The little girl ran out the back door and disappeared over the ridge of the dunes.

"Thank you again for having us over," Ben said. "Again, I hope this is a good time for you. I hate to impose on your Sunday."

"No, it's fine," Sally answered. "I have to get back down to the gallery this afternoon to help Gwen, but this will be just fine. Would you help me in the kitchen for a moment? We can bring some lunch out here."

A few minutes later they were back on the sun porch sitting around a table with a tray of food and a pitcher of iced tea mixed with lemonade.

"Sally, the boat parade last night was incredible," Ben said. "I'm sorry we couldn't spend more time with you and Gwen. I had so many guests, the night just seemed to slip away. I hope you had a good time, and thanks for dancing with Megan."

"No, we had a very nice time. I hadn't danced in years. It was a lot of fun," Sally said.

She poured them both a drink. "I saw the dining cabin and the space you mentioned for the painting of the *EmmaLee*. I'll have a few sketches to share with you by the end of the week."

"Great, I can't wait to see them."

There was an awkward pause in the conversation. Sally took a long sip from her glass. Ben was looking out at the lake.

She flinched in surprise when he suddenly spoke again, still looking out past the dune line. "Gwen seems so nice. How long have the two of you been...?" he paused, obviously embarrassed for bringing up the subject.

"How long have we been together?" she replied with a smile, trying to soften the edge of his discomfort.

"I'm sorry, it's really..."

"Ben, it's okay. Gwen and I have been together for quite some time now. She's originally from New York. We met when she was in town one summer on vacation with some friends."

"She seems very nice. Is she an artist, also?"

"No, she ran a small gallery in New York. She's been very helpful to the business here. She has a great sense for it."

"I can tell. You have a wonderful collection," he said, hoping to change the direction of the conversation.

"Are you hungry? Let's get some food started here."

They kept busy in silence for a few minutes, making the sandwiches and preparing plates with salad and some fruit she had cut up. Megan came running back over the hill and joined them at the table on the porch. They ate their lunch, making idle conversation about the boat parade and the party from the previous night. Sally watched Megan eat with enthusiasm and ask politely for more fruit. She chattered on about the boy she had danced with.

Sally struggled to keep her emotions in check. She could feel the dark tide building again within her. She tried to smile as Megan rambled on, but she was struggling to keep her composure, not really hearing what the little girl was saying.

"Sally, are you okay?" Ben finally broke in.

Sally sat back in her chair and looked across at him. Her eyes were growing moist and she knew she was going to start crying. "Could you excuse me just for a minute?" she finally said. "I'll be right back." She got up quickly and walked into the kitchen.

She ran water into the sink and splashed some on her face. She leaned on the counter, her head down, trying to hold back the flood of tears. She could hear Megan still chattering out on the porch. *She is such a beautiful child.*

She sensed Ben in the doorway to the kitchen.

"We've obviously come at a bad time," he said. "I'm really sorry."

She tried to find the words to protest and say everything was okay. She just stood there staring at him.

"We should really try to do this another time. Is there anything I can do?" he asked.

She didn't respond.

"I'll call you later to make sure you're feeling better," he said.

She nodded, feeling numb all over and still unable to speak.

"Thank you for lunch. I hope I didn't say anything..."

"No... no, it's not that at all," she answered, wiping tears from both cheeks.

"I'll call you," he said, and turned and walked away.

She heard them leaving and the front door closing behind them.

Chapter Eight

I never doubted my friend Jonathan would realize his dreams. You could tell just from looking into his eyes. He had a sense of purpose that was unmistakable. I often teased him about being so serious all the time. It's not that he wasn't fun to be around. He had a great sense of adventure and a spirit that was contagious as hell. It was more that he felt compelled to stay true to the course he imagined for his life. I think he was afraid if he let the dreams get even the slightest distance away, he'd lose them and never find them again.

He learned a love of building boats from his father and grandfather. They ignited the early spark that grew. He knew he had to go to college to study design and engineering if he was ever to build the boats he saw in his dreams. He wanted more than to run the family business and build a few small boats each year for the summer people. Every time he saw that boat, the EmmaLee, you could tell from his reaction he was watching his dream come to life right before his eyes. He was mesmerized by the damned thing.

During that summer before the war, we started to talk about what we would do if our country decided to enter the battle. Jonathan talked a lot about joining the Navy. I'm sure he wanted to be near the ships. It was all part of the dream.

Jonathan awoke from a deep sleep. He heard his brother knocking around their room. It was still too dark to see him clearly. He held the big alarm clock up to the little light coming through the window. It was five in the morning.

"Luke, where in the hell have you been?" he asked, sitting up and reaching for the lamp between their beds. His brother sat across from him on his own bed. Jonathan could smell the whiskey on him. "Luke, are you okay?"

"Just shut up and go back to sleep," his brother snarled. "And leave that light alone."

Jonathan had heard the slur in his talk and had seen him in this condition far too often. He turned on the light and both of them covered their eyes.

"Godammit, Jonathan! You're gonna wake the whole damn family," Luke whispered as he fell back onto the bed, trying to shield his eyes from the light. Jonathan squinted through the blinding glare of the light bulb. He saw his brother's clothes were torn and dirty. His hands were covered in dirt and what looked like dried blood.

He walked over to the bed and pulled his brother's arm away from his face. Luke tried to turn away, but Jonathan could see he had been badly beaten. There was dried blood all over his face and several welts and bruises. One eye was partially swollen shut. Some of the blood had dripped down unto his shirt.

"Who'd you get in a scrap with?" Jonathan asked.

"Just shut up and leave me alone!"

"Luke, we got to get you cleaned up before morning."

Luke turned toward his brother. "If you want to help, get the bottle out of my drawer there." He pointed to the dresser by the far wall.

"You don't need any more to drink."

"Just get it or I'll have to whip your ass, too."

Instead, Jonathan went quietly out into the hall and down to the bathroom. He brought back a wet towel. Luke had turned out the light and curled up on his bed facing the wall. Jonathan stood for a few moments thinking about how sad it had been to watch his older brother slipping away.

As a younger boy, Jonathan had always looked up to Luke. It had pained him to see kids teasing his brother and ostracizing him because of the crippling disability with his leg. Luke had always kept to himself and had few friends. But, he had been kind to Jonathan in those earlier years. He had been a good big brother, helping him out around the boatyard or making time to go fishing. It had been the past couple of years the decline had begun noticeably. The drinking just kept getting worse. The moods became darker.

Jonathan couldn't place any single event that may have touched off the fall. It became more noticeable when Luke finished high school and went to work full-time for their father in the boatyard. If ever he had expressed an ambition in life, it had been to join the military and get away from home. He had gone to Detroit that first summer after he finished school to take a physical for the Army. Apparently, there was no room for boys with less than two healthy legs. Luke received a letter a few weeks later informing him he had failed the physical. He never talked about the military again.

Jonathan threw the wet towel at his brother's back and climbed into his own bed.

Later that morning, Jonathan was working in the large boathouse sanding the hull on an old runabout they were restoring. The air was filled with sawdust that shown like a heavy sand mist in the sunlight streaming in the front door. He loved the smell of the wood and its smooth feel beneath his hands. He noticed something behind him and turned to see two people framed in the glare of the open door. He could see it was a large man and a smaller woman, but their faces were darkened in the shadows and he couldn't make out who it was. The man walked into the building.

"Good morning, son," the man said, gesturing for the woman to come in with him.

"Hey," answered Jonathan.

"We're looking for a boat. Can you help us or call someone in who can?"

Jonathan got up from his knees and stood facing the man. He was much taller and quite heavy around the middle. He was dressed nicely in a blue blazer and a white shirt open at the collar. Jonathan noticed his shoes. They were black leather and shined brighter than his best varnish finish.

The woman came up by his side and Jonathan saw it was not a woman, but a young girl. He recognized the face although he had never been this close to the Compton girl before. He felt the air sucking out of his lungs and tiny needle pricks all over his skin. His face felt hot and he was afraid he was turning red.

"Can you help us?" the elder Compton repeated.

Jonathan tried to speak but choked on his words. He was staring at Emily Compton and was struck by how much more beautiful she was up close than from a distance on the deck of her boat. Emily smiled at him and he thought he would melt right there into a big puddle in front of both of them.

"My...ah...my dad is around back," Jonathan was finally able to say. "He'll be able to help you. Hold on just a minute." He backed up slowly, feeling numb all over and embarrassed at his clumsy behavior. He walked out into the boatyard and called for his father. He looked in both of the outbuildings and then went into the house.

His mother was sitting at the desk in the kitchen. "Your father had to run up to town for a bit," she said. He knew Luke was in no condition to help the Compton's. He walked back down to the boathouse. On the way across the yard he tried to compose himself. *She's just a damned girl.*

He was feeling a little more comfortable when he came back in and saw the Compton's looking at the boat he'd been working on.

"My dad's off to town for a while." He didn't want them to leave. He wasn't responsible for selling boats but decided he could help get the process started. "So, you're looking for a boat?" he began.

The man came over and held out his hand. "My name is Stewart Compton. This is my daughter, Emily." She came over and shook his hand.

Jonathan looked into her eyes briefly, then looked away, angry at himself for being so unsettled. She was wearing dark slacks and tennis shoes with a white short-sleeved blouse. Her hair was held back neatly with a rolled-up scarf tied behind her head.

"It's nice to meet you," he said. "I'm Jonathan. This is my family's business. My dad usually works with our customers, but I'd be happy to try to help." He felt better, managing to get a coherent thought out without sounding and looking like a total fool. "What kind of boat are you looking for?"

"I love this old boat here," Emily started. "Is it for sale?"

"It is, but it needs some more work. I'm almost done sanding out a few spots on the hull that we've been working on. The engine's been rebuilt and runs like a charm."

"How much more time do you need with her?" Stewart Compton asked.

"Oh, I could finish her up pretty quick, I guess."

"Daddy, can I get up in the boat?" Emily asked.

He turned to Jonathan. "Would it be okay if we took a look?"

"Sure, let me get a ladder so you can climb up." He pulled a short step ladder over from against the wall and set it up next to the boat. He climbed up first and crawled over the side. Mr. Compton helped Emily up the few steps. Jonathan reached over and took her hand and helped her up. He could smell the soft hint of Lilac as she passed by. Her father followed, and Jonathan moved out of the way so they could get up to the front seats.

"She's a little dusty from all the sanding," Jonathan said, "but I'd get her all cleaned up for you."

"Oh, I'm sure you would," Mr. Compton said. "These leather seats are beautiful."

"Yeah, she's a dandy. We got her in from the Reynolds family from over in Boyne City. They wanted a bigger boat this summer."

Emily was in the driver's seat, holding the wheel and looking at all the instrumentation. "I love this boat, Daddy."

"Let's have Jonathan get back to work then, baby," he said, smiling at his daughter.

They all climbed down. Emily turned to Jonathan and captured him again in her big eyes.

"Do you think you could have her in the water pretty soon?" she asked.

"Not more than a few days to get the varnish coats on her."

"Why don't you talk to your dad when he gets back," Compton said. "Have him call me." He handed Jonathan a card from his wallet. "Thank you, Jonathan." Placing his hand on the boat, he said, "Appreciate your help. You're doing great work here."

Jonathan watched them leave. He took a deep breath and tried to keep the face of Emily Compton fresh in his memory. He looked down at himself and suddenly realized how badly he looked in his old work overalls and boots spotted with varnish and sawdust. He touched his face and realized he hadn't shaved or taken a bath this morning.

Then, he thought of Catherine and felt the guilt wash over him again for his feelings about Emily Compton. In his mind, he justified his feelings. Catherine was real and they really cared for each other. He could see a future with Catherine. Emily

Compton, on the other hand, was an illusion, a silly fantasy. There was certainly no future for him there. But for now, he thought, the fantasy was definitely a nice diversion.

It was close to dinner time and Jonathan was working hard to finish the prep work on the Compton's new boat, so he could start varnishing the hull. Throughout the afternoon he had worked without a break to finish the next phase. When his father came back, he told him about the Compton's interest in the boat. He gave him Compton's card, and his father left to go call the man. He hadn't seen him since.

Jonathan worked in such a frenzy, he was now covered from head to toe in a heavy coat of sawdust mixed with sweat. It was in his eyes, nose and ears and he had to spit frequently to clear his mouth. Throughout the work, his mind had been wandering back to the morning's encounter with Emily Compton. Her face and smell were etched in his brain and he couldn't stop thinking about her eyes and the softness of her touch when they shook hands. Her voice echoed in his ears.

Even working in the shade of the boathouse, his shirt was drenched in sweat. He took off his old brown fishing cap and pulled the shirt over his head, throwing it on the side of the boat. His body glistened with sweat and sawdust. He shook his head to break loose some of the sawdust from his hair.

He heard someone talking, coming up from the docks along the water. He watched as Emily Compton came back into the boathouse accompanied by another girl. Jonathan felt that familiar lump in his throat seeing her return.

"Jonathan, hello," Emily started. "I wanted to bring my friend Louise over to see the boat. Is now a good time?"

He stood there for a minute, embarrassed, trying to decide if he should dress himself. Emily didn't seem to react to his appearance in any noticeable way, although he could see the friend, Louise, was looking him over carefully. He looked for a rag to wipe more of the dust from his face. His sweaty shirt was the closest thing available and he reached for it and wiped it around his face several times. He noticed Louise wince.

"I'm sorry I'm such a mess," he said.

Emily smiled, "You look like you could use a dip in the lake."

"You know, that's a great idea," Jonathan said with relief. "Why don't you go ahead and show Louise the boat and I'll go rinse off real quick." He ran by them and out the boathouse door toward the lake. He ran as fast as he could out to the end of the main dock out over Round Lake. He sat down to take off his shoes and socks, then dove quickly into the cool water. He felt the soothing embrace of the lake's chill and could feel the dirt and grime rinsed from his body. He came back up to the surface and shook the water from his hair. Swimming back over to the dock, he pulled himself up on the wooden ladder tied to one of the main posts. He picked up his shoes and socks and walked back down the dock, leaving a trail of water dripping from his body.

When he got back to the boathouse the two girls were up in the boat, Emily Compton again sitting behind the wheel. He could hear them talking before they noticed he had come back.

Louise was whispering, "That boy sure is an eyeful."

"What do you mean?" Emily asked, not taking her eyes from the chrome plated instruments on the dash of the boat.

"Didn't you see the muscles in his arms?"

Emily turned to her friend. "Louise, I'm not blind."

Jonathan couldn't believe they were talking about him. He coughed to let them know he had returned.

"Oh, Jonathan, I didn't introduce you properly to my best friend, Louise Kelly," Emily said. "She lives over across the channel. We've been friends up here every summer since we were little girls. Louise, this is Jonathan...McKendry, isn't it?"

"Hello, Jonathan," Louise said with a big smile.

He nodded back.

"You look a lot more comfortable now," said Emily.

Jonathan had a sudden crazy thought and he wasn't even sure if he should say anything, but before he could second guess himself, he just blurted out, "We have another boat down at the docks. It's another Chris Craft, just a couple feet longer. It's not for sale, but I know the owner wouldn't care if we took it out for a ride. I'm supposed to check the engine anyway."

Emily didn't hesitate, "That would be great! Come on Louise."

He led them down to the dock and helped them into the boat. He jumped in behind them. The key was in the ignition. After a few minutes of preparation, he started the engine and the roar and sputter of it was loud, echoing off the trees across the channel. The smell of gas drifted over them. Louise and Emily sat together in the middle row of seats.

"Do you have time for a little ride?" he asked above the noise of the engine.

The girls looked at each other and nodded.

"I'll get us started, then you can give her a try," Jonathan said, looking back over his shoulder. He jumped back up on the dock and released the lines, then pushed the boat out from the dock as he climbed back in. "Any place you'd like to see?"

"No, you pick," Emily answered.

He headed slowly out into the main channel of Round Lake, pointing toward the mouth into Lake Charlevoix. Several boats were coming into the channel toward them and the girls waved as they passed.

Jonathan was feeling heady with the two beautiful summer girls in the back of the boat. He kept at low speed through the channel. H could hear the girls talking but could only make out a few words here and there over the sound of the engine. He turned and saw them pointing to something up on the hill.

"Emily, if you want to come up here in the front," Jonathan said, "I can show you how to drive this thing." Emily came

88

forward and sat next to him. Louise leaned over the seat from behind. Jonathan took her through the basics of the boat's mechanisms.

They were just coming out of the channel into the bigger lake. There was only a slight chop on the water and just a few other boats in sight. "Okay, hold on," he said. "Let's get her up to speed." He pushed the throttle down and felt the strong power of the boat push them back against their seats. The engine's noise roared louder as he continued to accelerate. The engine ran smooth and they were quickly up to half throttle.

"How fast will she go?" asked Emily, shouting over the engine noise.

"Here, you find out," Jonathan said as he stood and motioned for her to slide over into the driver's seat. She scooted over and changed places with him. She put her left hand on the wheel and pressed the throttle down. The boat surged ahead again. He felt the wind whipping at his face and bare chest. He watched the girls laughing out loud and the wind blowing their hair into their faces.

"Where should I take her?" Emily shouted.

Jonathan pointed down along the north shore of the lake and she followed his lead. He sat against the opposite side of the boat watching her drive. The wind pressed her blouse tightly against her and he couldn't help but notice the swell of her breasts. He realized Louise was watching him and he looked away quickly to the course up ahead.

"Have you been into Horton Bay before?" he asked.

"Where is that?" Emily turned to ask.

"Just up ahead a bit further. Just around that last point you can see up there."

She adjusted her course.

"Jonathan, will my boat run like this? Will she be this fast and smooth?"

"Sure will."

She looked at him intently and smiled. "I love this boat," she shouted out.

He smiled back and had to look away to keep from staring.

After about ten minutes of cruising down the lakeshore, Jonathan turned to Emily. "Slow her down as we come around the point here."

Emily slowed the boat and the big wake of water from behind pushed forward and caught them, lifting them up on the swell of it. They eased around the wooded point as the quiet harbor of Horton Bay slowly revealed itself. It was sheltered from the wind and the surface was a smooth shiny calm reflecting the greens of the cedar and hardwood trees surrounding the bay. There were no other boats and no one along the shore they could see.

"We've never stopped in here before," said Emily. "This is beautiful."

"It's so peaceful," said Louise.

"My friend George and I come here a lot to fish. There are some nice trout hanging out over there by the mouth of the creek." He pointed to the spot where the small creek made its way out of the woods and tall grasses into the lake. He decided *not* to point out where he and Catherine Hansen often sat and kissed on the beach.

They glided into the center of the bay. Emily cut the engine and the boat continued to drift slowly forward. The sudden quiet of the bay was soothing after the long ride with the din of the boat engine.

"This place is absolutely incredible," Emily repeated. "Have you ever seen a more magical place, Louise?"

They all watched a large brown hawk swoop down low over the water, then quickly upward before diving straight down into the lake. It splashed down hard, then lifted off again into the air with a small trout held firmly in its beak.

"Louise, we just have to take a swim," Emily suddenly decided.

"In our clothes?"

"Sure, we'll dry off during the ride back. Come on." Emily kicked off her shoes and moved to the back of the boat.

"Get ready," Jonathan said. "This water is darn cold from the creek coming in over there."

Emily climbed up on the back deck of the boat. She turned to her friend. "Come on, I'm not going in alone. Jonathan, you need to come in, too. Get some more of that sawdust out of your hair."

He watched her dive out and disappear in a splash.

Louise looked at him and cocked her right eyebrow. "Let's go!" She was over the side too, before Jonathan could answer. He walked back and stepped up on the rear deck. The two girls had come together and were holding hands as they kicked steadily to stay at the surface. Their hair was slicked back tight against their heads and their eyelashes sparkled with water drops. Emily looked up him.

"You're next," she said. "Come on! It's not that cold."

He took a small step back, then pushed forward, up and out over the water. He dove down headfirst just off to the side of the girls, spraying them with water as he slipped below the surface. He came up a few yards past them and looked back at the girls and the boat floating on the surface of the bay. It occurred to him just then he could never have imagined being in this place with two girls like this.

Emily pushed her wet hair back away from her face and said, "Jonathan, you're so lucky to live up here all year and have places like this whenever you want."

"It's a little cold to swim over here in February," he teased.

"You know what I mean. Louise, don't you sometimes wish summers would last forever?" Emily dipped below the surface for a moment, coming back up slowly with her head back, letting the water sweep her hair smoothly away from her face. "Could you bring us here fishing sometime?" she asked.

"Do you like to fish?" Jonathan asked.

"Daddy takes us out cruising on our boat and we stop to fish now and then. Have you seen our boat, the *EmmaLee*?" she asked without the slightest hint of bragging or pretention.

"The *EmmaLee*? Yeah, I think I've seen her," he smiled.

"Well, I do love to fish, and you just have to bring us back here sometime," Emily said. "Do you promise?"

Jonathan swam over closer to the two girls, treading water. "Have you ever been fly fishing?"

Louise broke in, "How do you fish when you're flying?"

Emily splashed her in the face. "No, I haven't. We'll just have to learn, won't we, Louise?"

"My friend George is going to be real unhappy with me telling you girls about our secret fishing hole." Jonathan said.

"Well, bring George along," Emily answered. "He can teach Louise." She gave her friend a sly grin.

"Well, let me talk to George," he said. "You know, we better start heading back."

He swam around them back to the boat. He kicked up hard and grabbed the top edge of the boat's deck, then pulled himself up and over, dripping all over the inside of the boat. He motioned for the girls to come over. Louise came first. He reached down and pulled her up along the side of the boat. She got a knee over the side and pulled herself up.

He turned back to offer Emily some help. She grabbed his outreached hand and held on firmly as he lifted her out of the water. He couldn't help but notice her blouse had turned transparent from the water and pressed tightly against her skin. The white of her bra showed through, and he tried not to stare. As she moved to slide over the deck into the cockpit of the boat, she caught her leg and fell into Jonathan. He caught her in his arms and they fell back into the leather boat seat below, Emily sprawled on top of him.

Emily was laughing and struggling to get herself up. "I'm sorry," she said. "I really am a klutz. Are you okay?"

He helped her up and watched as she sat down beside him. Their eyes met and lingered for just a moment. "I'm fine, nothing broken."

Emily shook her hair to get it out of her eyes. "Thank you for bringing us down here."

"Do you want to drive us back?" he asked.

"Let's let Louise take her back. Do you want to?" Emily asked her friend.

"Start her up for me!" Louise said.

Jonathan started the engine and moved back to the center seats, letting the two girls sit upfront to take the boat back to the boatyard. He let the warm wind dry him as they made their way back to Charlevoix. He watched the girls from behind, remembering everything about their trip with him this afternoon. *How can I tell George about this?* he thought. *First, he'll never believe me, and then... what about Catherine?*

As they approached the channel back into Round Lake, Jonathan moved up to take over the wheel. Louise slowed the boat and changed places with him. As he got behind the wheel, he noticed another boat coming out of the channel toward them. It was a large sailing yacht, about 40 feet, he estimated. It continued to draw nearer, and he heard Louise say, "Emily, that looks like the Harris boat. Isn't that the *Windrift*?"

Emily lifted up in her seat looking over the windshield of the Chris Craft. Jonathan had seen the boat before. It was kept at a dock just down from theirs. He didn't think he knew the Harris family. His father's business did very little work with sailboats. The two boats came alongside each other, about fifty feet separating them.

"Oh, look Emily, it is the *Windrift*. There's Connor," said Louise.

Jonathan turned and saw three young men in the rear of the sailboat. At the wheel, one of them was staring back at him with a face he knew only too well. He saw the girls waving next to him. When he looked back up at the sailboat, Connor Harris was glaring back at him. It had been a few days since their encounter on the street, but he could feel the scrapes from his fall start to burn again.

"Hello boys," yelled Louise as the boat passed.

Emily just waved, then looked ahead up into the channel.

Chapter Nine

It was close to 2 o'clock before Sally was able to get down to the gallery that Sunday afternoon. She walked along the storefronts down the main street of town, oblivious to people walking by her. She was caught up in her thoughts about the visit from the Clarks and how poorly she had acted. She sat for over an hour out on the sun porch after they'd left. She kept trying to sort out her emotions and make sense of her feelings.

When she got down to the gallery, she quickly walked to the back. She saw Gwen talking to some customers and nodded to her as she passed. She got back to her studio and closed the door. She walked slowly around the room looking at the work that was scattered in various stages of completion. She noticed a stack of several paintings in the corner and felt herself pulled in that direction. She kneeled and looked at the first canvas, a landscape she had started of the high bluffs along the lake near Cross Village. She sorted through the other paintings until she came to the last, leaning against the wall.

She felt her heart falling from her chest into the pit of her stomach. She sighed, "Oh dear..."

Before her was a painting that appeared about half finished, a small girl sitting on a porch chair surrounded by flowers. It was a piece she hadn't seen in years and she had clearly blocked it from her memory. She stared at it now and felt the familiar crush and weight of pain and mourning she had tried to put behind her so many years before.

The little girl in the painting stared back at her. Sally felt tears gathering in her eyes and dripping down over her cheeks onto the floor below. She looked at the familiar smile of the girl. Her mind took her back to the night of the accident as clearly as if it was all happening again... the night of the boat accident... the night she had lost everyone.

Gwen walked in and saw her crouched in the corner staring at the painting. "Oh honey, what's happened? Here, let me help you," Gwen offered as she went to Sally's side and put her arm around her. "Come on, let's put that away. Let me get you something to drink."

She helped Sally to her feet and the paintings fell back against the wall, the little girl's face disappearing behind the other canvases. They walked over and sat together at the desk on the other side of the studio.

Sally tried to keep from crying and she held a hand over her mouth, trying to get her emotions in check. She reached out for her friend and put her arms around her and sought comfort in her embrace. Through her tears she managed, "Ever since I saw the little Clark girl... I've tried to put it out of my mind for so many years. She's about the same age as ..."

Gwen interrupted, "Sally, please don't let yourself go back there. I could see this coming last night on the boat when we were with Ben and his daughter."

Sally squeezed her more tightly and buried her face in her sweater. "You would think after so many years..."

George Hansen was down at the docks speaking to a couple who had just tied up their boat. He noticed Ben and Megan Clark going by on the walkway along the docks and he called to them. They stopped, and Ben waved as George excused himself from the couple and walked over to the Clarks.

"So, what did you think of our little boat parade last night?"

"George, I've been to some pretty spectacular events over the years, but last night was really a treat. We may have to come back every year," said Ben.

"You're more than welcome to come back every year," George said. "It looked like you had quite a party going onboard the *EmmaLee* last night."

Megan answered first, "We had a band, and everyone was dancing. I got to dance with Sally and a boy."

George bent down and felt his old knees creak. "And what did you think of the Venetian boat parade, young lady?"

"The lights on all of the boats were so pretty" Megan said. "Did you see the *EmmaLee* when she was all lit up?" the little girl asked and before he could answer she continued, "... and the fireworks were great!"

"Well, I'm glad you had such a nice time."

Megan continued on quickly, "We went to see Sally's house this morning and I got to go down to the beach, but Sally got sick and we had to leave."

George stood up and turned to Ben with concern on his face, "Is she okay?"

"I'm not really sure. We were having lunch and we were going to look through some of her old photo albums of her family and the boat, and then she started to get very upset."

"What did she say?" George asked.

"She got very emotional and I could tell it was a bad time."

George reached out and touched him on the shoulder and began walking with them along the docks. "There's a lot of history in those old pictures and some not so pleasant memories for our Sally. She's a strong woman and she's made a great life for herself here, but there were some darker times she occasionally struggles with."

"I was afraid it was something I said. I made some reference to Gwen that seemed to upset her some," Ben said.

"No, I doubt that had anything to do with it. She and Gwen have been together for years and that part of her life seems to be going along just fine."

Ben looked at his new friend and shook his head, "Maybe you should check in on her. I told her I'd call later, but I'm worried."

George took a cell phone from the inside pocket of his jacket. He keyed in Sally's number from memory and listened as it continued to ring. He finally disconnected the call. "She may well be down at the shop by now. I'll head up there in a bit and see how she's doing. Thanks, anyway. I'll let you know."

Ben said, "Well, tell her we talked, and we certainly don't need to spend time with those old albums if it's going to upset her."

George stopped and said, "Call her later. I'm sure she'll be feeling better."

Ben nodded and turned with his daughter and continued along the walkway. George watched them move through the milling crowds, past all of the big boats tied up for the festival. He turned and started up the hill through the park to the main street of town. It was another incredibly hectic day in Charlevoix with traffic and shoppers moving in all directions. He crossed the road at a stoplight and walked down the block in the direction of Sally's gallery.

When he walked through the front door, he saw neither Gwen nor Sally anywhere in the shop. A few customers were walking around. He went to the back and knocked on the closed door to the studio. Gwen opened the door and he saw Sally sitting at the desk in the rear.

"Hello ladies," George said. "I just wanted to stop by and say hi." He saw Sally was wiping her face with some tissues.

"George, it's not a great time," Gwen said. "We're kind of right in the middle of something."

Sally sniffed in the background, looking away at the floor, "George, I'll call you a little later," she said.

"Can I help with anything?" he offered.

"No," said Gwen, "we just need a little more time here."

"Okay, but just call if you need anything. You promise?"

"Sure, thanks George," Gwen said. "We'll see you a little later." She closed the door and George turned and walked out of the store. He couldn't get rid of the helpless feeling he had inside. He wished there was something more he could do, but as he thought back on the years he had shared with Sally's family, he remembered how much of their fate had always been beyond his control.

Chapter Ten

There's an old saying about "trying to get out of a hole" that says you have to stop digging. My friend Jonathan found himself in one of those holes that first summer he met Emily Compton. Try as he might, he just kept digging himself in deeper and deeper.

He finally told me about his boat ride with the two summer girls. He tried to explain how he was selling a boat and had to give them a ride. I reminded him my sister was his steady girl, and he brushed the whole thing off as boat business.

After a while, he also told me the guy who almost ran him over on his bike was real interested in Miss Compton and not real happy with him about the boat ride.

I guess I wasn't too surprised to hear that. I remember quite clearly telling him again to come to his senses and get this girl and her boat out of his brain. I could tell my advice didn't seem to catch, as it went in one ear and quickly out the other.

Jonathan had walked by to pick up Catherine at her house just after dinner on Saturday night. He was taking her to the movies to see the new John Wayne film that had just come into town. They were standing in line out on the sidewalk with about twenty other people.

Jonathan had been working hard on the Compton boat for the past three days and figured he would have it ready to deliver by Monday. He had tried to keep Emily Compton out of his thoughts, but it had been damn hard with her new boat there in front of him hour after hour. He had called Catherine last night to ask her out and to try to ease the burden of his guilty feelings. She had a babysitting job for Friday night, but they had agreed to get together tonight instead.

Catherine was dressed in a simple cotton print dress and brown loafers and she had her hair pulled back in a ponytail. Jonathan thought she looked great and he was grateful to be around a girl he was comfortable with and could make easy conversation.

"I should have guessed you'd bring me to a Western," Catherine said. "What ever happened to Clark Gable and a good love story on a Saturday night?"

Jonathan put his arm around her and pulled her closer. "John Wayne will kiss the girl tonight," he said. "You just watch."

Catherine rolled her eyes and elbowed him in the ribs. He pushed away and looked back over her shoulder. He saw a group of people coming down the sidewalk that included Emily Compton. Louise Kelly was with her and two other girls he hadn't seen before. Louise spotted him first. He felt a mild panic come over him and he turned back and looked ahead at the line into the theatre in front of them. He held his breath, waiting for the inevitable.

"Hey, Jonathan." It was Louise. "Hey, Jonathan, how are you?"

He turned and watched as Catherine turned to see who was calling. Emily now saw him standing there and smiled back. The two girls broke away from their group and came over.

"Hi, Jonathan," said Emily. "How's the boat coming? I meant to stop by earlier today."

Catherine squirmed a bit and Jonathan could tell she was not pleased with this new development. He started to make some introductions. "Emily and Louise, this is Catherine Hansen." To Catherine, he said, "Emily and her father are buying a boat from us."

"Hello, it's nice to meet you," Emily said with a gracious and genuine smile.

Jonathan couldn't help but notice how terrific she looked... the hair, the light make-up and the clothes.

Catherine nodded and tried to manage a smile in return. She turned and gave Jonathan a look that clearly said, *I'm not very happy about this. Make them go away!*

"Emily, I put a last coat of varnish on the hull this afternoon," Jonathan said. "I have a little more bottom work to do tomorrow and I should have her ready for you by Monday. My dad will call yours as soon as it's ready."

He was sure they were going to mention something about Horton Bay, or going fishing. He was just waiting for it to bring this nice evening with his girlfriend to a crashing halt. He could tell Emily was trying to be sensitive to his situation, but looking into the eyes of her friend Louise, he could tell she wasn't going to be able to resist. *Sure enough...*

"Will you be able to take us out on a test run?" Louise began.

"Sure, sure," he interrupted before she started in on their previous voyage. "Look, we need to get into the show or we're going to miss the beginning. We'll call as soon as the boat's ready, probably Monday morning."

"Okay Jonathan, thanks," said Emily. "It's nice to meet you Catherine. Enjoy the show." She smiled again at Jonathan. "Good night."

Louise backed away with her friend with mischief clearly burning in her eyes. "Night, you two," she said, then turned and walked away.

Jonathan stood for a moment trying to sense Catherine's mood and what he should say next. She beat him to it.

"You certainly meet some nice people down at the boatyard. I take it they're summer girls? That dress must have cost a fortune."

"Yeah, I think," Jonathan stammered. "Hey, we need to get inside."

She looked him square in the eyes, as if she was looking for some further clue to what had just transpired. "Now you wouldn't let those summer girls catch your eye would you, McKendry? I hear they chew up local boys and spit them out just for fun." She had a look that he hadn't seen before. He couldn't tell if she was really mad or just digging to see how he'd react.

"Come on, what's a rich summer girl like that going to see in some poor boat painter?"

"Oh, I think they see plenty." She elbowed him in the mid-section again, then pulled him by the arm up to the ticket window. "He's buying, two please!"

Luke McKendry was sitting at his customary stool down at *The Helm*. It was just past 10 o'clock. He looked down at the glass of beer in front of him. It was about a quarter full. The rising bubbles from the bottom of the glass caught his attention. He felt the comforting effects of the night's beers working through his body, numbing the pain and dulling the senses. He was oblivious to the people around him at the bar. The bartender came over.

"Another round, Luke?"

He nodded and swallowed the rest of the beer, sliding the glass back across the bar. The old man filled the glass from a tap in front of Luke and put it back down on a small square napkin.

"You remember much about the other night...that scrap you got in?" Bud asked.

Luke looked up and tried to focus on the man and what he'd said.

"Those boys tore you up pretty good, son. You need to watch your mouth when you're drinking like this. I tried to get you home, but there's no reasoning with you on nights like that," the old bartender said.

Luke finally realized what he was talking about. "Those sonsabitches got more 'n they gave, Bud. You seen 'em back in here since?"

"No, they were boat people, just passing through. They were as drunk as you were. You took an interest in one of their women. You remember?"

Luke didn't remember anything, except waking up back at home, feeling and looking like hell. "Thanks for trying to help. What we do, go out back?"

"Yeah, I didn't want you knuckleheads tearing up my bar," Bud said. "I was about to call the sheriff over, but I figured you didn't need to spend another night down at the jail."

Luke looked at himself in the mirror across the bar. The image had become a familiar scene. Even in the dark light of *The Helm* he could see the bruises under his left eye and the cut along his cheek. The rest of his body was starting to heal up. His ribs were still sore.

His father had thrown him out of the house that next morning. Luke hadn't even protested. He just got up and walked out the door and hadn't been back. He'd been staying with an old friend over on Clinton Street. He needed to find a job. *Maybe old man Burt needs some help on one of the fishing boat crews?*

"Luke, I heard your Pop throw'd you out," the bartender said. "You need anything until you get set-up? I'll try to do what I can."

Luke nodded without looking up from his beer.

"Why don't you get the hell outta here tonight? You've had plenty. I don't want to be scrapin' you up out back again," Bud said.

"Yeah," said Luke. "Hey Bud, I gave those boys a good go the other night, didn't I?" Luke looked at the old man through drooping eyes.

"Luke, there was three of 'em. I tried to help, but they was about to kick my ass, too. You didn't have much chance, son. You got to watch yourself. Don't want to hear about them putting you in the ground someday for the long sleep. You hear me?"

Luke shook his head slowly, trying to remember what had happened that night. He picked up his glass and drank the whole beer in one long drink. He put the glass down and took a deep breath. He felt the beer hammer his brain and work through the rest of his body. He stood up and held on to the bar with both hands to steady himself.

"I'm gonna go," he managed to say.

"You go straight home to Bobby's place now."

He walked out the front door without answering.

Catherine and Jonathan came out of the movie theatre with their arms around each other. They walked through the crowd out onto the street. The night air was still warm, and the town was lit up with all the familiar lights in the stores and restaurants. Cars moved along Bridge Street at a slow pace, many with boys hanging out the windows calling to girls.

"How about some coffee or a shake?" Jonathan offered.

"Sounds good, but I need to be home by eleven."

They started walking down towards the park.

"You thinking anymore about going to school next fall?" she asked.

"Thinking about it," he answered, looking away across the park lawn to the boats down below.

"Still thinking about engineering school up at Tech?"

"Uh huh."

"You know, I'm probably not going to be able to go. There's just no money and I don't know how I'd do it."

"I haven't got that all worked out yet either," he said. "Figured I'd be working my way."

They had been through this conversation before. Jonathan knew she was worried about him leaving her. He had tried not to think that far ahead, but the issue was looming out there.

"You know I love you?"

"I sure do." He stopped and pulled her to him and kissed her.

He was looking into her eyes when he heard a voice interrupt them from behind.

"You sure have a way with the women, son."

Jonathan turned. It was Connor Harris, sitting on a park bench with two of his friends. He felt a chill course through him, and he held Catherine behind him. He could see a look in Harris's eyes that spelled real trouble.

"Catherine, I want you to go on over to the restaurant and order those shakes," Jonathan said.

"Jonathan..."

"Now!"

She backed away slowly, then crossed the street reluctantly. "I'm calling George..." she said.

"Just go, now!" he demanded.

Connor Harris got up from his seat. His two friends followed. He walked over and stood just a few steps away, staring Jonathan straight in the eyes. He could smell they'd been drinking. "Well, boat boy, you're just getting all kinds of women chasing after you now, aren't you?" Connor said.

Jonathan held his ground and didn't answer. He sized up the two others and saw they were set like a hair trigger, ready to go off. People passed on the street, paying little attention to the confrontation.

Connor moved another step closer. "It seems every summer we need to put boys like you in your place. You know what I'm talking about?"

Jonathan didn't answer. He could see a wild rage in the eyes of Connor Harris. He looked around quickly to see if he could find any familiar faces for support.

"What the hell were you up to with Emily Compton the other day?" Harris asked. "You know she's my girl, don't you?"

Jonathan was breathing faster now. He could feel the adrenaline working through his system. There was a ringing in his ears and a pressure building there. He kept his eyes on Harris. "You seem to want trouble over this no matter what I'm gonna tell you."

"You're the one who wants trouble when you start going after girls you have no place with," hissed Connor.

"If we're gonna do this, it's between you and me, unless you need these two to fight for you," Jonathan said, not giving an inch.

Connor looked around at the crowds of people continuing to walk by. "Down by the docks. Let's go."

Jonathan's gaze was fixed on the face of Harris. He had been in his share of fights growing up, as any kid would, but he thought to himself he had never looked into the face of someone this dangerous.

Then, he sensed a blur of motion coming up from behind Harris, but he couldn't take his eyes away. The pressure building in his brain kept on and it seemed all he could hear was the ringing in his ears. Harris said something to him, but he couldn't hear him.

He watched as Harris turned slowly to see what was coming up behind him. One of the other boys suddenly lurched to the side and fell to the sidewalk. Jonathan heard a sort of muffled roar, almost animal-like, through the noise echoing in his brain.

Then, he saw Connor Harris' head jerk backward towards him. He felt, more than heard a concussion of sound and watched as blood from Connor's head flew across the space between them and splattered down the front of his own face and shirt.

Jonathan stepped back in disbelieving shock as Harris spun around to face him again. His eyes had gone blank, almost looking right through him. The left side of his forehead was a bloody pulp. He hung limp for a moment and his feet moved as his body instinctively tried to gain balance. His left leg gave out and he crumbled in a lifeless heap.

Jonathan saw his face hit the sidewalk and watched as a pool of blood began to spread slowly out over the pavement and into the grass. He felt lightheaded and thought that he was going to fall or pass out. He looked up and saw Luke standing in front of him. His brother had a crazy, dangerous look on his face and his eyes were glazed-over and vacant looking. In his right hand he held an old weathered piece of lumber.

When Luke saw his brother looking down at the board, he dropped it on the legs of Connor Harris.

A crowd began to gather now, and Jonathan heard someone scream and someone else yell for help. He staggered backward and tripped on something and fell into the grass. He came up into a sitting position. Luke was still standing there staring at him. He looked for Harris's two friends but couldn't find their faces in the crowd of people.

He managed to speak, "Jesus, Luke." He wiped at the blood that was dripping down his face.

He saw Emily Compton push through the crowd. Emily saw Harris lying still on the pavement in the pool of his own blood, then she turned and saw him sitting there. He could feel tears starting to run down his face.

Emily knelt down next to Connor and yelled out, "Someone get a doctor!"

Louise came into the circle of people and got down on her knees next to her friend and held her as she started to cry. "Someone please get some help!" Louise pleaded.

Jonathan managed to get back to his feet. He looked over and his brother was gone.

"Emily, please try to eat something," her mother said. The two women were sitting at the long oak table in the kitchen of the Compton home. A cook was working at the sink and clattering some pans as she cleaned up, but otherwise they were alone. Margaret Compton had her arm around her daughter's shoulder.

Emily looked down at the eggs and toast on her plate but had no inclination to try to eat. She had been up most of the night trying to sleep, but not able to get the images of the past evening out of her mind. A doctor had finally come down to the scene of the fight in the part, then an ambulance. They had taken Connor away. She remembered a policeman being there and seeing him leave with Jonathan and two of Connor's friends. She hadn't spoken to Jonathan. She just remembered the fear she had seen in his eyes and the tears streaming down his face.

Her father walked into the kitchen. He had left for the hospital an hour earlier.

"Connor is still alive," he said, joining them at the table, sitting across from his daughter.

"Oh, thank God," she heard her mother say.

"He's heavily sedated and apparently in a coma, but they say he's stable, whatever the hell that means." He asked the cook to bring over some coffee.

"Did you see him, Daddy?"

"No, they wouldn't let me in, but I spoke with his parents. His father had been down at the police station. They've arrested McKendry's older brother, Luke."

"Luke? But, I thought..." Emily started.

"Yes, it was the older brother," her father said. "Apparently, he had been told a fight was about to start by Jonathan's girlfriend, I guess. He came up from behind and smashed Connor on the head with a piece of lumber. Jonathan and the two boys with Connor were both questioned, but they weren't held. Connor's father is meeting with the prosecutor later this morning to determine what kind of charges will be filed."

"Is Connor going to be okay?" she asked with a pained voice.

"I really don't know, Honey. Let's just pray that he'll come out of this."

Emily's mother began, "Your daughter was just telling me she was out in a boat with this McKendry boy and Connor had seen them."

"When was this?"

"It was a couple of days ago," Emily answered. "Louise and I stopped by the boatyard so I could show her my boat. Jonathan offered to take us out on another boat they had that was like the Chris Craft. We ran down the lake, then Connor saw us when we were coming back in the channel."

"Stewart, we're going to get dragged into this mess, you know that don't you?" her mother said.

"Let's just pray Connor is going to be okay," he said. "And Emily, I want you to stay away from the McKendry place and from that boy. It sounds like he's not responsible for what's happened to Connor, but it won't do anyone any good for you to be seen with him. Is that clear?"

Emily nodded.

Jonathan was sitting in the Compton's Chris Craft when his father came into the boathouse.

"Get down out of there!" his father yelled. "I've been looking all over for you. "I've just been down to the police station.

They've got Luke locked up and they're not sure what he'll be charged with yet."

Jonathan climbed down out of the boat. "Pop, he didn't have to help me. I could have handled it."

"You've done enough already. Didn't I tell you to keep your distance from those people?"

"I was out with Catherine. I didn't know I was gonna to run into this guy. I told you what happened. I didn't start anything."

"You started it when you went off with that Compton girl the other day." His father moved over and slumped down on a bench next to the boat. "Luke is in a hell of a lot of trouble. If that kid dies..."

"Pop, he was itchin' for a fight. We were about to go at it when Luke came up."

"He had no right to hit that boy like that. He may have killed him, for God's sake!"

Jonathan looked down at the dusty floor of the boathouse. He had been out here all night trying to sort through what had happened. Catherine had met him after he came out of the police station. She was really upset and told him she ran into Luke and warned him about the fight. She was crying and tried to apologize for getting Luke involved. He walked her back to her house before he came home.

Catherine asked him why this person wanted to fight. He told her he was just too tired and upset to go through the whole story, but she kept pressing him. When they reached her house, they sat on the front porch step. George came out and joined them. He told them the whole story about the bicycle crash and the day in the boat with Emily and Louise, and Harris passing them on his sailboat.

Catherine had got even more upset and wanted to know how he felt about the Compton girl. Her words stuck in his mind, "Jonathan, I can't be what this girl is for you."

He tried to explain he was just showing her a boat. She wouldn't listen and ran into the house in tears. George just shook his head and walked in after his sister.

His father's words interrupted his thoughts. "Your brother was drunk again. I guess he was down at *The Helm* again all night. That's not gonna help him."

"I have to go see Luke," Jonathan said, walking toward the door.

"No, you're going to stay right here! Do you understand me? don't want you settin' a foot away from this boatyard."

He looked at his father and saw desperation in his face like never before. He looked older and it made him ache to see the pain he was causing him and his family.

Jonathan walked down the hill to the docks and out to the end of the pier. He sat down with his legs hanging over the side. It was still early and there were no boats out yet. It was very quiet except for a few ducks paddling by. He looked down the channel toward Lake Charlevoix and thought about the day in the boat with Emily and Louise. He wanted to go back to Horton Bay alone, to take a swim or catch a fish, to just make all of this go away.

Chapter Eleven

The phone next to Sally's bed rang and the jarring sound caused her to sit up quickly. She pushed the hair away from her face and tried to wake up enough to answer the call. She saw how late it was on the alarm clock and felt comfort in knowing she had been able to get some sleep. She finally picked up the telephone.

"Hello," she answered dully, still not fully back from a deep sleep.

"Good morning, Sally, it's Ben." She didn't respond. "Sally, I hope I'm not intruding. I just wanted to call and see how you're feeling."

"I'm okay, thank you," she answered, pulling her legs over the side of the bed. She wondered where Gwen was.

"Sally, I thought you might like to join us on a boat ride this afternoon. We're taking the *EmmaLee* out to Fisherman's Island. We thought you might like to come along and get some fresh air."

"Oh, I don't know how I could today, Ben, but thank you," Sally said. "I need to get down to the gallery. I'm late as it is."

"I already tried to reach you down there. I spoke with Gwen and asked her about the boat trip. She thought it would be good for you. I asked her to come along as well, but she said she had some things she needed to stay in town for, and one of your assistants was covering the store. Why don't you come with us?" he asked.

Sally sat without responding for a few moments. Looking out the window she could see it was going to be a beautiful day and she really did need to do something besides sitting around. "What time are you leaving?"

"Can you be down here by noon? We'll have some lunch prepared and Megan's made some cookies for you."

Sally closed her eyes and thought of the little girl and how sweet that was. "Ben, this is very nice of you. I'll be down around noon. Thank you."

"Terrific," Ben said. "Bring a swimming suit with you."

"Okay, I'll see you soon." She hung up the phone and sighed.

She went downstairs and made coffee and a quick breakfast. She tried to call Gwen, but their assistant, Patty, answered and said she was out running some errands. Sally left a message she was going out with the Clarks for the afternoon. She walked into the living room and couldn't help but see the photo albums on the shelf against the far wall. She walked over and reached for the one on the far left.

When Sally got to the boat, she saw George and Elizabeth Hansen were on deck and she returned their wave. Ben met her as she came onboard. He took her hand and helped her onto the deck of the *EmmaLee*.

"I'm glad you could join us," Ben said. "You're looking much better today." He hesitated, "I mean... I'm just glad you could get away."

They walked forward to join George and Elizabeth who both gave her a hug.

"What would you like to drink?" Ben asked.

"Oh, lemonade would be fine," she said.

Ben signaled for someone to come over and gave the crew member the drink order. Megan came running up to join them with a plate filled with her cookies. She had a red bathing suit on and a towel wrapped around her middle. Her hair was tied back with a white ribbon.

"Hi Sally! These are for you to help you feel better," the little girl gushed.

Sally crouched down. "What kind did you make, Megan? They look great."

"They're peanut butter!" She held the plate up for everyone to take one.

"These may be the best cookies I've ever tasted, Megan," said George, as he rubbed his generous belly. "And you can see I've been able to sample a lot of cookies in my day."

The little girl laughed, then said, "I'm going to go back and help with lunch." She ran back towards the main cabin.

"The winds are going to be fairly calm today, so we thought we'd head over to Fisherman's Island, anchor off and maybe catch some fish or go swimming," their host said.

Ben signaled, and the crew began scurrying to free the lines and get the boat underway. Within a few minutes they were away from the docks and slowly heading out into the calm harbor of Round Lake toward the channel to Lake Michigan. It was right at 12 o'clock when they heard the bells start clanging on the drawbridge up ahead. The traffic barriers were coming down to halt the cars on Bridge Street. Two sailboats were waiting in front of them for the bridge to open to allow them to pass. During the summer, the bright blue metal bridge opened every thirty minutes on the half hour to let the larger boat traffic through. The bridge quivered, then parted in the middle, two large sections rising up towards each side of the channel.

The *EmmaLee's* skipper positioned her behind the sailboats and had her follow them through the open bridge channel. Dozens of people lined the sides of the channel and many waved as they passed. Sally looked over the side. The water of Round Lake was a deep emerald green and clear enough she could see bottom near the side of the channel as they passed under the open bridge.

Two small boys were sitting on the pier watching the bobbers on their fishing lines. They smiled at her when they saw she was watching them. Up ahead, she saw the two piers on each side of the channel reaching out into Lake Michigan. There was a lot of boat traffic going both ways through the channel on this warm summer day. The big red lighthouse at the end of the south pier stood as a familiar beacon.

As they reached the end of the channel, the water's surface began to undulate in slow gentle swells coming in from the lake. Sally felt a breeze freshening on her face. She looked back to the right at the beach in front of her house. The house was hidden from view behind the tall dunes and trees. It was such a clear day that out on the far horizon she could just make out the gray mass of Beaver Island. She was standing with the Hansen's and Ben Clark and they were silently enjoying the beautiful sights coming out into the big lake.

She felt the rumble from the boat coming up through her shoes as the captain powered her up. She looked over at Ben and he smiled back. She thought again of her mother and similar trips she had made on this boat out to Fisherman's Island and other wonderful places in these northern lakes. Reaching for the heavy bag hanging on her shoulder, she felt the hard lines of the photo album she brought along.

The ride out to Fisherman's Island was calm and uneventful. Soon they were anchored a hundred yards off the western shore of the small island that rested in shallow water not more than a long stone's throw from the mainland. At times of low water people could wade easily from the beach which was part of a large state park. It was heavily wooded and edged by a long sandy shoreline.

Ben came forward and invited them all to come down below for lunch. It was a wonderful meal and Megan helped serve. The wine was cold, and Sally couldn't help but indulge in a second glass when offered. The conversation ranged from the past weekend's boat parade to Ben's plans for the *EmmaLee* for the rest of the summer.

When they finished, everyone went back up on deck for dessert and coffee. They were all sitting around a table on the rear deck in the shade from the sun. As they finished the dessert of apple pie and more of Megan's cookies, Sally reached into her bag and brought up the photo album.

"I thought we might try again to take a look at some of these old photos today," she said.

Megan ran around the table and hugged her. "Do you have pictures of your mom on the *EmmaLee*?" she asked.

"There are several, little lady," Sally said. "Pull a chair over here and we'll take a look."

The Hansens, Ben, and his daughter positioned themselves around Sally at the table so they could all see. She placed the old book down and rubbed its worn cover before she pulled it open to the side. Everyone pressed closer to see the first picture. It was a shot taken of the *EmmaLee* from another boat as it made its way across Round Lake. It was a magnificent shot of the boat showing several uniformed crew members and other passengers at the rail. The boat's ornate bowsprit pointed out ahead. Several small flags were flying from the foremast.

"She looks like a miniature Queen Mary from this angle," George Hansen said, with admiration in his voice. The written caption read, *The EmmaLee, Round Lake, 1939.*

Sally turned the page. There were two more black and white photos of the ship. The first was taken from the city docks back across Round Lake to the EmmaLee, docked at her boathouse on the south shore. The other showed the boat coming out of the channel toward Lake Michigan and had been taken from the south pier. You could see the tall dunes of the lakeshore back in the distance behind the ship.

She turned the page again and they all looked down at a picture of a family posed in front of the main cabin of the ship. "This is my mother's family," Sally explained. "That's her in the middle with her two brothers. She must have been around eighteen when this was taken."

The boys wore dark sport coats and ties with white pants and shoes. Sally's mother, Emily, was dressed in a long frilly white dress with toes of white shoes peeking out. Her hair was styled up on top of her head.

"Your mother was beautiful, Sally," said Ben, "and your grandmother."

George chimed in, "Yes, she was quite a looker, if I may say so."

Sally laughed and pointed. "And my grandparents, Stewart and Margaret Compton. He was in the car business in Detroit."

"Yes, I've heard of his career," Ben said.

On the opposite page was a close-up shot of Emily Compton taken in the same dress, probably on the same day. It was a shot from her waist up and she was standing at the rail of the ship with a glorious smile and loose strands of her hair blowing across her face in the wind.

"This is my favorite picture of my mother," Sally said.

"It's quite beautiful," Elizabeth Hansen said.

"Your mom was so pretty," little Megan said. "Do you know which cabin she stayed in when she was little?" she asked. "I wonder if she stayed in my cabin."

"I really don't know, honey," Sally said. "I do know they went on many trips like the one we're on today as a family. In fact, there's a picture somewhere in here of the children playing on the beach over there on the island. You can see the boat in the background." She turned several pages until she found it.

George shook his head, "It's like time has come back around and we're here again in 1939."

"Sally, these photos are incredible," Ben said. "Would you mind leaving the book onboard for a few days?" he asked.

"No, not at all."

Megan interrupted, "Daddy, you said we could go fishing. Can we now?"

Everyone agreed, and Ben called a deckhand over to round up the equipment. In a few minutes, they had poles over the side off the stern of the boat. Within moments, Megan shrieked with joy, "I've got one! I've got one! Look, Daddy, it's a big one."

Her father helped her reel in a nice green-sided smallmouth bass. It was about fourteen inches long. Sally quickly got a camera from her bag and took a picture of the fishing party with Megan in front holding her fish.

"I was thinking of having the dinghy lowered and going ashore to check out the island," said Ben. "Would anyone like to join me?"

"Daddy, I want to keep fishing."

The Hansens declined and said they wanted to stay and help Megan.

"Sally, how about a little treasure hunting excursion over to the island?" he asked.

"Sure. You really don't want to come along, Megan?" Sally asked.

The little girl shook her head, intent on watching her line down below.

Sally and Ben agreed to put on their swimming suits and were soon in the small boat, Ben rowing over to the island. The water was bright and crystal clear and Sally could easily see the many-colored stones on the bottom of the lake. The boat hit shore and they both climbed out to pull it up on the sand.

They started off along the shoreline, walking together. "Thank you for bringing the pictures out today," Ben said.

"I hope it gives you a better feel for the ancestry of your boat and how much it meant to my mother's family back in those days."

They walked along for a while in silence, then Ben stopped to pick up a stone he saw in the shallow water. "Is this a fossil or something?" he asked.

She came over and looked at what he was holding. "It's a Petoskey Stone, and yes, it is a fossil. They're all over up here along the rocky lakeshores. People collect them and polish them and make them into all kinds of crafts. I can't believe you've never seen a Petoskey Stone."

"I don't think we have these back East."

"Just look how much you're learning," she said, and smiled. She enjoyed being with Ben and she refused to feel guilty about it. Gwen had been invited, so it wasn't as if she had been sneaking off with him this afternoon.

"I don't want to dredge up darker times, but I was worried about you yesterday. I'm really glad to see you're feeling better," Ben said.

"I'm fine," she said, leaving it at that. "How about a swim? It's getting hot up here on the beach. Let's swim over across the channel there to the main beach."

He followed her into the deeper water, taking his time to let his body acclimate itself to the cooler temperature of the big lake water. He watched Sally dive in and porpoise out into deeper water until she couldn't touch anymore and then she started to swim in a slow, graceful stroke. He held his breath and prepared for the shock and then followed her toward shore. He caught up with her about half-way across the narrow channel.

"God, that water's cold!" he said. They reached the shallows and he watched her walk up onto the sandy shore. He couldn't help noticing the pleasing proportions of her body in the swimsuit. As he joined her on the shore, the warmth of the sun on his back was a welcome relief. They walked along down through the water's break for a while without talking.

Sally stopped and looked out over the water. They could see the *EmmaLee* resting calmly out past the small island.

"Ben..." she paused. "Ben, yesterday was about old memories I've tried to keep hidden away for a long time."

He came up beside her. "You don't have to talk about it if..."

"No, I think I really do need to talk about it." She stepped back and sat down in the sand. Ben joined her. She started to speak in a slow, quiet voice. "I had a daughter. Her name was Ellen. She was nine years old when she died in a boating accident." Sally stopped and swallowed, looking down at the sand, digging a small hole with her feet. "My parents were also lost."

Ben put his hand on her shoulder in comfort. "Sally, I'm so sorry. I had no idea."

"Ellen had gone on a trip to Chicago with my parents on their sailboat. She was so excited to go. They were taking a couple of weeks to go down there, then cruise back up the Wisconsin coast. I couldn't get away to join them. I was already divorced at that time. I had the gallery and I just couldn't get away. My ex-husband was living in Chicago and Ellen got to see him when they were down there."

The hole at her feet was growing deeper and she had pushed a large pile of sand out in front of her. Ben just listened and let her proceed at her own pace.

"I talked to her almost every night of their trip. She was having a wonderful time. My parents were treating her like a little princess and taking her to all kinds of interesting places along the way." She paused for a moment. Ben could see the pain in her face and the tears building in her eyes. She covered her face with her hands. "I haven't talked with anyone about this in so long."

Ben put his arm around her shoulder and pulled her over next to him. She put her face on his shoulder and let the tears finally break loose. They sat for several minutes without speaking.

She looked up at him, "I'm sorry."

"I think you've needed to get this out for a long time."

"My old photo albums... the ones we were going to look at yesterday," Sally continued. "The last one is filled with pictures of my parents and my daughter. I haven't opened it since they've been gone. I had wanted to take it down yesterday and share those pictures with you and Megan, and let you see my daughter." She paused, catching her breath. "I just couldn't do it."

"Being around Megan must be hard?" he asked.

"Well, it sure caught up with me yesterday," she said. "But Megan is a wonderful little girl...," she couldn't finish.

"Can you tell me what happened?" Ben asked.

Sally took a deep breath. "The day my father chose for the crossing back over the lake from Wisconsin looked like it was going to be a good weather day. He was very cautious about the big lake and he was a good sailor. They had a very good boat. It was fifty or so feet, a really nice boat my dad had designed and built. They sailed all over the Great Lakes on it for years.

About mid-afternoon, they were somewhere near half-way across the lake. They radioed the Coast Guard they were having engine problems. An hour or so later they called in to say they were underway again. About twenty miles out from the Michigan coast they ran into some weather, just fog at first. Apparently, a weather system had shifted and pushed down farther than expected from the north." She had to stop for a moment.

"Are you sure you want to go on?" Ben asked.

She nodded. "The Coast Guard told me the next morning that a freak thunderstorm had blown up over the northern part of the lake with extremely high winds. They had been out in it and seen waves and swells as high as ten feet. My father radioed in an emergency call just before dark. He said they were trying to make it over to the shelter of the Manitou Islands down from Grand Traverse Bay. Then he called to say he was having engine problems again and they were adrift. He couldn't keep the boat into the weather, and they were taking on water." She looked over at Ben. "He gave them coordinates of their position. They were apparently still about ten miles out from South Manitou. The man with the Coast Guard told me they were out in water over 400 feet deep." She picked up some sand in her hands and watched it sift down into the hole she had made. "We never...we never heard from them again."

There were no more tears now. She sat looking out at the water. Ben didn't know what he could possibly say. He held her more closely to him.

"The Coast Guard received a call in the early morning from a freighter in the area. They called in to report a collision with a small boat during the storm. My dad's boat had apparently drifted into the shipping channel. The Coast Guard searched the area that night after the storm passed and into the next morning. They finally found some debris on the water about midday, some cushions and a few other things. Then, they found floating wreckage from the boat, smashed fragments from the hull."

She paused for a moment, rinsing her hands in the shore break of the cool water. "We never found them, Ben. We never found the boat. The water was too deep for a salvage crew. They're still out there."

"Sally, I'm so sorry. I can't imagine."

"I've always felt I should have been with them," Sally said. "I know I wouldn't have been able to do anything, but I should have been there with her. I just can't help but think about how frightened she must have been."

Ben sat with her there on the shore trying to hold back his own tears. He knew her pain after losing his wife. He knew nothing he could say could begin to make it go away.

Chapter Twelve

I grew up with the McKendry boys. Jonathan, of course, was my best friend. I have memories as far back as kindergarten with him. We were always running as a pair. For the most part, we kept our noses clean, but we got into a few scrapes. His brother, Luke, was just enough older he wouldn't spend much time with us, even as little kids. We looked up to that boy anyway. Even though he had been born with a weak leg and he often took abuse from older kids in town, there were times he seemed larger than life to me and Jonathan.

One summer, Luke must have been eighteen or so, he took me and Jonathan out in one of their boats. We headed down to the South Arm of Lake Charlevoix. It was pretty exciting to be out there all alone with no adults onboard. We were laughing and sitting up on the seats, feeling the wind blow our hair back and yelling at the top of our lungs. It made us feel grown up just being out there alone with Luke. I remember him sitting there quietly driving the boat, keeping a lookout for other traffic. Every few minutes he'd light up another cigarette.

We slowly cruised down into the South Arm, this narrow little stretch of lake that runs a few miles down to East Jordan. We passed the old car ferry at Ironton and waved to the Captain. A little further on we came to Holy Island and pulled around into a small cove behind the island and the west shore of the lake. It was getting on into early evening by then. The wind had died, and the light was shining that soft brilliant glow in the trees you see just before dark.

Luke pulled us up on the shore next to the short bridge that connected the island to the mainland. Luke had me throw an anchor over and we sat there below the bridge listening to the day slip away, and the frogs and crickets taking over.

Luke took out his pack of Camels and lit another smoke. He handed the pack over to me and Jonathan. I guess we were about twelve and taking the cigarette pack was like we were suddenly ten years older and living in a man's world. Jonathan and I looked at each other and tried to act cool like this was no big deal. We both took a smoke. Luke lit a match and held it for us to light up. I'll never forget the taste of that first smoke in my mouth. We started talking about all sorts of stuff with Luke, like we had always been running with him.

"You boys been gettin' any women this summer?" he asked.

Me and Jonathan just started laughing like two kids would. He just shook his head.

"You two ever do a back flip off thbridge?" he asked.

I remember looking over at Jonathan. He gave me this look and I knew we were in for it. He looked so strange sitting there with a cigarette in his mouth. Jonathan said, "Hell yes!"

Well, we all stripped down to our shorts and jumped over the side onshore. It was kind of weedy and muddy, and we mucked our way up to the road and onto the bridge. The road was gravelly and hurt my feet to walk on it. We were tip-toein' and holding on to the rail of the bridge to keep our balance. We got out to the center and Luke climbed kind of awkwardly up onto the rail, dragging his bad leg along with him. He motioned for us to come up next to him.

Me and Jonathan climbed up and we were all three standing there on the top of the rail, looking down at the water. It felt like we were so high in the air, but it couldn't have been more than ten feet.

Luke slowly turned around, his arms out to help keep his balance until his back was to the water. He looked over at us, "Back flips, boys."

Jonathan elbowed me in the ribs, "Come on."

We both turned and stood there with Luke with our backs to the lake. My legs were shaking, and I thought I was gonna fall.

"Tuck your legs boys, nothin' to it," Luke said.

I looked over at Jonathan and he had this big smile on his face like he was having the best time ever. We looked back at Luke and he was staring straight ahead, concentrating hard. He took a deep breath, then squatted down with his arms held straight out. It was like slow motion watching him.

It seemed like it got real quiet, like the frogs were all watching us, too. I started wondering about how deep the damn channel was and getting scared about sticking my face in the bottom and breaking my neck.

He started up kind of slow, then at the last minute pushed hard and leaped up off the rail of that bridge. Jonathan and I both turned to watch him and almost fell in ourselves. He tucked his legs up under him just like he had done this a hundred times before. We watched him roll over backwards in a slow, smooth arc and then his legs came out just as he got to the water. He threw his hands up over his head and slid down into that water without hardly making a splash.

I remember my jaw hanging down like I had just watched Ted Williams hit a grand slam. We stood there watching the hole in the water Luke had disappeared down into, the ring of waves heading out in all directions. He didn't come up for what seemed like the longest time. We stood there waiting for him to come up. I looked over at Jonathan and he was leaning out as far as he could trying to see his brother.

"Holy shit, George!" he said, then he yelled out, "Luke! Goddammit, Luke!"

The water grew calm beneath us. We stood there a few moments longer, trying to see into the depths, trying to hear something. Jonathan grabbed my arm and jumped, pulling me along with him. We fell down through the air screaming at each other. It seemed like we were falling through the air forever. We hit the water with arms and legs flapping. I sunk down deep, and my feet squished down into the soft mucky bottom of the lake. It felt like I was stuck there. I half expected to see Luke stuck next to me. I wiggled myself free and swam to the surface. Jonathan came up about the same time. We were gasping for air and looking around for Luke. We were both spinning around in the water trying to spot him.

"Luke, goddammit..." I heard Jonathan yelling again.

Then, we both got quiet and listened, paddling to keep up on the surface. The frogs were going again, but otherwise there were no other sounds. I looked over at Jonathan and saw real fear in his eyes for his brother.

Then, right between the two of us, there was a giant explosion of water that scared the shit out of both of us. I know I damned near crapped my pants when Luke jumped from up on the rail again and crashed down between the two of us. He came up about ten yards away, facing us, the boat anchored out behind him. He just shook his head, smiling, like we were two of the biggest chumps he had ever seen.

Connor Harris regained consciousness at the hospital three days later. He was looking around the room when a nurse stopped by on her rounds. She called in a doctor, then went to call his parents.

An hour later his room was full of family and friends including Stewart Compton and his daughter Emily. Connor was awake and aware of people in the room, but he hadn't spoken or moved. His left eye was swollen shut, hidden by an ugly bruise the color of an angry sky in a summer storm. He had a puzzled look on his face as people milled around and talked about him.

The doctor told his parents earlier it wasn't clear whether their son had suffered any permanent brain damage from the blow he'd received. He said it would take a few more days to really be sure about his recovery. Emily was standing by her father listening to Mr. Harris describe his son's condition.

"That damn drunk nearly killed him, Stewart. I don't know how the boy survived after taking a blow like that. They've still got that animal down at the jail. The judge reluctantly granted bail, but nobody's come forward to post it."

"What has the prosecutor's office told you so far?" Compton asked.

"I'm insisting he do whatever's necessary to put that boy away where he can't hurt anyone else. They're talking about aggravated assault. He could get some serious jail time and he deserves every bit of it," Harris said with a bitter tone. "I brought my lawyer up from Chicago and he's pressing the court for attempted murder. The fact Connor was in a confrontation with this McKendry kid's brother will probably prevent that kind of charge."

He stopped and shook his head and looked over at the lifeless form of his son. "You know, it's one thing for boys to be fighting, and God knows that Connor's been in his share of them over the years, but it's another thing for a boy to try to kill someone like that."

Emily listened to the men and didn't know what to think. She hadn't seen Connor get hit and had come up too late to really see what the altercation was about. She knew Connor had a temper because she had witnessed it on several occasions. She couldn't get the image of Jonathan's face out of her mind and the shock and disbelief as he sat there in the grass that night. After Connor had been taken away to the hospital, she tried to talk to Jonathan, but he was too stunned to even reply. His girlfriend, Catherine, had come between them and led him away. She found herself wondering about how he was dealing with all of this.

"The boy's trying to convince the police it was self-defense and he was only coming to the aid of his brother," Mr. Harris began again.

Emily spoke before she realized what she was saying, "There were three of them against Jonathan..."

"That's enough, Emily!" her father interrupted. "Nothing justifies what the boy did out there that night."

Emily moved away and walked over to the side of Connor's bed. He noticed her coming up and looked up at her. He looked right into her eyes without the slightest hint of recognition. She took his hand and held it in hers. "Connor, I hope you can hear me. We're all praying for you to get better." She smiled at him, but his expression didn't change.

Jonathan finally got permission from his father to go down to the jail and visit his brother. The police officer led him back and placed a chair for him in front of Luke's cell. The officer moved away a few steps and stood watching the two brothers. Luke was sitting on the bed next to the wall looking down at the floor. He hadn't acknowledged his brother's arrival. Jonathan sat looking at him for a few moments.

Finally, he spoke. "Luke, what you did the other night... what I mean is, I appreciate you trying to help me." There was no response. "Those three boys were about to tear into me, and I was trying to get that Harris fellow off by himself to make it a fair fight. Then, well... I don't know what woulda' happened."

Luke didn't look up, but grumbled in almost a whisper, "Just get out of here, you hear me?"

Jonathan looked at the guard who didn't change expressions. He looked back to his brother and pulled the chair closer to the bars. "Luke, I'm tellin' them the truth... that Harris fellow was trying to start the fight and you were just protecting me from those three guys. Dad's trying to get a lawyer from up in Petoskey to take your case. We're gonna get you outta here, Luke."

His brother finally looked over at him. He stood up and walked over to the bars. Jonathan stood to face him.

"What did I just tell you?" Luke asked in the same hushed tone.

"Luke, you gotta let us help you."

"Don't waste your time." He turned and went back to his bed.

The guard touched Jonathan on the sleeve and motioned with his head it was time to leave. "Luke, Dad's tryin' to get bail together. We'll be back to get you outta here." There was no response. "Luke, I'm sorry you got into this. I coulda taken those boys, then none of this would have happened."

Jonathan watched as his brother turned his head slowly sideways to face him. They just looked at each other for a few moments, then Luke shook his head and turned away, lying back on the bed.

Catherine Hansen was waiting outside the jail when Jonathan came out. The sun was bright after his time in the dark building. He squinted at her through the glare.

"How's he doing?" she asked.

Jonathan just started walking down the sidewalk. She joined him and asked again, "Is he doing okay?"

"Yeah, just great," he said with obvious sarcasm.

"Jonathan, we need to talk about this Compton girl."

He didn't respond. He just kept walking back toward home.

"You need to tell me if you have feelings for that girl, Jonathan."

His mind was spinning from the visit with his brother and his patience was as thin as December ice. He was in no mood to be challenged about anything. He had tried to put the thought out of his mind, but he couldn't help but think none of this would have happened if Catherine had just left, as he had told her and not gotten his brother into the middle of it. He stopped and turned to face her. The familiar prettiness of her face softened his mood some and he fought to calm himself. Finally, he said, "We need to be thinking about Luke now, Catherine. There's no more time for this nonsense about girls. You know how I feel about you."

She grabbed him by his arms and made him look at her. "I always thought I knew."

He pulled away and started walking. She didn't follow.

When he got back to the boatyard, he heard someone working in the big building. When he walked in, he saw his father up on a ladder sanding the hull of a large cabin cruiser. Jonathan looked around and saw another sanding block and picked it up and went over to the boat next to his father. He started sanding the wood in slow circles, not really paying attention to his work. His father didn't look down and just kept working.

"Pop, I'm afraid for Luke. I'm afraid he's gonna go to prison, and it's really all because of me. If anyone should go to jail, it should be me. I'm the one caused all this."

Still nothing from his father.

Jonathan threw the sanding block against the boat's hull in anger and the crash echoed against the close walls of the boathouse. He looked up the ladder at his father. He never stopped sanding.

Jonathan turned in disgust and walked up to the house. He went into the kitchen and got a bottle of milk from the ice box. He was pouring a glass when his mother walked in. She took the milk from him when he was finished pouring and put it away. The curtains in the small kitchen window were pulled back and the hot sun poured in making the room just a little too warm to be comfortable. He went over and sat at the kitchen table and watched as his mother moved about, cleaning up the kitchen.

"Ma, I just saw Luke." She stopped and looked over at him. "He's ah... he's not doin' so well. I told him we were all tryin' to help. He just chased me away. I can see in his eyes he's given up, Ma." Jonathan could feel tears in his eyes, and he wiped them away in embarrassment. "We've got to help get him outta there, Ma. I shouldn't have let this happen. I've got to help him!"

"Jonny, you've done nothing to be ashamed of, and you need to stop this kind of talk. Your father's doing everything he can now for your brother. Despite all that's come between those two, your father loves Luke and he's gonna do what's right to help him." She wiped her hands on a towel and came over and sat at the table with him. "There's going to be a hearing in the morning and Dad's got a lawyer coming over tonight to meet with us and to talk to Luke. He's a good lawyer, son."

"What about the bail?" he asked.

"I don't know. That's a lot of money. I know your Dad's been down to the bank to try to borrow some money on the house, or the business, but he hasn't got an answer yet."

Jonathan watched his mother get up and go back to her work. She had her uniform on from the hotel. He looked at the clock on the wall. She'd be leaving for work soon at the big hotel down at the Belvedere Club. She'd be cooking food for families like the Harris's and the Comptons. They'd be sitting down to their fine meals and their fine wine, and Luke's gonna be sitting over in that jail.

He finished the milk and took the glass over to the sink. He walked out the back door and his mother didn't say another word.

He walked down around the boathouse to avoid his father. When he got down to the piers at the waterfront, he turned and headed up towards town, making his way along the water between the boat houses and along the docks. He could see the

EmmaLee tied up at the Compton's dock and he turned and walked up through an alley away from the water. Walking with his head down, watching his feet kick stones and thinking about his brother, he didn't notice the girl coming down from the road.

"Jonathan?"

He looked up to see Emily Compton. She stood there facing him in the alley. He noticed her face looked different. She appeared drawn and tired, and her hair was all askew. She was dressed simply in black slacks and a red blouse. He stopped and just stared at her.

"Jonathan...."

He started to walk on past and she grabbed gently at his arm. He stopped reluctantly.

"Jonathan, I can't believe this has all happened, and I'm just so sorry it's because you and I were together. I never thought anything bad would come from it, or I never would have gone near the boat with you that day."

He looked into her eyes and felt a flood of emotion he couldn't sort out. There was a depth in her eyes he struggled to look away from. He hated himself for his feelings about this girl and he started walking again, pulling his arm away.

She caught up with him and walked alongside. "Connor's hurt very badly," she said. "He came back today and regained consciousness, but he doesn't know where he's at and he can't speak." She waited for a reply and didn't receive one. "They're not sure how much he'll recover from all this. I know he brought this on himself and I'm not standing up for him, Jonathan. It's just he's been hurt so badly. I think he almost died."

Jonathan finally spoke, "I know he's a friend. I know you two have feelings and for that I'm sorry about what happened," he said honestly, sorting out his feelings while he talked. "But in a way, you know he was looking for trouble?"

"Yes, I know."

"My brother was just trying to help me. He wasn't trying to kill anybody. He was just trying to help me," he said, the desperation clear in his voice.

Emily tried to change the conversation. "My father picked up my boat for me," she said, almost ashamed to bring it up.

"I know."

"It's a fine boat, Jonathan. You did a beautiful job getting it ready for us. Thank you."

He stopped and looked at her again. He couldn't help but look into those eyes. "I can't be around you anymore." He felt an emptiness in his gut and fought to keep his voice from cracking.

"Jonathan," she said, reaching out to take his hand, "Connor and I, well... we've been friends for a long time."

He just stared back.

"We've grown up together here in the summers." She paused. "I want you to know Connor is just a friend."

"A friend," he repeated.

She looked at him and found herself caring, more than she would have imagined, that he understand.

He stood there, surprised at her confession.

"Jonathan, I know it will be hard for us to spend any more time together."

He remembered his father's warnings and he thought of his brother sitting down in the jail. "Thanks for coming over, but I need to go." It was the last thing he wanted to do, but he knew it was the right thing.

She let go of his hand. "I understand," she said.

He turned and kept walking on toward town without looking back.

Chapter Thirteen

Sally sat across from Gwen. They had managed to get a table on the first floor of the restaurant on Bridge Street, even though it was a busy night. It was dark, but warm and welcoming and on this particular evening, packed to capacity. The bar along the wall was two-deep in patrons. The noise from the crowd was continuing to get louder, and the two leaned across the table so they could hear each other.

"We haven't had a minute to catch up," said Gwen. "How was your boat ride with the Clarks?"

Sally had been thinking of little else since returning from the trip the previous night. Talking about the accident and her daughter, Ellen, had been painfully difficult, but as the boat was returning to Charlevoix and she was standing on the deck looking out at the waves, she felt a sense of true healing begin again. For so many years there had been this great dark place in her mind, standing between her and some sense of normalcy on the other side. Ben Clark had made it easier, certainly, and it amazed her at how easy it had been to open- up to someone she had known for such a short time.

"The boat ride?" she finally answered.

"Yes, the boat, the rich guy and his daughter."

Sally reached for her wine glass and took a long drink. "We were walking on the beach and somehow we started talking about Ellen and my folks." She took another swallow. "It's been more than ten years now, hasn't it?"

Gwen nodded.

"So many times, I've felt like I've put those memories away, then something triggers this flood of emotion and pain all over again."

"You know you'll never truly escape that. The feelings and the love are just too deep. She reached for Sally's hand. "You've been incredibly strong."

The waiter came out and set down their plates of grilled whitefish and salads. He asked if their wine glasses needed freshening and they nodded. Sally looked around the old restaurant she had spent so many evenings in during her life. She saw a few local friends here dining, and she knew most of the help.

It was like every place in this town for her, comfortable and familiar. Year in and year out, the routine just continued to run on with the seasons. She had never been away for any extended period after she'd returned from school. It occurred to her she needed to think seriously about getting away for a while.

She noticed a look on Gwen's face she had come to recognize over the years. Something was bothering her. "Are you upset about the time that I've been spending with the Clarks?" Sally asked, then immediately regretted bringing it up.

Gwen was watching the wine swirl in her glass as she spun it around slowly on the table. "Sally, we've been together long enough now I'm pretty damn secure about us. I will tell you though, at times this past week I've almost felt guilty about being here and being with you."

Sally interrupted, "Oh, please don't say that."

"What I'm trying to say is I feel guilty you've had a chance to meet this man and he appears to be such an incredibly nice man, and if it weren't for us..."

"If it weren't for us, what?" Sally asked.

"It just bothers me that I can't give you a more normal life and a family again. Does that make any sense at all?"

Sally just shook her head and looked intently into the eyes of the woman she had spent so many of the past years with. They had been good for each other and found great joy in each other's company. On occasion though, one of them would drift off course. Gwen would get thoughts of returning to the city or moving to Europe. With Sally, there had never been any specific haven or new place that seemed to be pulling at her, but she had to admit to herself there had been times when she had felt to get away.

"A more normal life," Sally repeated. "What the hell is a normal life anymore? You need to stop feeling guilty about us. I'm the one who should be feeling guilty for leaving you so much this past week with the festival and the *EmmaLee,* and the Clarks."

Gwen smiled and reached across the table and touched her cheek. "We're a helluva pair, you and me. Why don't we take George's sailboat out tonight? He always offers. We can run down the lake, maybe anchor out somewhere and just get away."

"We've got to be back in the morning to open up."

Gwen reached for her cell phone to call George Hansen.

Sally had been taught to sail from the time she was a small child. Her parents had kept a sailboat for years and she had been on many long cruises with them. Their first boat was a forty-foot *Pearson* that was outfitted for big water and long trips. They had sailed the North Channel many times and up through Lake Superior. Her father had fixed up a small step for her to stand on when she was younger, so she could take the wheel and skipper the boat. She could vividly remember the thrill and sense of power and control, standing on that step, taking the helm, holding that big wheel and seeing such a long powerful boat out ahead of her with full sails set.

She was at the helm again now, steering George Hansen's sailboat through the channel into Lake Charlevoix. Gwen was up front preparing the jib sail to be raised. The main had been hoisted and the boom swung loose as she steered the boat out under power. She could see the wind was coming out of the southeast and it blew up to meet them as they cleared the last buoy of the channel. She turned the wheel slowly and fell off to port. Gwen came back and took the big winch handle from its cradle. A minute later they were under sail, the motor turned off. The boat heeled over just slightly, and it cut smoothly through the waves.

Sally looked back and saw the bright red intensity of the sun just barely above the trees in town. She reached down to turn on the running lights as the day slowly faded to dusk. Gwen went below and came back up with two glasses of wine poured in clear plastic cups. She sat down on the high side of the cockpit. Sally steered with one hand, holding the wine in the other.

Gwen was looking up ahead. "Where do you think, Oyster Bay or Horton?"

"Let's see how we do in getting all the way down to Horton Bay," Sally answered. "The wind looks like it's going to hold for a while, and we can almost beat on this tack all the way there." She looked down at her friend and as usual, was caught by her simple beauty and the elegant lines of her face. Her short hair was blowing back from the wind. She wore white shorts and an old gray sweatshirt with "NYU" imprinted on the front.

In her mind, she could hear Gwen's words from dinner. It hurt her to think the time she had spent away with the Clarks this week had caused Gwen to doubt their relationship. Was Gwen serious in thinking she could be happier in a more traditional relationship and having a family again? Her wreck of a first marriage certainly didn't give her great expectations. There had never been another man who interested her after the divorce. She had many male friends, but none she had ever developed more serious feelings about.

Sally took a sip of wine and felt it warm her as it went down. She thought of Ben Clark. How did she really feel about the man? They had spent some nice time together and he was incredibly thoughtful and pleasant to be around. It had been such a short time for the two of them together she had only a vague sense of what he was truly like. He seemed to be a devoted father and to have done a great job raising Megan after his wife had passed. Physically, she had to admit, he was an attractive man. When they had been together on the beach yesterday, she found herself comfortable in his embrace as she shared the dark memories of her past.

Gwen spoke up above the noise of the wind in the sails, breaking Sally's thoughts. "Every time I feel this damned town is getting just too small and I want to bust out and head for more concrete and tall buildings back east, I'll have a night like this out on the lake, or some other incredible place up here and wonder how I could ever consider leaving." She lifted her wine up to Sally. They touched glasses, and each shared a toast to the night and the beautiful lake.

An hour later they dropped the sails as the boat eased into Horton Bay. Darkness had come quickly. Sally could see the lights from four or five other boats anchored in the calm harbor of the bay. This had been a favorite spot for her since she was a little girl. It was such a quiet escape, even with the other boats here tonight.

She turned the big sailboat up into what little breeze was still blowing. They got the sails down and the anchors positioned to hold them for the night. Gwen brought the wine bottle up from below, and they sat next to each other on the soft cushion. They could hear the sound of classical music coming from one of the boats off across the bay. Sally looked up at a sky filled with so many stars visible on a dark night, out away from the lights of any town. Over the trees she sensed a moving glow of lights that within minutes revealed itself in the full glory of the Aurora Borealis, the Northern Lights.

The wine and the quiet of the night were soothing. Sally, at least at that moment, felt a comforting peace of mind. She reached down for the bag at her feet and pulled out a sketch pad and a folder that held several photos she had taken of the *EmmaLee*. She spread the photos on the seat next to her and watched as her hand began guiding the pencil across the blank page.

Chapter Fourteen

Even with some tough lawyering on behalf of the Harris family and the slowly recovering Connor Harris, Luke McKendry managed to get off with only ninety days in the county jail that fall. Luke's old man had managed to come up with the bail money and Luke had been out of jail for a month before the trial. I remember he kept pretty much to himself during that time, and he didn't say much during the trial either. It was October when he started his sentence. The Harris's, Comptons and all the other summer people were back home down south by then. Mr. Harris had come back for the trial, but Connor evidently wasn't up to the trip. We heard he would make almost a full recovery. Apparently, he had a slight slur in his speech, but they thought it would continue to improve.

Jonathan and I went back to finish up our last year of high school. We didn't talk much about the fight and life had returned somewhat to normal, particularly after all the summer folk had moved on. My sister, Catherine, changed more than anyone after that summer. She had her life so set on making her way with Jonathan, the shock of it possibly not happening hit her awful hard. She and Jonathan kept seeing each other, but I could tell it was different. I'm not sure if he saw Emily Compton again that summer, but I could tell she wasn't far from his thoughts.

Jonathan and I were coming home from an afternoon hunt that Sunday in December when the Japanese attacked Hawaii. We heard the news playing on the radio when we walked into Jonathan's house that night. His parents were sitting in the living room listening. I'll never forget the look on their faces. With two sons, both who would soon be of military age, they were dealing with that great fear parents and wives and brothers and sisters felt across the whole country that day.

By the time Jonathan and I finished school the next spring, we had already decided we were joining the Navy together to fight the Japanese. As it turned out, we got separated after basic training. Jonathan got sent west to join the Pacific Fleet. I was sent to New York and served on a troop transport that ran across the Atlantic. Luke tried to enlist again, but Uncle Sam just couldn't use him with that leg of his.

I lost touch with Jonathan after a while and only got news from Catherine who would get an occasional letter from him, or news from his parents. From the tone of Catherine's letters to me it was becoming clear their relationship was fading.

Jonathan was assigned to an aircraft carrier and worked on the flight deck as part of the launch crew. I received word in 1944, he had been wounded severely and was recuperating in a hospital in Pearl Harbor. I had been sent home earlier that year after surviving a German sub attack on our ship that killed many of our crew. I had some bad burns and a broken leg, but I managed to hold on until we were eventually fished out of the water.

I tried to get word to Jonathan in Hawaii, but I didn't get answers to any of my letters. His parents told me he had broken his back during the attack on their ship. The details were sketchy, but he apparently had some paralysis in his legs.

There were a lot of things to get used to when I returned home from the war. One of the most difficult was discovering my sister had been seeing Luke McKendry for over a year. Luke *had gone to work for a boat manufacturing company in Charlevoix that was making landing craft for the Navy. He had moved out of the McKendry house and was renting a small place out south of town. Catherine had gone to work there as well, along with many of the women in the area whose men were away at war.*

I never was clear on how Luke and Catherine got together. My sister seemed happy enough with the situation when I got home. Luke wasn't drinking as bad as he had in the past. There didn't seem to be any talk of marriage, but she was spending a lot of time over at Luke's. I tried to talk to her about Jonathan, but she told me that was all in the past.

Then, in the winter of '45, the McKendry's got word Jonathan was well enough to get shipped back home. He was being sent to a V.A. hospital near Detroit to finish out his rehabilitation. I finally got a letter from him written just before he left Hawaii. He told me he was feeling much better and his back was healed, but he was still having trouble getting his legs to cooperate. He said he was looking forward to getting home soon, hopefully for the trout opener in the spring. He didn't mention anything about Catherine.

Jonathan had been at the V.A. hospital in Ann Arbor for over a month since returning from service in the Pacific. He was in a ward with a dozen other veterans who were in various stages of repair. His days consisted of dealing with the monotony of confinement, bad food, too many war stories from those around him and an ongoing series of painful therapy for his legs.

He had little memory of the day he was wounded. Japanese planes had attacked their battle group. He had been on deck helping to get a squadron of fighters into the air. Later, he was told the ship had taken several direct hits from enemy torpedoes. He had been knocked over in one of the explosions and fallen nearly thirty feet to a deck below. He regained consciousness two days later on a hospital ship. His back had been broken in the fall and he had bad wounds on his face and arms. He was put on heavy painkillers and the first weeks of his recovery were a blur.

Eventually he was transferred to Pearl Harbor. Even the time spent there was a series of scattered memories, dulled by the morphine and other drugs. It was during his time at the hospital at Pearl he learned he couldn't walk. It was a blow more devastating than anything he could have imagined. Doctors tried to reassure him there was always a chance when his back was fully healed, he would regain some function in his legs.

The trip back to Michigan had been a long and painful ordeal. The train from California, in particular, had seemed like an endless series of washboard bumps that sent pain shooting through his back. One evening, lying in the portable hospital bed they had loaded him onto the train with, he threw the covers back and looked down at his bare legs and feet and with all of his concentration and energy, he willed his toes to move. At first, he thought he was imagining a slight movement, then he was sure the large toe on his right foot had, indeed, moved ever so much. He had whooped in joy and a nurse came in to check on him. He woke several of the other soldiers in the car with him. He tried again and three of his toes moved. The nurse screamed, too and leaned over to give him a hug.

Each day since he had arrived in Ann Arbor, he had worked hard at getting his legs to respond. With the help of a physical therapist named Gerome from Albuquerque, he worked relentlessly. Gerome was a combat veteran who had been wounded in Europe in 1942. After his recovery, he had stayed on to work for the Army at the hospital. He was a tough, no nonsense sergeant, who gave Jonathan a severe regimen to follow. Within days, he had him standing between two rails where he was able to drag his legs along, supporting himself with his arms. Soon, his legs began to respond as well. Each day he found he was getting stronger and needed to support himself with his arms even less.

Gerome had come to get him on this morning for their daily session. He helped Jonathan down from the bed and into a wheelchair. He was excited to work as hard as he could today. His parents were driving down from Charlevoix to see him this afternoon. Gerome wheeled him down the hall to the therapy room and left him at the doorway for a moment while he went back to get Jonathan's folder. He sat there looking down at his legs, feeling more hope he would be able to return to a somewhat normal life. He thought often of getting back north in time to go fishing with George on the trout opener, of wading up the shallow waters of Horton Creek and casting to that first rising trout. At times, he thought of Catherine. They hadn't written in over a year and her last letter was a vague warning she wouldn't be waiting for him.

He felt a touch on his shoulder and thought Gerome had come back. He turned and saw a nurse's aid uniform. When he looked up, he saw the deep green eyes of Emily Compton looking down at him.

"Jonathan? Is that you, Jonathan?" she said in utter surprise.

He reached down for the wheels and slowly turned the chair to face her. "Oh my God" was all he could manage to say.

She crouched down in front of him. "It is you. Jonathan, what's happened?" She placed her hands on his knee.

He had thought of Emily on occasion during his time at sea. She had become a distant and fading memory of a time he thought would never return. He looked at her without responding. Her face had matured in his years away. She had grown into a young woman. Her hair was cut shorter and she had little or no makeup on, but her face still glowed. He reached down and touched her hands.

"Emily, what are you doing here?" he finally managed.

"I'm going to medical school at the university and I volunteer several days a week over here at the V.A. I can't believe it's you!"

Gerome came back down the hall and walked around to take the back of Jonathan's wheelchair. "So, McKendry, you're chasing nurses again. You sailors never stop. Would you like to introduce me?"

Jonathan was still trying to compose himself. "Gerome, this is Emily Compton," he said.

She stood up, still holding on to his hand. "I met Jonathan years ago up in Charlevoix. We bought a boat from his father."

"Nice to meet you," Gerome said. "Jonathan, you need to tell your friend here we have work to do."

"I'll come by to see you later," she said as she backed away slowly. "I'll stop by." She turned and walked down the hall.

"Well, McKendry, I will say you have good taste in broads. So, you used to chase that skirt up there in Charlevoix, or wherever it is you're from?" Gerome asked.

"No, it wasn't like that. It wasn't like that at all," he said, still looking down the hall as she disappeared around a corner.

"You ready to go get some work done?" the old sergeant asked.

Jonathan nodded, and they turned and went through the door into the therapy room.

His parents came that afternoon. There was a lot of crying and hugging. He was struck by how much they had aged. He was sure his appearance had been a shock to them, as well. He had lost considerable weight and his face had a sunken look with deep black circles under his eyes and a red scar that was still healing across the side of his forehead.

They spoke all afternoon about his time away and his injury and recovery. They told him about home and a few of the new things happening in town. He was pleased to hear Luke was doing okay and had a good job. They stayed through dinner and promised to come back in the morning. His mother's sister lived in Detroit and they were spending the night with her family.

It was after dinner that evening when he saw Emily walk through the door into his ward. The other men in the room gave her approving looks and a few comments as well. She just smiled back at them. She came to the side of Jonathan's bed. "Do you feel up to a walk, or a ride, I guess I should say?" she said, a little embarrassed.

"Sure."

She went to bring over a wheelchair. She helped him into the chair, then pushed him down the long row of beds out into the hall. All afternoon she'd been thinking back to that summer in Charlevoix. She had heard Jonathan had been away at the War. She thought about him from time to time. She remembered his young innocence. She remembered the feelings she began having for him and how it all came crashing to a halt after Connor had been hurt.

There was a large lounge down at the end of the hall and they stopped there. Emily sat beside him in a chair at one of the empty card tables. "Can you tell me what happened?" she asked.

He couldn't help himself from saying, "You're the most beautiful thing I've seen in so many years, I can't even remember."

She smiled and her even white teeth surprised him. They were so perfect and smooth, and he had been among so much that was broken and destroyed. Her smell was fresh and clean and noticeably different from the hospital and ship smells he had grown so accustomed to.

"Jonathan, do you want to talk about what happened?"

He nodded his head slowly and said, "It seems like it's been twenty years since we were up at the lake. There were times I thought I would never see the lake again, or catch a fish, or drive a boat."

"You're home now and you're safe."

"I'm walking better now," he said. "Gerome and I are working harder every day. I almost walked without holding the rails today. I know I'm getting stronger and I know I'm going to walk out of here."

"I heard you were away at the war. We've been up to Charlevoix these past few years, although last summer I stayed here at school. My father let the Navy take the *EmmaLee*. She's out on the East Coast somewhere."

He went on to tell her about his ship and his job, and the action they had seen. He told her what he could remember from the day he was hurt and then about his recovery and trip home to Michigan. It was over an hour before he finished, and it felt good to tell her of his time away.

"My friend George is back in Charlevoix," he said. "He got a little banged up, too. The Germans got a piece of him, but he's home and he's okay. I'm going to get up there to fish with him this spring, one way or the other," he said.

"My brothers shipped over to Europe last year," she said. "They finished school, then went to OCS to get their commissions. They're in England with a support group for the Air Force." She paused and smiled at him. "Jonathan, I'm really glad you're back home safe."

Her words comforted him, and he wanted to reach out and hold her hand, but he held himself back.

Emily said, "I've always felt so badly about what happened that summer to your brother and all. I heard he went to jail for a time."

He nodded, feeling the regret coming back.

"Connor is much better these days. He was able to go back to school and he's working for his father in Chicago."

"I hope he's had sense enough to stay away from my brother," Jonathan said, quietly.

"I haven't heard of anything," she said. "Do you think you'll be able to go home soon?"

"I'm trying hard to get stronger. Gerome is working me to death and I'm doing better every day. I want to get home by the end of April for the trout season opener with George. I know I'm going to make it. Gerome won't say, but I know he's working hard to help me."

"Is there anything I can do?" she asked.

He smiled. "You're doing enough right now."

Over the next several weeks, Emily stopped in to see him every day she worked. She pushed him around the grounds when the weather was nice enough to get outside, and she would eat lunch or dinner with him in the cafeteria. They shared stories of their childhoods and the times they had both spent in Charlevoix. They had not spoken much in the short time they had been together that summer so many years earlier, and they found they had so much to learn about each other.

Jonathan looked for her each day he knew she was on duty. The hours she was away passed slowly. At times, he wondered if her interest in being with him was just her compassion for a wounded soldier and part of her job, or did she really enjoy being with him?

It was a sunny morning in early March when Emily came in pushing a wheelchair. He sat up to greet her and put the book he was reading on the nightstand beside the bed.

"Good morning, Seaman McKendry," she said with a wonderful smile.

"Hello, Emily," he said, brushing his hair back with his fingers.

"I have a surprise for you," she teased.

"And what would that be?"

"I have permission to get you out of here for a while," she said, obviously pleased with herself.

"You're kidding!"

"No, I'm not. Tonight, we're going out on the town and I'm buying you the biggest steak you've ever eaten."

"Emily, you really didn't need to do that," he said and paused for a moment, "but, I'm sure as hell glad you did! Where do you want to go?"

"I'll be back around six to pick you up and we'll head into town. I have a great place picked out and we have reservations for around 6:30."

She helped him down into the chair, then down the hall to meet up with Gerome for his morning session. Jonathan was so excited he felt like he could jump up and run down the hall.

He turned his head to look at her. "You don't know how much I appreciate what you've done to help me."

She rubbed his shoulders and continued to push him on down the hallway. She had been up most of the past night thinking about Jonathan and her feelings for him. He was so unlike the other boys and men she had known. Physically, she had always been drawn to him, but she also felt a deeper connection. For a while she had thought it was just their love for the water and boats, but now she was beginning to feel it was more. These past weeks working with him to get well had allowed her to get to know him so much more deeply. She often remembered the day she met him in the boathouse with her father. She realized now, even from that first day, there was something special about Jonathan McKendry.

About two hours before Emily was to return, it occurred to Jonathan he didn't have any decent clothes to wear to dinner. He asked Gerome about it and they agreed his old Navy uniform just wouldn't do. Gerome volunteered to help and took some clothing sizes from Jonathan and left. A little over an hour later he returned with his arms full of new clothes.

Jonathan had showered and was ready to get dressed. He looked through the items Gerome had purchased for him. There was a navy-blue sport coat that he slipped on over his tee shirt to see if it fit. The feel of the jacket felt strange on his body after so many months in hospital pajamas. It fit fine, and the new smell was a welcome change. There was a white shirt and a striped tie. Gerome had picked out a pair of gray wool slacks and they fit well enough to get by for the night, maybe just a bit long. He had also found some black leather loafers. When Jonathan slid his feet into them, he was surprised how well they fit and how comfortable they felt.

Within a few minutes with Gerome's help, he was dressed. There was a large floor length mirror in the bathroom down the hall and Gerome helped him stand in front of it. Jonathan looked at the image staring back at him, standing there with real civilian clothes and standing, by God! He felt the lingering dull ache of his wounds continue to ebb.

"Gerome, I don't know what to say."

"You look like a million bucks, man."

"We better get down to the lobby. I told her I'd meet her there." He took one last look in the mirror at the stranger looking back at him. For so long he had seen a broken and pained image stare back. More and more in the last weeks, he had begun to feel like the long climb out of this deep and terrible hole was nearing an end. He could see the edge now and he saw light shining from the real world that was waiting for him again.

Emily arrived on time as promised. She drove up to the front of the hospital on the circle drive in a black convertible with a tan canvas top and stopped by the front door to get out. Jonathan was waiting on the front walk with Gerome. He was helping him stand as she arrived. She waved as she got out and came over.

"Jonathan, you look...well, you are a sight to see," she said. She came right up and hugged him, then she kissed his cheek. The feel of her next to him was the most wonderful thing he knew he had ever felt. She stepped back.

"Let me look at you," she said.

"Gerome did a little shopping for me," Jonathan said. "I didn't really feel like putting on the old Navy dress whites."

"I told him he looks like a million bucks, don't you think, Emily?" Gerome said.

"Two million, easy," she said with a big smile. "Let's get you into the car. Are you ready?"

"Absolutely." With a cane and Gerome's help, he was soon sitting in the front passenger seat of the car.

"Thanks," he whispered to Gerome as Emily went around to the other side of the car. "I owe you big."

"You have a great time. You've earned it," Gerome said, and then he pulled back and closed the door.

Jonathan watched him wave as they pulled away. He saw the big hospital behind his friend and felt happy to be leaving it behind, if only for a night. He watched the trees along the drive pass by, and he felt like he was moving down a corridor from the past into a new future.

When he looked over at Emily, she was smiling at him. She turned to watch the road. "Jonathan, we're going to Dominic's tonight," she said. "It's a great place out on the south side of town. They have a Porterhouse steak there as big as a plate and garlic mashed potatoes that are unbelievable."

Jonathan sat silent for a moment. He was enjoying the feel of the new leather seat beneath him, the smell of the new car and Emily's perfume. He was mesmerized by the traffic and people walking on the sidewalks. Finally, he said, "Emily, you're the one who's unbelievable. I'm not sure I'll ever be able to tell you how much this means."

He watched her smile again, and he noticed the dress she was wearing, red and black with a white scarf around her neck and black and white high-heeled shoes on her feet. Her hair had been curled and styled, and it shined even in the soft fading light. Her lips were bright red and so were her nails, as he looked at her hands on the steering wheel. He couldn't help but think of her when he had seen her as a young girl years ago on the deck of her father's boat with her hair blowing in the wind. She had grown into a beautiful woman and she was here with him in one of the nicest cars he had ever seen, let alone sat in. He shook his head in amazement as he thought about how far he had come in the last months from his small confined bunk on the ship and the series of hospital beds and long hours looking at the ceiling.

He watched the small college town of Ann Arbor slip by as they drove. Young people were walking together, boys and girls holding hands, sitting together and talking on benches, going in and out of stores. He was finally beginning to feel like he was really home in America and life was returning to normal.

Later, they sat across the table from each other at dinner. The restaurant was dark and noisy, and filled nearly to capacity. The waitress had taken their order for drinks and he watched as she put a glass of white wine down in front of Emily and a frosty cold mug of beer in front of him. He looked at the bubbles rising from the bottom of the mug and the icy cold condensation on the outside as he reached out to touch it.

"Do you have any idea how long it's been?" he asked her.

"For a cold beer?"

"For a cold beer." He held the mug up and proposed a toast, "To America's prettiest Florence Nightingale. Thank you for everything you've done to help me get back... to get back home."

They touched glasses and drank. Jonathan savored the cool chill and taste of the beer as it foamed inside his mouth and down his throat.

"Jonathan, you deserve so much more. You served your country and you almost gave your life. I can't begin to imagine what you've seen and what you've been through."

Listening to her words, he began to see images of the War and his ship and friends, some who were now dead. He closed his eyes to block the thoughts and opened them again to see Emily Compton. The contrast was overwhelming, and he put the drink down. He felt like he was short of breath and his heart was pounding in his chest. He breathed deeply for several moments but couldn't seem to find the right words. He just stared into the beer, watching the bubbles lit from behind by a candle on the table.

Emily seemed to understand and didn't try to speak. They sat in silence for a while, then the waitress brought menus and they had a welcome diversion.

They ordered a short time later and as the waitress walked away, Emily asked, "Will you be going back up to Charlevoix, I mean as soon as they say you're ready?"

"My folks were here again yesterday."

"Oh, I didn't know. How are they?" she asked.

"Well, I can't believe how much my dad has aged, so much more than my mother. They want me to come home as soon as possible. My dad needs help with the business. My brother's working over at a plant in town." He looked for a reaction from her when he mentioned Luke, but didn't notice any change of expression. "The old town's been going along just fine they say... a little quieter in the summers than before the war."

"And your friend George is home?"

"Yeah, he's back and almost put back together. I guess I told you about his ship. He's doing just fine. My parents said he's planning to come down to visit in the next week."

"I'm sure it will be great for you to see him."

"I've been thinking about college," Jonathan said.

She was taking a sip from her glass of wine and after she swallowed, she said, "That would be great. Do you know where you want to go and what you want to study?"

"Engineering, I think," he said with hesitation. "I want to build boats and I have a lot to learn," he said, feeling a bit clumsy about the whole discussion.

"My father's an engineer. You should talk to him about it. He could give you some great advice, I'm sure of it."

He felt a little embarrassed at the thought of talking to Stewart Compton about his education, but he put the thought aside for now. "I've been thinking about Michigan Tech up in Houghton. They have a good engineering school. I was looking into it before the war."

"Houghton, Michigan? Way up in the U.P.?"

"Right. It's way up there, but it's a good school I'm told. I think I'm going to be able to get some money from the Navy to help with the tuition. Gerome's been helping me with the whole process."

"What would you do without that man?" Emily said. "You're so lucky to have him."

"I've been very lucky all around, to get back home, to have enough left of this body to put back together, to have friends like Gerome... and like you."

"Well, thank you," Emily said. "It's been my pleasure. I still can't believe we met again after all these years, even though the circumstances aren't what you would have hoped for."

The waitress brought salads and placed them down in front of them. They went through the motions of placing their napkins on their laps and reaching for silverware and tasting the food. Jonathan's thoughts were far away, however. He suddenly couldn't help but think of men and friends who had been with him back on his ship in the Pacific, sitting in the mess, eating bad food, waiting for the next engagement, wondering if they would ever get home again. He looked again at Emily Compton and knew he was truly blessed to have survived, to have returned and to be sitting here with this girl, in this place.

When the dinner was finished, and Jonathan had reluctantly agreed to order a second dessert, they sat facing each other with napkins askew in front of them on empty plates.

They had talked about their families and school and how Emily was planning to finish medical school at the University of Michigan and start a family practice. While they talked, Jonathan had been thinking about how different their lives had been and probably would be in the future and yet, for this time tonight they seemed to have so much common ground and they were together as if it was the most natural thing. He knew George Hansen would never believe it.

"That is the best meal I'm sure I will ever have in my entire life. Thank you," he said as he pushed back from the table and put his hands on his stomach.

"You're welcome. You had quite an appetite, which I can understand after eating that hospital food." The waitress brought the check and Emily reached down for her purse and left some bills on the table. "There are some friends of mine I'd like you to meet. They're going to be down at this little bar off campus tonight, and I said we would stop by."

Her invitation caught him by surprise, and he didn't answer right away as he thought about the prospects of meeting her college friends. It seemed too awkward and too overwhelming. *What could he possibly have in common with them?*

"Would you like to come, or is it just a bit much on your first night out?"

"Some friends?" he managed to say.

"Yes, a couple of girlfriends from my sorority and some boys we hang out with. I know they'd like to meet you."

Her words cut through him and he knew she wasn't trying to hurt him, that she was just trying to include him in her circle of friends to have some more fun on his night out, but... *some boys*

157

that we hang out with. He felt foolish for assuming she didn't have a boyfriend or that she might even be interested in him as more than just a past acquaintance and patient at the hospital. He tried to hide the disappointment in his voice. "You know, this has been a great time and thank you for dinner. It was incredible, but I'm really running out of steam and probably better get back."

"Oh, of course," she said, clearly disappointed.

When they pulled up in front of the hospital, she got out and got a wheelchair from inside the door. She helped him out of the car and into the chair. A nurse came out to meet them. Emily came around to face him before the nurse wheeled him inside. She took his hand. "I'm really glad we could do this, and you could get out of this place for a while."

Jonathan felt her soft hand in his and looked into her eyes and tried to block out all the jealousy and uncertainty he knew was unfair. He wanted to tell her to stay but finally managed, "This was really great. Thank you. You'll have to let me return the favor someday."

Emily knelt down in front of his wheelchair and took both his hands in hers. "I'll take you up on that offer, as soon as you feel up to it."

"Will I see you tomorrow?"

"I'll be back after classes in the afternoon. Good night, Jonathan." She leaned over and kissed him again, this time on the lips, then pulled away and walked to the car. He watched her slowly drive away out into the street. The moist hint of her kiss lingered on his mouth.

Chapter Fifteen

Sally was drifting through a dream. Strangely, she knew it was a dream, as if she was watching herself. She was on a large boat and could feel a cold wind in her hair. The waves were large and crashing up over the side of the boat, drenching her. The cold wetness caused her to shiver uncontrollably. She could hear shouting and looked around her to see who was calling. Out in the water she saw a hand disappear behind a large swell of waves. She kept looking to see it again.

She tried yelling to the person to get them to answer, but she couldn't seem to get the words out clearly. The harder she tried to speak the more difficult it became. Only every other word seemed to come from her mouth in any clarity. She saw the arm rise out of the water again in the heavy waves, then it fell out of sight. She climbed up over the rail of the boat and jumped down into the water. It was icy cold, and she couldn't breathe. Her clothes felt like they were crushing in on her. The waves swept her up to their crests, then washed over her, sending her downward into a dark green hole, only to be lifted up again.

She heard a voice calling again. When she tried to answer, a wave hit her and filled her mouth with water and she was coughing and trying to catch her breath. She felt the weight of her clothing pulling down on her and she fought and kicked hard to stay above the surface.

She screamed again and this time the sound came out clearly and she found herself sitting upright in her bed, her real scream echoing through the house.

Two hours later she was walking down the sidewalk toward her gallery. It was a little past ten and the other shops along the street were open for business. Gwen had gone down to Traverse City for the morning to look at some work they were considering showing. A storm front was making its way in from Lake Michigan. Dark purple clouds passed quickly above, and the wind kicked debris along the walkway. She could smell the rain in the air.

She reached the storefront to the gallery and stopped for a moment to look at the sign on the door...*The Thomason Gallery*. She stepped back and looked at the pieces she and Gwen had selected to display in the windows.

She unlocked the front door and entered the shop. Walking to the back in the dark shadows of morning, she found the light switches on the back wall and pushed them all quickly. The room exploded in the brightness of color and shape. She looked around at the life she had chosen and the business she had built. There were beautiful pieces of art all around her, paintings, sculptures and several pieces of her own work. It had always pleased her to surround herself each day with such beauty. She walked among the work and felt its familiar lines and colors begin to reach her and comfort her.

The quiet of the shop was suddenly broken by the small bell hanging on the front door. The door pushed open and Sally saw a woman and small girl walk in. It was Mary Alice Gregory and she was holding the hand of the little girl. Sally heard the familiar voice of Megan Clark.

"Hi, Sally!"

"Good morning, Megan. How are you?"

Mary Alice Gregory cut in, "Hello, Sally. Isn't it just a dreadful day out there?"

"Yes, I'm afraid our week of great weather has passed for a while."

"Well, Megan and I are out on a shopping spree this morning. When I talked to Ben, he said he had some business on the phone all morning so I offered to take Megan, and we're having just a wonderful time," Mary Alice said, holding up several plastic bags of merchandise.

Sally could sense that tone in the woman's voice that always set her on edge. She was relishing her role as guardian for little Megan today and wanted the whole town to know about it.

"Sally, look at my new sweatshirt," Megan said. She reached down into one of the bags and pulled out a blue sweatshirt with a large white "Charlevoix" sewn in across the chest.

"Why, Megan, you're a true local now," Sally teased. "Come over here and show me what else you've bought."

The little girl spread the bags out on the floor and started rustling through them.

"We have a few more shops to check out down the street," Mary Alice said, "then we're meeting Ben for lunch. Depending on his schedule, Megan and I may run up to Petoskey this afternoon. As you know, Sally, there are some darling shops up there I know Megan would just love."

Sally swallowed hard and fought to control her words, "Won't that be nice," she managed.

"Look, Sally, a new bathing suit. Isn't it great?" Megan said.

Sally reached out to take it from her and held it up. "It's beautiful, sweetie," she said. She remembered the sketches she had worked on the previous night on the sailboat down at Horton Bay.

"I have something for you and your father." She noticed the sour look on Mary Alice's face as she got up to go get her bag. She had drawn several simple sketches of the *EmmaLee* in different settings and from different angles. She wanted Ben to agree on a direction before she proceeded. "Megan, come over here and I'll show you."

Sally spread the drawings out on a table. Mary Alice and Megan walked over and stood beside her. "These are some sketches of the *EmmaLee* I'd like you to share with your dad. After you've talked about them, have him call me so I can get started on the painting."

"These are neat!" the little girl said.

"What are you working on now?" Mary Alice asked, looking at her watch impatiently.

Sally couldn't help but feel the pleasure in giving Mary Alice some of her own medicine. "Ben has commissioned me to paint the *EmmaLee*. He wants to hang the piece at the head of the table in the dining cabin."

"Well, isn't that nice," Mary Alice said.

"Sally, you're such a good drawer," Megan said. "Could you teach me sometime?"

"I would love to."

The phone in the shop rang at four that afternoon. Gwen was closest to the counter and picked up the receiver. "Thomason Gallery, this is Gwen, can I help you?"

"Why hello Gwen, this is Ben. How are you?"

"I'm just fine, Ben. Are you looking for Sally?"

"Well, actually, I have the sketches Sally sent over of the boat. I was calling to see if you and Sally had plans for dinner this evening and if you were free to join us here on the boat for dinner at around seven."

Gwen looked around the shop for Sally but couldn't see her. "That's very nice of you. Let me see if I can find Sally. She seems to have stepped out, or maybe she's out back. Let us call you right back."

"Sure. I know it's last minute, but let me know if it will work out," Ben said. "The chef's putting together a wonderful meal, and I have a couple new wines I would love to share with you. And we need to talk about the sketches."

"Sure, Ben, that sounds nice. We'll call you right back." Gwen hung up the phone. She looked out at the people passing on the sidewalk, holding umbrellas against the rain and wind, and down to the boats across the road moored along the city docks. *Sure, Ben, that sounds just great.*

Sally came out of the back room looking through some papers in her hands. They had been quite busy in the shop today since she had returned from her trip down to Traverse City. Gwen had wanted to talk to Sally about her nightmare from earlier this morning, but there just hadn't been a good opportunity and she had been wrestling with whether she should bring it up at all.

"Oh, there you are," Gwen said. "You just missed Ben. He's invited us over to the boat tonight for dinner. He wants to talk about your sketches."

Sally slowed and looked back at her. Gwen could see the sudden indecision across her face.

"Dinner?" Sally said.

"Yes, he said around seven."

"What do you think?"

Gwen looked down at the floor, then out onto the street again, thinking through the conversation with Ben and the look on her partner's face. "I think that... I think you should go. You really don't need me. He wants to talk about your sketches and—"

"Gwen," she heard Sally interrupt. "Gwen, he invited us both, didn't he?"

"I just happened to answer the phone and..."

"...and he invited us both to dinner, didn't he?" Sally asked with a hint of uncharacteristic irritation in her voice.

"Yes, he did."

"Why don't we pass on dinner and I'll just plan to stop by there sometime tomorrow to go over the drawings with him?" Sally offered.

"Okay, I don't mean to make this into too big an issue," Gwen said. "I'm sorry, why don't we go? It sounds like his chef is preparing a great meal."

Gwen watched as Sally came over and put the papers down on the counter. Sally reached out and took her in her arms and held her close. Gwen felt her face get lost in her blonde hair and she held her tightly. She pulled back and saw tears forming in Sally's eyes. "Why don't we go?" Gwen said.

Ben looked across the table at the two women who were his guests for the evening. The steward was clearing the plates and the chef had come out to serve another wine. He was filling everyone's glasses. He couldn't help but notice Sally and Gwen and been subdued and quiet for much of the dinner. He found himself staring at Sally. When he realized she was looking back at him, he reached down for his wine glass.

"This is a wonderful new Shiraz from Australia I would like you to try," he said. He looked back at Sally and noticed sadness in her eyes he hadn't seen earlier. He watched Sally and Gwen taste the wine.

Gwen spoke first, "It's wonderful, Ben. Can I see the bottle?"

He handed it across the table to her. "Some friends in New York had this one night at a dinner and it was so good we ordered some for the boat the next day," he explained. "It's becoming one of my favorites. What do you think, Sally?" he asked.

He watched as Sally took another drink, longer this time.

"It's lovely," she said as she looked over at Gwen and smiled slightly. "And the food was... well, delicious. Thank you again for having us over."

Megan had eaten earlier and now came into the dining cabin and joined them at the table. "Hello, everyone," the little girl said. "I've been watching Disney on the TV. I love the little boy that plays Beaver in the movie."

Ben reached over and scruffed his daughter's hair as she sat down beside him. "Would you like to join us for some dessert, Megan?" he asked.

"What are we having?"

"How about... strawberry shortcake!" he said and watched the smile grow on his daughter's face.

The dessert was served, and everyone was quiet except for Megan who kept on about the movie and how she thought that maybe Wally was cuter than the Beaver. When the dishes had all been cleared, Ben got up and walked around to fill his guest's wine glasses and then he went over to get the sketches from the sideboard.

"Sally, as I was saying earlier, these drawings are terrific. I don't know if I could pick any one I like better than the others."

"Ben," said Gwen. "This had been a great dinner and thank you for having me, but I really do need to get back down to the gallery to catch up on a couple of things before morning. Sally, you can stay to go through these, can't you?"

Ben watched as Sally gave her friend a long and inquiring look.

Finally, Sally spoke. "Sure, why don't you go on ahead. I'll see you later."

"Ben, thank you, this has been very nice," Gwen said.

He walked up the stairs with her and out onto the deck of the ship. He watched Gwen walk on ahead along the deck toward the walkway down to the dock. She stopped at the opening in the rail and turned to face him. She reached out to shake his hand and he leaned forward to kiss her on the cheek. "Gwen, I'm sorry you have to leave."

"It's getting late and I really have to get caught up." She paused and then said, "Ben, can I be totally honest with you?"

He hesitated for a moment.

"Ben, I can tell you have... that you have feelings for Sally."

Her frankness caught him unprepared and he couldn't respond.

"Sally is a wonderful woman... all I really care about is her happiness. Do you understand what I'm trying to say?" she asked.

All he could do was nod.

"Good night," she said and turned and walked down the ramp.

He stood watching her walk away, illuminated by the lights along the dock. He sighed and turned and was surprised to see Sally standing in the dark shadows of the ship's cabin.

He walked over toward her. She stood motionless and he could just see the outlines of the features of her face, but he could tell she was crying. He came up in front of her and stood awkwardly for a moment, then he held out his arms and moved into her to hold her. He felt her come slowly into his embrace and sink down into his body. She placed her head on his shoulder, looking away across the park, watching Gwen walking up the hill into town.

They stood there together. Ben could feel her gentle sobs, her tears soaking down through his shirt. He felt her arms wrapped around his shoulders and the closeness as their two bodies pressed together.

"Sally?" He couldn't find words. "Sally, please don't..."

She pulled her face back to look at him. He could see the incredible sadness in her eyes, and he could feel his own tears starting to come. He heard Gwen's words again in his mind. *I can tell you have feelings for Sally.*

She put her cheek up against his and he felt her tears slide between them. Her face was warm and wet, and he held her close.

After a few moments, he began to feel her relax in his arms and she grew still. She placed her face down on his chest, then after a while she looked up directly into his eyes. "Ben, this is so unfair. I'm sorry that—"

He put his hand gently on her mouth and he looked into her eyes. They shined back at him, reflecting the lights from the dock. He let his hand slowly drop from her mouth, then he pressed forward and let his lips brush hers. The touch was electric, and he pulled back and looked at her again. Her eyes were closed, and he could feel her tremble. He moved his hand behind her neck and up into her hair and pulled her close to him again. He felt the soft wetness of her lips press against his and he kissed her deeply now. He felt the closeness of her, and he moved with her in a long, slow embrace. He tried not to think, just feel.

She pulled back and now her eyes were open. She smiled at him through the tears on her cheeks and flooding her eyes. They stood looking at each other and he felt a dozen emotions racing through him. He just wanted to hold her and to be in this place.

A large raindrop fell and splashed on his nose and it startled them both. Then, more drops began to fall and suddenly it was raining hard. He felt the rain soak into him, and he watched as it splattered on her hair and her face. It was a cool rain that echoed hard against the boat deck. They both started to laugh, and he kissed her again as he felt the rain wash over their lips.

Sally could still feel the touch of Ben's lips on her mouth as she walked home across the bridge over the channel. She stopped at the center of the bridge and looked out to Lake Michigan. It was raining lightly, and the clouds were sweeping low over the town in the darkness. She could see the lights along the piers and the large white light sweeping the horizon from the lighthouse.

She had left Ben standing there on the deck of the ship. She had to leave him, to get away to think through her emotions and the implications of it all, and the words she had heard from Gwen. *All I want is for her to be happy.*

She placed her hands on the cold metal rail of the bridge. A car thundered by behind her and she turned to watch the red taillights drive slowly down through the town. A boat was coming in the channel now from the lake and she watched the red and green running lights coming toward her. She turned to keep on along the bridge, then up the hill toward her house. *All I want is for her to be happy.*

Chapter Sixteen

I had been down to see Jonathan in the hospital in Detroit a month before he was ready to come home. When we had last seen each other, we were boys going off on a new adventure to fight in a great war to protect the world from unspeakable evil. When we reunited that first day back in Michigan it was striking to see how much we had changed in those few short years, not just physically, but in a much more profound way. We had returned not only as men who had matured far beyond our early years, but also as friends who could relate to each other at a much deeper level. We still had our childhood experiences and bonds. Now, we also had the shared experiences of war and death and survival that brought us together more closely than ever before.

I stayed with Jonathan for two full days on that trip to the hospital. We both shared our time away at war and the time of recovery after our wounds. We talked about the new worlds we had seen and the new people who had become our friends. We cried together as we talked about the pain of war, injury and of death that became so much a part of our daily lives.

When I left him that last day, we both knew we were fortunate to be back home together and alive. We were both excited about the lives that lay before us and the promise the future now held, when only a few months earlier it had been so hard to find hope of any kind.

We also spoke of home in Charlevoix and I tried to fill Jonathan in on what had changed since we had been away. Certainly, there were new people and places to talk about, but I also tried to help him understand how much the war had also changed those who had stayed behind. What I noticed most in returning was the change in attitude and spirit in the friends and family I had seen since my return. Many seemed to share a more resolute sense of purpose, while others still struggled to find their way. All clearly had a renewed love of their country and appreciation for those who had left to defend it.

I found it hard to talk about Luke and Catherine and I was surprised Jonathan didn't ask. In the end, I wasn't able to find the right way to tell him his brother and his best girl were now together. That would have to wait until Jonathan came home to us in Charlevoix.

Jonathan sat uncomfortably in the firm seat of the passenger train carrying him on the final leg of his journey home. He rode in his Navy dress uniform and his cane lay against the seat at his side. He looked out across the countryside of northern Michigan, the pine forests and rolling hills coming slowly to life as spring continued to press her will upon the land. It was mid-April and there were still pockets of snow back in the shade of the deep woods. Where the sun could reach the land, fresh green colors from sprouts and buds were beginning to take over the dull grays and browns of winter. Through the morning he had seen deer in the meadows and ducks and geese flying low over the trees. As he pulled through towns, he saw families waiting to meet loved ones, many soldiers like himself who had been away far too long.

He would be in Charlevoix by mid-afternoon. His family was coming down to the depot on the lake to meet him. His friend George would be there. He wondered often about Catherine, but he didn't expect she would come out to see him, and frankly, he wasn't sure what he would say to her.

He saw Emily Compton the day before he was being discharged from the hospital. He was able to stand on his own and walk up to her with his cane when she came in to see him for the last time. They both stood there awkwardly for a moment, then she came to him with her arms open and hugged him tight. There had been little left to say. She wasn't certain if she would be coming up to Charlevoix for the summer. She had tentative plans to stay in Ann Arbor and take classes and continue to work at the hospital. She left him that morning with a kiss on his cheek. There were tears in her eyes as she wished him good luck and said goodbye.

His reflection in the train window stared back at him, but he could also see Emily's face in his mind and the tears in her eyes. He could hear her words and the soft tones of her farewell... *Good luck, Jonathan. Please write to me.*

He had searched for deeper meaning in her embrace and kiss and in her parting words, but he knew he was fooling himself. Their worlds had come together for brief periods, but there was so much dividing them in what lay ahead. She had friends and family in a world so different from where he had come from and where he was going. She had a career in medicine that would surely consume her and guide her path. His plans were only tentative possibilities. One step and one day at a time, Gerome had so often reminded him.

The train slowed as it approached the depot platform in Charlevoix. The skies had grown dark in the past hour and it was now raining hard. He looked out across Lake Charlevoix as he passed in front of the Belvedere Club property and the fine homes up along the hill. The train rattled over the old bridge across the channel and its brakes squeaked as it was brought to a stop at the station. He looked across the aisle and out through the window toward the depot. The platform was empty. If anyone had come, they were inside trying to keep dry from the storm. He pulled his bag down from the overhead shelf and with his cane, made his way slowly up the aisle to the exit door. A conductor took his bag for him and helped him down the steps onto the platform.

George Hansen came running out from inside with an umbrella up to shelter him from the heavy rain. "McKendry! Welcome home, you sonofabitch!"

He smiled as his friend swept him up in a big hug.

Then he saw his parents standing together under the shelter of the depot's roofline and he walked together with George under his umbrella to meet them. His mother came forward first and fell into him with a tearful greeting. He stood facing his father. The elder McKendry held out his hand and they shook formally, a firm grip of affection between father and son.

His father smiled at him and said, "Welcome home, son."

Jonathan moved forward and hugged his father and felt him squeeze back. It was the first time he could ever remember hugging his father.

"Your mother has prepared a big feast, and we have a whole bunch of friends and family coming over to join us for dinner," his father said, as they separated.

"That sounds great, Pop."

"You're walking so well," he heard his mother say.

"Well, you met Gerome when you were down in Ann Arbor. Without him I'd still be lying in that bed back in the hospital."

His father reached his arm around him and said, "Let's get you home now."

The reception had been a loud affair with everyone trying to talk at once and beer and wine flowing freely. His family had planned an open house and there was food on every table and countertop and a steady procession of people coming through the house to welcome the young sailor home.

Jonathan was standing in a corner of the living room talking to several old friends. George came up and joined the conversation with two fresh beers for himself and Jonathan. After a few minutes, the others moved away leaving the two old friends together again.

"Jonathan, how many times did you think about this day when you were away overseas?"

"Oh, at least every day," he answered. "I'm having a hard time believing I'm really here now. I know I'm going to wake up soon and still be in that damned hospital back in the Pacific."

George looked around the room. "I imagine Luke will be by any time now. I wanted to talk to you about Luke when I was down in Ann Arbor, but... well, I don't know."

"What about Luke?"

"Well, it's really Luke *and* Catherine," George said.

Jonathan shifted his weight on his cane. "Yeah, Catherine... you know your sister and I have not kept up very well."

"I know," said George. "But what you don't know is what's been going on between Luke and Catherine."

Jonathan stared into his friend's eyes. "Luke and Catherine?"

"They've been together for some time now. I'm sorry I didn't tell you about this earlier."

Jonathan looked down at the glass of beer in his hand, then took a drink. He shook his head and a smile slowly spread across his face. "Well, I knew there was someone. It never crossed my mind it was my own brother, but what the hell, does it really matter who? I knew it was over between us a long time ago. I really didn't expect her to wait for me after all this time." He paused for a few moments. "But Luke, that is a surprise."

"You don't seem too shook up?" George said.

"No... no, I guess not. Has Luke cleaned up his act? Is he treating her okay?"

George sighed before he answered. "It's really hard to say. He still spends a lot of time down at *The Helm*, and Catherine's there more than I would like to say. He's working steady over at the boat factory, but I'll be honest with you, he hasn't changed much."

"I haven't heard about any more trouble with the law."

"I guess there have been a few minor scrapes. Since I've been home, what bothers me most is how much Catherine has changed. I swear you won't know her when you see her."

"Why is that?"

"She's just a whole different person," George said. "God, I don't know exactly, but it's like Luke has crept inside and all the joy's gone out of her. She doesn't even look like you remember. Her hair and face are usually a mess and her clothes, well... it's just a damned shame."

"Have you talked to her about it?"

"You can't get two words out of her anymore."

Jonathan saw the crowd around the door into the kitchen moving aside as his brother, Luke, walked into the room. He saw Jonathan and George over in the corner and slowly made his way in their direction. Jonathan looked at his brother and was amazed at the deeper lines of age he saw in his face. His hair was cut much shorter and there were traces of gray already beginning to show. He had a half empty beer in his hand.

"Welcome home, war hero," he said with a slur in his voice Jonathan remembered well.

He reached out to put his arms around his brother, but Luke just put out his free hand and shook Jonathan's with a weak grip.

"How are you, Luke?"

"Bout the same." He nodded his head slowly, looking his brother up and down and at the cane in Jonathan's left hand. "So, looks like we both got bum legs now, huh?"

Jonathan just nodded.

"Hey look, I can't stay. I got a couple of things I need to get to, but I'm gonna be down at *The Helm* tonight. Stop by and I'll buy you two war heroes all the beer you can drink. How's that?"

Jonathan hesitated.

"Well look, really, I gotta go," Luke said, "but stop by tonight, okay?"

"Yeah, I'll try to come by," Jonathan said. He watched his brother turn and walk out of the room. He felt George put his hand on his shoulder.

Catherine was waiting at the bar at *The Helm* when Luke walked in. She finished her cigarette and put it out in the full ashtray in front of her. A nearly empty glass of beer rested in her other hand with red lipstick on the rim. Her dress was a faded print that looked far past new. Her hair was pulled back and collected with a green rubber band, and the ends lay in ragged clumps down her back. She saw him come in and turned on her stool to make room for him to slide in next to her. She leaned over and kissed him on the cheek as he sat down. "Hey honey," she said.

Luke didn't answer. He got the bartender's attention and just nodded for the usual. The clock on the wall behind the bar showed a little after four in the afternoon. There were a few customers down at the other end of the bar and no one was sitting at the tables yet. Luke got his drink and drained half of it before he spoke. "Just got back from seeing your old sweetie."

"Now Luke, don't start," she said. "He's old news and you know that."

"Yeah, I suppose. I asked him and your brother to stop down later after all the folks get their fill over at the house. I figure I owe him a cold beer or two, goin' out and fightin' for the country and all."

She didn't answer and just looked at the bottles lined up along the shelves behind the bar.

"I guess he got pretty tore up over there," Luke said, looking down into his glass. "He's got a cane and... God, it looks like he's lost 50 pounds."

Catherine turned to face him. "Luke, you know I don't have those feelings for your brother anymore?"

He nodded.

"There was no way I was waiting. Besides, he always had eyes for that Compton girl," she said. "I've got my own life now and I've got you."

Luke didn't look at her. "I suppose he knows about all that by now."

"I suppose," she answered softly. "There's something else." She finished her drink and signaled for another. Luke still didn't look up. "I've been late about five days now, Luke."

He finally turned to look at her. "What do you mean, late?"

"My period."

He just looked at her without answering and then looked back to his drink. "You sure?"

"Of course I'm sure, goddamit!" she said. "I've never been late a day before."

"Okay, then."

"Just okay?"

"Well, just what I said, okay."

She grabbed him tightly by the arm and pulled him around to face her. "I'm telling you we're gonna have a baby, Luke."

He wouldn't look her in the eye. "Yeah," he said, "I heard you." He pulled his arm away and took his drink and finished it.

Catherine sat staring at the side of his head for a few moments. She sighed deeply then grabbed the empty glass in front of her and threw it as hard as she could against the far wall. It crashed into the liquor bottles. Glass and alcohol splattered in all directions. The noise echoed through the empty bar.

Bud, the bartender, came scrambling over when he heard the crash. Catherine got up and walked quickly out of the bar without saying another word.

"What in hell was that?" the old man asked.

Luke looked up and said, "It's just the bitch drunk again. Put it on my bill."

The guests had left the McKendry house and Jonathan was sitting at the kitchen table eating a sandwich. His mother was scurrying around cleaning up. His father came in and sat across from him.

"It's good to have you home, son."

"Thanks for going to all this trouble. It was good to see so many old friends and faces."

"Sure, sure. Did you see Luke? He wasn't here more than a few minutes."

"Yeah, I saw him."

"You've heard about him and Catherine then?" his father said.

"Yeah."

"You gonna be all right with that?"

He just nodded, looking down at the table. He noticed his mother looking at him over her shoulder at the sink. She looked away when their eyes met.

"So, how's the business been, Pop?"

"It's been pretty slow, honestly. The past few years have been real quiet up here. Mom's had to take another job up in town cause things have been so slow over at the hotel."

"This summer should be better, don't you think?" Jonathan asked.

"I hope so." His father paused. "I hope so."

He took another bite from his sandwich and when he swallowed said, "I'll be around this summer to help out, Pop. I've been thinking about going away to school next fall, but I haven't been accepted yet."

His father was looking out the small window over the table, seeming to consider what his son had just said. "I was hoping I could count on you a while longer than that, Jonny."

"What do you mean?" He noticed his mother turn to watch them.

"I'm gonna need your help, son. I've been runnin' a little slower these past couple of years. We didn't want to tell you about it because you had enough to deal with."

"How bad? What is it?" Jonathan asked with alarm in his voice.

"There's no reason to get all worried," he answered. "I'm not gonna check out any time soon, but my heart's been on the blink and I've had to slow way down. I'm just not going to be able to keep up with the business if it comes back at all this year."

Jonathan rubbed his eyes and was quickly trying to consider the ramifications of all this. "You're sure you're gonna be all right?"

"Yeah...I got this medication and your mom's been cooking all this special food for me."

Jonathan tried not to show his disappointment. He was both shocked at the news of his father's health but also glad it apparently wasn't a dangerous condition. But, he couldn't help think about school and his own future. He pushed those thoughts aside. *There will be time for all that.*

"Have you talked to Luke about this?" Jonathan asked. "Has he been any help?"

He watched his father shake his head and he could tell from his expression what the answer would be.

"Your brother hasn't been much help to anybody, including himself. I honestly can't tell you why Catherine took up with him and for the life of me, I can't see how she stays with him. He's been lucky to keep his job over at the plant these past years with the drinking and all."

His mother came over and joined them at the table. "Jonny, your brother needs help. Maybe you can get through to him. God knows we've tried."

George came by to pick him up around seven that night. He had his father's old Chevy pickup with tools and lumber stuffed in the back. Jonathan had changed out of his uniform for the last time, he figured.

"How about a little look around town before it gets dark?" George asked as Jonathan slowly eased himself up into the truck.

"Sounds good. Can you take me out to the pier? I want to see the big lake again."

They slowly cruised up Belvedere Avenue, then north through town. It was warm enough to roll the windows down and Jonathan was enjoying the fresh smells of spring and the sights and sounds of his hometown.

They drove slowly up Bridge Street, waving to a few people along the way. They passed *The Helm* and Jonathan could see his brother sitting at the bar through the open door. He looked away, thinking about his conversations at the kitchen table with his father.

Down to the right the city docks on Round Lake had a few early boats tied up and a few moored out on buoys on the lake. They passed the place at the park where Luke had attacked Connor Harris on that summer night. Jonathan stared at the spot as they passed. He could still see Harris lying there on the sidewalk. He remembered Emily Compton kneeling there looking at him, the terror in her eyes and the helpless feeling that overwhelmed him that night.

George must have sensed his thoughts as he turned up the volume on the radio in the truck to divert his attention.

"The old town looks pretty much the same, don't you think?" George asked.

"It looks pretty damn nice," he said, looking back.

They turned off the main road and headed over to the city park beach on Lake Michigan along the pier. When George parked the car, he asked, "You sure you can walk out there?"

"Let's give it a try."

Slowly, the two friends walked across the sand toward the pier. Jonathan could smell the big lake and feel the breeze coming in on his face and he welcomed the familiar memory of it. The sun was falling low over the far horizon and turning a pale red among scattered clouds of gray and purple. George helped him up onto the pier and they began walking out toward the lighthouse at the far end. A couple of old men were sitting on stools holding fishing rods over the rail.

When they got to the end, Jonathan stopped and rested with his arms on the railing, looking over the water to the sharp edge of the horizon and the sun just now touching it. Wisconsin was out there, too far to see, and in closer, Beaver Island, although not visible through the low haze and growing dark of night.

"George, there were nights out on our ship I would look out over the ocean and imagine I was really back here, looking at the lake and I was home and safe."

"I had those same moments."

"Do you ever think about why we made it back and so many others... well, so many others didn't?" Jonathan asked.

"I just counted my blessings every single day. We could easily be at the bottom of one of those big cold oceans."

"So, God decided to keep us around a bit longer. What the hell do we do about it?" Jonathan said, as much to himself as to his friend.

"We better damn well make the most of it."

Later, they parked downtown and walked into the bar to see if Luke was waiting for them. It had grown dark and Bud had closed the door as the evening's chill set in. Jonathan and George walked into the dimly lit bar and saw Luke still sitting where they had seen him earlier.

Jonathan walked up next to his brother and pulled a stool back to sit down. Luke's eyes were closed, and he didn't move. George sat down on the other side and nudged Luke. He lifted his head in surprise and turned to see first George on one side and then his brother on the other. He reached out and examined what was left of his drink and then swallowed it. His head swayed slightly as he tried to gain focus.

When he spoke, the words were more than slurred, they were almost unintelligible. "So, we got ourselves both a you damn war heroes, huh?"

Jonathan thought for a moment about staying to help his brother get home, but then he thought to himself, *to hell with him.* "George, let's get out of here."

"You sure?"

"Yeah, I'm sure." They left without saying anything to Luke and he didn't look up to notice they were leaving.

They walked out onto the sidewalk. Jonathan looked up the familiar street of his youth and looked back at the door to the bar. "God, he's a mess."

"I tried to tell you it's been bad."

"And Catherine's been putting up with that?"

"She's been as bad at times."

"How could that happen?"

"My folks are just sick about it. After we left, she just kept slipping downhill and before they knew it, she was too far down the wrong path."

Jonathan stood silent for a bit. He turned to George. "Let's get some cold beers and a boat and go down to the old bay."

"Horton?"

"Yeah, come on. Let's go."

"It ain't fishing season yet."

"I know. I just want to go and sit and look at the stars and drink some beers with my best friend."

"Your dad got any boats in the water yet?"

"If he doesn't, we'll get one in. Come on."

An hour later they had a cooler filled with ice and a case of long neck beers stowed in the back of one of his father's old runabouts and they were cruising out through the channel into Lake Charlevoix. The sun had been down for a while, but a full moon was coming up over the hills across the lake and the reflection cast its way back toward them on the smooth surface.

Being in the boat, smelling the gas and feeling the chill of the night coming off the lake, Jonathan felt like he was really home. The beer was cold in his hand and he held the wheel in his other as they made their way slowly through the channel past all the boathouses and the big houses up on the hill, then the Coast Guard station on their left. When they cleared the pilings from the railroad bridge, Jonathan pressed the throttle down and the old boat surged up with a throaty roar. They were soon planed out and sliding smoothly across the surface of the still lake. The sky was clear, and the moon was so close you could see the sharp shadows across it. Every minute more stars burst out and sparkled in the growing darkness.

They sat up on the back of the seats with their feet on the cushions. Their heads were up above the windshield and Jonathan savored the feel of the wind in his face and through his hair.

"Goddamn, this is nice!" George yelled over the roar of the engine.

After a while, they could make out the point coming out from Horton Bay. Jonathan made a wide circle and then slowed the boat and turned off the engine to let it slide silently into the bay. There were a few lights on in the cabins up in the woods, but it was dead quiet. The boat kept gliding across the calm surface.

George reached in the back and grabbed two more beers. Small chunks of ice clung to them and they were almost too cold to hold on to. He found the opener in his pocket and popped the two tops, handing one bottle to Jonathan. Without speaking, they touched the necks of the two bottles together and then both took a long slow drink.

"Welcome home, Hansen."

"Welcome home, McKendry."

"Do you think the fish are still here?" Jonathan asked.

"No one's been around to fish 'em now for years. There should be some monsters in there by now," he said, motioning with a nod of his head up towards the creek in the middle of the bay.

"What, two weeks till opener?" Jonathan asked.

"Yeah, two Saturdays from now."

"Let's camp out down here like we used to and get at 'em before sun-up," Jonathan said, taking another long pull from his beer. "The Hendersons will let us use their beach again, don't you think?"

"Sure, I'll call 'em about it."

Jonathan looked up. "George, these are the same damned stars we were looking at out there in the middle of the oceans, but they sure as hell look a lot better back here in the bay, don't you think?"

"They look swell to me."

They both sat in silence awhile.

"George, we gotta do something to help Luke... and Catherine, too, huh?"

"They may be past help."

"Yeah... I guess. I talked to my dad today. He wants me to stick around and help out with the boatworks. Did you know about his health?"

"Yeah, I just heard from your mom a couple of weeks ago."

"Shit, I don't know what to do about school now, George."

George put his beer down on the deck of the boat and looked over at his friend. "Well, the way I see it, after what we've been through, we damned well deserve to make our own way. I know your dad probably needs help, but there's got to be another way."

"There must be something." Jonathan tipped the beer bottle to the sky and felt the cold beer flow down into his gut and a numbness starting to build in his cheeks. When he finished, he threw the bottle in the back of the boat and reached for another. "You ready?" he asked.

The two men sat back looking up at the stars and the moon that was now almost straight overhead. A few bats were out and darting around the boat trying to catch up with an early hatch of bugs. Tree frogs up in the hills sounded like a chorus of banshees and broke the stillness of the night.

"I told you about Emily Compton?" Jonathan asked.

"Yeah, we talked about her when I was down in Ann Arbor."

"She said she won't be comin' up this summer," Jonathan said and then paused, taking another drink. "Probably just as well, huh?"

"Probably just as well."

Chapter Seventeen

It was just past ten o'clock in the evening and the crowds along Bridge Street were beginning to thin out. Those few who remained in town had made their way into the bars and restaurants, and the sidewalks were nearly barren. As Ben Clark walked alone down past the closed shops and darkened windows, he was oblivious to the sounds of laughter and loud voices coming from the night establishments. His mind was wrapped around the earlier events of the evening and the two women who had shared his dinner table.

The stoic Gwen, leaving early, then parting with an admonition. *I only want her to be happy.* Her words continued to repeat in his mind. He tried to decipher whether this had been a gentle warning to stay away from the vulnerable Sally Thomason, or an invitation.

The face of the beautiful and tormented Sally remained clear in his mind. Her tears still burned on his cheeks from the moments he had held her, and then the kiss.

As he walked, he tried hard to sort through his feelings for the woman. These few days in this small town, and the events that had transpired had been so unexpected. He had to admit he felt a strong attraction and connection to Sally from the first moment they met. What he had been unable to sort out was why. Certainly, she was an attractive and talented woman. She had a wonderful way with Megan, but he wasn't looking for another mother for his daughter, and he honestly hadn't given any serious thought to a new relationship either. The pain of their loss was still too near, and yet he felt drawn to Sally.

When they had parted earlier tonight, she left without an explanation or a promise of any further discussion. She had just walked away up the hill into town.

The lights were out throughout the house. Sally sat out on the sun porch, looking into the darkness. The glass of wine in her hand remained full and it almost spilled in her lap before she placed it on the table beside her. She had been home for over an hour now trying to make sense of what had just happened with Gwen and then Ben. The house had been empty when she returned, and she had no idea where Gwen had gone. She needed to talk to her and get this all out. The thought of losing her was like a sharp stake through her heart.

What in the world was happening? Everything suddenly seemed to be moving so fast. All she could think of were the few moments she and Ben had held each other and the feel of his body tight against hers and the taste and lingering feel of the kiss. She couldn't push aside the guilt inside.

She got up and walked back into the house. There was enough light coming in from streetlamps that she could make her way. She got to the kitchen and picked up the phone. She dialed the gallery and listened as it continued to ring with no answer. She clicked the phone dead. She dialed again, this time the bar downtown where she and Gwen often stopped for a drink in the evening. Their friend Max answered. He hadn't seen Gwen all night. She hung up again. She dialed her cell phone, still no answer.

Back on the porch, she picked up the glass of wine and took it with her out the back door and across the lawn. In the darkness, she made her way down the path to the lake. The lights from the end of the pier cast their glow across the water and the bright beacon from the lighthouse continued to sweep the water and up over the land.

She made it down onto the cool sand of the beach and continued on down to the sound of small waves rolling along the shore. The rain had passed, and a few stars were showing through the breaks in the clouds. The sand was still wet and dappled from the falling rain drops. She stopped when she reached the water and let the waves wash over her bare feet. She held the wine glass to her cheek and felt the cool moisture soak into her. She took a short sip.

In her mind, she heard Megan's laugh and she thought of the young girl and her wonderful spirit and energy. Then, she could see her own daughter running along this same beach, splashing into the water, building sandcastles where she now stood.

She shook the images from her mind and walked along the shore toward the pier. A large sailboat was coming out through the channel, and she could see the lights from the boat moving slowly out toward Lake Michigan. People onboard were laughing, and music was playing loudly.

When she reached the pier, she climbed up on the steel and cement structure and began walking out toward the end. The large green navigation light blazed ahead of her on the end of the pier, and every few seconds the light house beacon would blind her as it passed. Sounds and faces continued to flash through her mind, and she tried not to think but just take in the night around her.

She slowed as she approached the rail. The sailboat was now rolling gently out over the swells as it penetrated the dark waters ahead beyond the pier. She put the wine glass to her lips and finished it in one long drink. She placed the glass by her feet and held the rail and looked out over the blackness of the lake and the sky.

It was midday before she was able to get herself down to the gallery. Her assistant had opened the shop and welcomed her as she walked in. Sally scanned the store for Gwen but didn't see her.

"Have you seen Gwen this morning?" Sally asked.

"No, I had to open when I got here."

Sally nodded and walked back into the studio. She saw the note folded in a tent on her desk as soon as she walked into the room. She stood staring at it for a few moments, unable to convince her body to move forward and pick it up. "Oh no," was all she could manage.

Finally, she walked over and sat at the desk and picked up the note. She unfolded it and turned on a small lamp, so she could see. It was written in Gwen's hand.

Sal,

It's better if I go away for a bit and let all of this sort itself out. I'm leaving for New York to spend a couple of weeks with my sister. I just want you to know I love you and I care for you, and most of all, I want you to be truly happy.

Whatever happens, I will always love you.

G.

Sally read the note again and let it fall on the desk. She wasn't surprised. In her heart, she had known Gwen was gone. She had left this all for her to figure out, when what they needed most was to talk and help each other work through all of this. The emptiness grew within her and she felt the clouds of doubt and confusion continue to build.

She looked down at the pictures of the *EmmaLee* she had taken, spread haphazardly across her desk. She reached for one she had taken when the ship first came into the channel last week. Ben and Megan were up at the front rail, waving to the crowds along the pier. The magnificent ship sprawled back behind them and shined in the midday sun, its crew spread along the deck.

She took the photo and put it in her pocket. She walked back out to the front of the gallery and through the front door without speaking. She turned to her right and bumped into a couple coming down the sidewalk from the other direction. They both apologized to her as she continued on without acknowledging them. She needed to walk and think. A few friends recognized her as she walked down the crowded sidewalk. She just nodded as she passed.

She walked without direction or a conscious sense of where she was going. She tried to bring her mind into focus on the changes that were suddenly presenting themselves in her life. She thought of Ben and Megan and where they might be this morning.

After walking for a while, she looked up and realized she was in front of her grandparent's old house. She stopped and looked up at the old Victorian. The front door was closed and there was no one around. Compelled to go up the walk and onto the porch, she heard the old wood steps creak beneath as she walked up, then over to a grouping of wicker chairs on the porch. She sat down without thinking about who might be home or how they might feel about her being there.

Looking across the street, she saw the row of familiar houses shaded by tall oaks in the summer sun and then down the street across the vast expanse of blue lake. She closed her eyes and felt the presence of her mother and her grandmother all around her. She could almost hear their voices.

Chapter Eighteen

It was the Friday before Memorial Day weekend, 1945. Jonathan and I had managed to settle into the flow of home and community since we had both been back. I was working with my father on a house he was building over on Walloon Lake. Jonathan had taken up at the boatworks, helping his father get ready for the summer season.

This weekend would begin the first flow of summer people back into Charlevoix. Boats would start showing up in the slips along the shores of Round Lake. Traffic would become heavier again and the shops and stores would begin hearing the bells on their doors ringing more frequently.

Each year there was a new sense of excitement with the coming season. There was a feeling of rebirth after the long slow crawl of winter, a feeling of promise for the lives and businesses of the locals.

Jonathan and I had got all our fishing in. We knew it would be a busy summer and neither of us was sure where we would be next fall.

He and I were able to make it down to Horton Creek for the trout opener back in April. We camped down on the shore the night before, just like we planned. It had been a wonderful night of retelling old fishing stories and times away during the War. We slept out in the open with the stars all around us up above. When we woke in the morning, the dew lay heavy on our faces and in our hair. Jonathan got up first to get the fire going again and to make coffee. I lay there a bit longer under my blanket trying to get warm and thinking about other mornings in April when we had been out like this as kids growing up. I thought of the fish we caught and the laughter. It felt so good to be home again and back among the trees and the lakes.

After coffee and a quick breakfast of donuts, we grabbed our gear and walked along the shore to the creek mouth. Jonathan was moving pretty well on his legs without a cane by then. The light was just coming up noticeably behind the hills to the east. The bay was calm and smooth except for the trail left by a mother duck with eight small ones behind her. Another pair of ducks swung in low from around the point. We watched them come toward us and then flare out their wings and slow gently to the surface of the bay. Their webbed feet splayed out and touched the water and they glided smoothly to rest, leaving small wakes behind them.

There would be no bugs for the fish to feed on this morning, at this time of year. The fish would be sulking on the bottom, waiting for the season and the sun to warm the water and the land and to get food moving again for them. We tied on big streamer pattern flies that looked like bait fish and leeches.

I remember watching Jonathan wading out into the bay at the mouth of the creek, moving slowly, trying not to make a disturbance on the water. I just stood on the shore for a while and watched. It was his first time with a rod in his hand since those years before the War. He got into position and I watched him hold the rod and reel out in front of him. Pulling out line from the reel, he was scanning the water coming out of the creek, trying to decide where to place his first cast. Making up his mind, he began the familiar rhythm of the cast and I was struck by how smooth and sure the rod moved after so many years away.

The heavy fly and line landed out across the surface of the water and he waited for the fly to sink before he began retrieving the line in slow pulls. I stood there watching, waiting for the sudden electric jolt of his rod with a fish connected. He just continued to strip the line and then he was casting again.

I had looked away for just a moment trying to pick a spot to fish for myself when I heard him shout. I looked out and saw the hard bend in his rod. He turned and I saw the smile across his face. Even in the low light that morning, I saw a face captured in the pure joy of the moment with no thoughts of where we had been or where we might be tomorrow.

Jonathan sat on the worn seat of the pick-up truck, looking over his shoulder as he backed another boat trailer down the ramp at the boatyard. His father was up on the dock giving directions and shouting advice. They had been working long hours for weeks getting the boats ready for the summer clients. In his side mirror, he watched the wheels of the trailer ease down into the water and he stopped the truck and set the brake. He walked around and released the winch on the trailer to let the boat slide back. He threw a line to his father and pushed the long wooden boat back along the dock.

"That's good, Jonny," his father yelled. "I've got her. Why don't you take her out for a quick run?" It was a welcome invitation to Jonathan to spend at least a few minutes out on the lake. "I left the keys in her," his father said.

It was late May and the weather was looking promising for the coming holiday weekend. Sunny skies through the past week had seen temperatures up in the seventies. The McKendrys had been receiving calls all week from clients to make sure their boats would be ready for the weekend.

Jonathan watched his father climb into the truck and slowly pull the trailer up out of the ramp. He tied the boat off front and back, and then climbed in to prep the boat and start the engine.

It cranked several times before he choked it enough to get it to fire. It rumbled a bit unevenly for a minute and then began to settle. He released the lines and jumped in behind the wheel. He guided the boat back out of the slip and then turned her out toward the open lake. He gave her just a little gas to slowly cruise out along the shoreline of Round Lake.

The air was fresh around him and the sun shining down high overhead made it hot in the cockpit of the boat. He took his shirt off and threw it down on the seat behind him. The sun felt good as it warmed his shoulders and back. He stood at the wheel, looking over the windscreen, taking in the sights along the shore and the other boats out on the water. As he made his way out of the channel into Lake Charlevoix, a large sailboat was coming toward him off to his port side from the direction of Oyster Bay. She had a full spinnaker flying and was making good time running with the wind. He fell off to give her room and watched as the big boat passed.

Along the beach, a few children ran into the water, braving the early season temperatures as their mothers sat in beach chairs watching them. The rail bridge was open across the channel and the big hotel up on the hill was a flurry of activity with cars pulling up to drop off weekend visitors.

Memorial Day was always one of their busiest times. Jonathan watched the uniformed doormen coming out to greet the cars and collect the luggage for the guests. His mother would be working long hours this weekend in the kitchen there.

He pushed the boat up to half throttle and ran in a big circle out across the lake. He knew he had to get back quickly to help his father. He navigated around the channel buoy and headed the boat down the center of the channel toward their boatyard. A breakwall ran along to his left protecting the lawn of one of the houses. There was a group of people gathered on the fresh cut grass with drinks in hand, watching the boats come by.

A face in the crowd caught his eye and he looked closer. The man turned to watch Jonathan's boat go by. It was Connor Harris. The two made eye contact. Jonathan showed no emotion but continued to stare back. He watched a subtle change of expression on Harris's face. His smile slowly faded, and a surprised look came over him as he realized who he was looking at. Jonathan remembered those eyes all too well, even after so many years.

The boat continued on and soon Harris was out of sight. Jonathan thought about whether he should be concerned with Harris back in town, or not. He certainly wasn't afraid. He had faced much worse since their last encounter. He thought about Luke and whether his brother had seen Harris since the fight. He was more concerned those two would cross paths again. Emily came to mind again. He wondered if she still stayed in touch with Harris.

He hadn't seen or talked to Luke since that first night down at the bar. He hadn't seen Catherine either and he wasn't going out of his way to try to find her. He heard one night from George there had been some trouble between Luke and Catherine. She had come home with a bruise under her eye. She said she had an accident down at work. George had been pretty upset about it.

Jonathan thought to himself he really didn't know his brother very well anymore, but he found it hard to believe he would hit Catherine. The way he had been drinking though, who knows how he might be treating her.

He came along a row of boathouses. A fleet of small sailboats for the kid's sailing classes was already out and tied up at one of the docks. Several big sailing and cruising yachts were already in their slips ready for the summer season.

He continued on down into Round Lake. He saw their docks up ahead on the left. His father was waiting for him. He pulled into one of the slips and threw the lines to him. When the boat was secure, they walked together up into the big boathouse. The shady cool felt good.

"Who else do we need to get in today?" he asked his father.

"We've got three more, including the Benander's 35-footer. Can you call George to come by tonight to help us with it?"

"Sure, he should be back from Walloon after dinner."

"Jonny, you know how much I appreciate your help around here. I don't know how I would have pulled everything together. I just seem to run out of steam."

Jonathan walked over and sat on a stool next to the tool bench. "Pop, it's just good to be back."

"This may not be the best time, but I've been meaning to talk to you about school," his father said. "I know you want to start this fall."

"Yeah, I really do. I'm waiting to hear from the Navy on the money they promised, and I've been getting my application for Tech together."

"You know we can't help you with the money. I wish we could, but..."

"Pop, I know."

"The thing is son, with Luke not around, I don't have anyone to take over the business in the next couple of years. I'm not gonna be able to keep this pace much longer."

Jonathan hesitated. He knew this discussion was coming, but he wasn't ready to discuss yet that he didn't want to take over the business. He loved boats and the lake, but he didn't want to run a boatyard and scrape around for the summer people year after year. "Pop, let's just see what happens."

There was no reaction from his father.

"We better keep moving with these boats, or we won't get done before dark," Jonathan said.

His father just nodded and walked out of the boathouse to the truck.

It was after dinner before they could get to the last big boat. Jonathan was down on their docks straightening out some lines and making sure all of the boats were secure when George came down through the boathouse and out onto the dock.

"Hey, buddy," he yelled.

Jonathan waved. "Thanks for coming down. We got that cruiser out back to put in for the Benanders."

"Not a problem," George answered. He walked out onto the dock and stooped down to help his friend untangle some lines.

"Guess who I saw today?" Jonathan asked.

George looked up. "I couldn't begin to guess."

"Our old friend, Harris."

"Oh, that's just great. I can't believe we've got that sonofabitch up here to deal with again."

"A lot of time's passed. I'm just a little worried he and Luke are gonna run into each other."

"Maybe Luke can finish the job on that asshole this time," George said.

Jonathan laughed, but he could see George was really upset about this.

"You know, Jonny, most of the people who come up here every summer are the nicest folks, and God knows, we love their money, but every summer it seems like there's a handful of assholes looking for trouble."

"The trick is steering clear of the assholes, friend," Jonathan said. "We better get up and help Pop with that cruiser."

Later, they had the big boat positioned to back down the ramp. Jonathan was driving the truck and George was down on the dock with Mr. McKendry, holding lines to secure the boat off the trailer. Jonathan slowly backed down the ramp, pressing hard on the old brakes to keep control of the heavy boat. He heard a loud crack and looked back to see the boat beginning to slide. The winch strap had broken loose and the boat was going back into the water whether they liked it or not.

Jonathan heard his father yelling at him, but he couldn't make out what he was saying. He could see in the side mirror of the truck, the trailer wasn't deep enough for the boat to clear bottom, so he let up on the brakes and let the rig slide faster down the ramp.

The big boat quickly gained momentum under its own massive weight and crashed back into the water. Jonathan jumped out of the truck and ran back to try and grab something on the boat. His father was yelling at George to try to secure the lines.

"Jonathan, get up here!" his father shouted.

"Pop, we'll get her. Just relax."

Jonathan's father and George were running along the dock, trying to wrap their lines around a piling.

"Pop don't. We'll get it," Jonathan yelled. Before he could get over to help, he saw his father lose his balance and fall over the side into the water.

"Jesus, Jonathan, I'll get the boat," George called out. "You help your dad."

Jonathan jumped down into the water. It was only four or five feet deep, but icy cold. His father was struggling to get to his feet. He had rarely heard him curse, but there was a whole stream of good ones flying at the moment. Jonathan reached him and helped him stand. His father started laughing and Jonathan couldn't help but join him.

As they started to walk out together, he felt his father stumble and he reached to hold him up. He saw a vacant expression come across his face and saw him grimace in tremendous pain as he went limp in his arms.

"Oh my God... Pop!"

"Jonathan, what's wrong?" George yelled.

His father lay limp in his arms, groaning in pain. The cold chill of the water was biting into his legs. He struggled to pull his father up onto the ramp and he laid him down as gently as he could next to the boat trailer.

"George, let the damn boat go. We gotta get Dad to the hospital now!" he screamed.

Another boat was coming in and George yelled something to them about securing the boat for them, then he ran to help Jonathan. By the time George got over to them, Jonathan was talking quietly to his father who was mumbling something unintelligible.

"We've got to get him in the truck," Jonathan said. Both men were able to lift him and carry him up the ramp. They placed him across the bed of the pickup. George offered to drive while Jonathan stayed in the back with his father.

As the truck sped away, Jonathan held his father's head in his lap. "Pop, we're gonna get you some help."

Somewhere around midnight, the doctor came out. Jonathan had been sitting with his mother for the past hours, waiting for an update on his father's condition. It was Dr. Webber, who had delivered both Luke and Jonathan. He was a good friend of the family.

"The old bird is still chirping, but he's pretty weak. I think we've got him stabilized, but he's had two more minor heart attacks since you brought him in, Jonathan. We're going to have to watch him close all night. I can't tell you we're out of the woods yet."

His mother thanked the doctor and walked over to a row of chairs along the wall in the waiting room. Jonathan watched her defeated figure sink low into the seat. She was still dressed in her uniform from the hotel. He felt the real fear he saw in his mother's eyes. His parents had been married for over thirty years. He sat beside her and held her hand, sharing the sorrow and grief she was feeling.

They called Luke earlier in the evening, but no one had answered at his house. Jonathan thought about his brother as he stood helplessly looking over at his mother.

"Mom, I'll be back in a bit. I need to get some air," he said. She looked up and nodded.

He felt the cool night air on his face as he walked out of the hospital. He got in the old truck and pulled out of the parking lot. He drove slowly through the dark streets of town with the windows open. Lights were still on in a few of the houses, but the town was mostly done for the day.

He found himself down at the intersection with Bridge Street and the lights of the main street in town still shone brightly, although the streets were mostly deserted. He looked down to his right and saw the neon sign out over the sidewalk for *The Helm.*

He pulled the truck out and headed slowly down toward the old bar. There were plenty of open parking spaces and he pulled up and stopped. He sat for a few moments, both hands on the steering wheel, looking out through the windshield at the sign for the bar and flickering neon Budweiser sign in the window. The front door was wedged open and he heard music from the jukebox playing inside. He turned off the truck.

Luke was sitting at the bar. There were a few other people sitting against the far wall and two men playing pool at the back. Smoke hung heavy in the darkly lit room and the smell of stale beer and vomit was overpowering.

Jonathan walked over to the bar and sat down next to his brother. Luke turned and recognized who it was, then turned back to his beer without speaking. The bartender came over and Jonathan ordered a beer. Bud drew a cold draft from the tap in front of the brothers and placed it down on the bar.

Looking straight ahead, Jonathan took a long drink, then said, "Pop is pretty sick, Luke. He's down at the hospital. It's his heart and he's pretty bad."

He heard Luke sigh, then watched as his brother took another drink.

"Luke, do you understand what I'm saying?"

Luke turned and faced him, and Jonathan looked into blurry eyes that were trying to focus. Luke nodded. His head was weaving, and he held on to the back of his bar stool to steady himself. It looked like he was trying to find words, but then he gave up and turned back to his beer.

"Luke, why don't we go get a cup of coffee? You need to see Pop tonight. I don't know if he's gonna get through until morning."

Luke turned again and gathered himself full-up on the stool. "I don't have a damn thing to say to the old bastard." He picked up his beer glass and drained it. He slammed it down, then stood, threw some bills on the bar and walked out the door.

Jonathan looked around the bar and tried to imagine the life of Luke and Catherine that revolved around this place. A deep empty sadness bore through him as he thought about his brother and Catherine, and about his father lying unconscious in the hospital. He started to cry. They were tears held back for too many years and he didn't try to stop them. He put his head in his hands and let the emotion and pain flow out in the tears that splashed down on the bar.

Old Bud came over and asked if he was okay, but he didn't look up. He turned and walked out of the bar. Luke was nowhere to be seen. He got in the truck and drove back to the hospital. As he walked into the waiting room, he saw his mother sitting and talking to the doctor. From her expression, he knew his father was gone.

Chapter Nineteen

Sally sat at one of the small outside tables at the coffee shop, sipping from a large ceramic mug, looking blankly out at the traffic and people passing by in front of her. She had sat on her mother's old porch for more than an hour before one of the new owners came home and saw her. The woman recognized Sally and had invited her in for a cup of tea, but she had thanked her and declined. The woman seemed to understand her need to be there and asked that she come back any time.

She heard her name and looked up to see George Hansen standing beside her. He placed his hand on her shoulder.

"Can I join you?" he asked.

"Of course. How are you?" she managed.

"Sally, I saw Ben this morning down at the docks. He told me a bit about last night. He's very worried about you and Gwen."

Sally squirmed a bit in her chair. "How much did he tell you?"

"Only that he was afraid he's come between you and Gwen. He feels terrible about it."

"Gwen is gone, George," she said with a slow and heavy sadness in her voice.

"What do you mean, gone?"

Sally sighed deeply. "She's gone back to New York. I'm not sure when she'll be back, or if she plans to ever come back."

A young girl was cleaning the tables around them and she asked George if he would like some coffee. He gave her his order and then turned back to Sally. "Tell me what's happened."

"Ben invited us both to dinner on the *EmmaLee* last night. I gave Ben some sketches for the painting of his boat he's asked me to do. He wanted to go over the drawings with us and finalize plans for his new painting."

Sally took a sip from her coffee. "Gwen is no fool. She knows Ben and I have been spending a lot of time together and that something is happening. I'm not sure exactly what, to tell you the truth."

George reached over and took Sally's hand in his. "Honey, no one can ever blame you for falling in love with this man. From what I've come to know about him these past days, he's a fine man."

"Falling in love with him...?" Sally shook her head. "I don't know what it is, George. I haven't felt this way in so many years, I can't begin to understand it. I know how much I enjoy being with him and with Megan. I've definitely grown close to both of them in these few short days."

"What have you said to Gwen about all this?" he asked.

"She is being either incredibly noble and understanding, or she's doing a great job of hiding her emotions," Sally said. "At times, I think maybe she's had enough of all this. Maybe this is her chance to get away and get back to the city and her old life."

"That may well be the case." His coffee came, and he blew on it to cool before he took a sip. "You should feel real fortunate to be loved by two such wonderful people."

Sally turned and looked at her friend. His wise old eyes sparkled. She squeezed his hand tighter.

She left George, promising to call later and walked across the busy traffic into the park and down the grassy slope to the boat docks along Round Lake. She saw the *EmmaLee* was away from her dock and nowhere to be seen in the small lake. She couldn't remember which day Ben said they were leaving.

George's words continued to play in her head...*to be loved by two such wonderful people.*

Was he gone now before they had a chance to really find out what was happening between them? She stood at the gangplank where the boat had been tied up for the past week. She thought of last night, the kiss and embrace they had shared. She thought of Megan's smile and the incredible energy and joy of the little girl.

As she turned to head back up to go home, she saw a large ship coming in through the channel from Lake Charlevoix. She could tell right away it was the *EmmaLee*. She felt frozen for a moment. Should she run before they saw her, or stay and see where all of this might lead? She reached in her purse and pulled out her cell phone and address book. Looking up the number for Ben's phone, she walked up through the crowd in the park and dialed the number.

He answered after two rings.

"Ben Clark."

"Ben, this is Sally."

"Good morning... how are you?"

"Honestly, I'm not sure."

"We're out on the boat. We took a breakfast cruise to watch the sun come up. Can you meet us down at the dock?"

Sally hesitated. "Why don't you come to dinner tonight at my house? I would ask you to bring Megan, too, but I think we need some time together to talk, don't you think?"

"I think it's a good idea. What time?" he asked.

"How about seven?"

"I'll bring some wine. Sally, about last night?" He paused.

"Yes?"

"I've obviously been thinking a lot about what happened, about... about what happened with us."

Sally interrupted, "Let's talk tonight."

She heard him take a deep breath on the other end of the line. "Okay, I'll see you tonight."

Sally's doorbell rang, and she looked at the clock in the kitchen. It was five minutes before seven. She pulled a tray out of the oven and placed it on the granite countertop, then went out to answer the door.

She saw Ben standing on the porch through the sidelight window to the front door. He was dressed in tan slacks and a black short-sleeve shirt. He held a small cooler at his side. She opened the door.

He looked up and smiled. "Hi."

"Hi, come in." She moved back to let him in.

She had put on a simple white sleeveless dress that buttoned up the front. She had leather strap sandals on her bare feet and her hair was pulled back loosely with a blue ribbon.

He reached out with his free arm and put it around her and kissed her on the cheek. "It's good to see you. Thank you for calling for dinner."

She returned his embrace and led him into the kitchen.

He put the cooler on the counter and took out two bottles of wine, dripping in an icy sweat. "Would you like a glass?" he asked.

"Yes, please." She got two glasses down and watched as he opened the wine and poured. "Let's go out on the porch," she said. "I've got some chicken in the oven. Let me get these appetizers on a plate."

He helped her with the food, and they walked together out through the back of the house to the sun porch. The sun was still showing high in the western sky out over the lake. It sent shimmering sparkles back across the water. A few sailboats were still out, and a large freighter was making its way south with a heavy load.

They sat in two wicker chairs, looking out at the lake.

"Do you ever take this incredible view for granted?" he asked.

"I suppose I do at times. It gets pretty cold and bleak up here on the bluff in February."

"Sally." She turned, and he held up his wine glass and she touched it with hers and they both tasted the wine. He paused a moment, looking again at the lake. "I've been thinking over and over again about last night." He turned back to her. "Is Gwen all right?"

"She's gone back to New York for a while. I'm not sure how long."

"Oh no... I'm so sorry if I've done anything..."

"You don't have a thing to be sorry about." She took another sip from her wine. "Ben, I don't know any other way to get at this than just come out and be as honest with you as I can." She looked into his eyes and felt her resolve starting to fade.

"Okay," he said, then taking a sip from wine, his hand trembling some.

"You know this past week has been a roller coaster of emotions. Meeting you and Megan and the ship coming back, sparking all of the old memories of my family and ... and of my daughter, Ellen."

He reached over and put his hand on her arm. "I know."

"Then, Gwen and I... well, there's a lot of history there as well."

"Sally, I..."

She stopped him. "I'd better get all this out, or I know I won't be able to later."

"Okay."

She took another sip of wine. "Ben... it's been a long time for me... but I may well be falling in love with you."

She felt him squeeze her arm more tightly.

She stood up and walked over to the edge of the porch, looking at the water, holding the wine glass in both hands. "Gwen and I haven't spoken since last night, but I think she's had enough of me and this town, and the business. She's gone back to New York and I don't think she'll be back." She turned to face Ben. "I don't even know how you feel about what Gwen and I have been to each other."

"All I know is you cared for each other very much and I'm sorry if I've come between you." He walked over beside her and took her hand. "Sally, I've been fortunate to meet an incredible person this week. I haven't felt this way about someone in a very long time." He looked away out over the lake for a moment, trying to gather his words. "When we kissed last night and I held you, I felt this sense of comfort and peace. It just felt right... and I think you felt that same thing."

Sally just nodded.

"We both have a past and we've loved before, but that shouldn't stop us from finding someone again."

She saw in his eyes how sincere his words were. She moved forward and put her arms around his neck. She felt his arms enclose her and she put her face on his shoulder and just let the feeling of the two of them together linger. Looking up into his eyes again, their lips came together slowly, and they kissed almost motionlessly for a time. She pulled back and smiled.

"So, you think you've fallen in love," he said, and paused, returning her smile. "I know I have."

They kissed again, this time with more urgency.

"I want to be with you and spend more time with you," she said, "but you're leaving soon."

"I want you to come with us."

Chapter Twenty

The passing of Jonathan's father was a terrible blow for the family but particularly for his youngest son. Jonathan loved his father and was deeply moved by his death. He also found himself caught in the difficult situation of having to take control of the family and the business, as his older brother Luke was going to be no help in either regard. With considerable guilt, he struggled with the priorities of his own ambitions and dreams, and the realities he and his mother were now facing.

All of this was compounded when another tragedy struck our small town. A summer of so much promise and expectation, suddenly turned to only sadness and fear.

The sounds of the gulls first woke him. Jonathan sat up quickly as the birds flew overhead, screeching at one another over some important bird issue. At first, he wasn't sure where he was. His hand knocked over several beer bottles sitting next to him, then he saw he was sitting in a boat down at their docks at the boatyard. As he tried to sit up, his head revolted, and a searing pain shot from his temples back through to the inner core of his brain. His mouth was so dry it was nearly stuck shut and he tried several times before he was able to swallow.

Fragments of memories from the past evening began to come back to him. Then, he knew his father was gone. He remembered the final scene with the doctors at the hospital and his mother and the quiet ride home. He recalled the talk he had with his brother down at the bar. From there it was all a haze of blurred images.

He stood and took off his clothes down to his shorts. He walked out to the end of the dock. It was so early that no one was around, and he honestly didn't care. He looked down into the clear green water and then jumped out and slid headfirst down into the icy depths. The sudden shock of the early summer water temperature cut through him like a thousand little knives, but it worked quickly to help cleanse the past evening's overindulgence. He came back up to the surface and allowed his body to float up horizontally. He drifted motionlessly on his back, looking up at the early morning cloud cover and letting the cold chill work through the ache in his brain.

His ears were underwater, but he thought he heard someone yelling. He looked up and turned back to the dock. A woman was standing there alone. He rubbed his eyes to clear them of the lake water. As he was able to focus, he saw it was Emily Compton.

"Jonathan, is that you?" she yelled.

He began swimming slowly toward her.

"Jonathan, I heard about your father this morning. I was up in town early, taking a walk and getting some coffee when I heard some people talking about it. I'm so sorry. I wanted to find you to see how you're doing."

How am I doing? He made his way back to the stern of the boat he had slept in and stopped there, treading water.

Finally, he said, "Hi, thanks for coming down. It's been a hell of a night. What are you doing here? I thought you had school this summer."

She came over and sat down on the dock just above him. "I decided to take one more summer for myself. There is still plenty of time for school. What happened with your father?" she asked.

"Pop had a bad heart and I guess he just tried to do too much getting all the boats ready for the season."

"If there is anything I can do to help…" she said.

"Yeah…thanks. God knows what we're going to do at this point. I was talking to my dad just yesterday about starting school in the fall, but now…I really don't know."

She looked down at him and her face and hair shined bright, even in the dull morning light. She had on shorts, white sneakers and an old gray sweatshirt with "University of Michigan" imprinted in blue.

He finally realized his teeth were chattering and his limbs were going numb in the cold water. "I need to hop out before I freeze to death. Sorry, I only have my skivvies on."

"I've been working as a nurse, remember?" Emily said. "I've seen more than you can imagine."

"Yeah, I suppose." He climbed the ladder on the side of the dock and walked, dripping, past her to the boat to retrieve his clothes. He used the shirt to dry himself as best he could, then slipped on his jeans and the damp shirt. He noticed Emily watching him, unashamed. "So, you're going to be up here all summer?" he asked.

"Yes, school starts again in late August. I have some papers to work on before I get back, but I'm planning to take some time for myself before the grind in the fall."

Suddenly, it just seemed right to ask, "I'd sure appreciate it if you'd come to the funeral with me."

She didn't hesitate, "Of course, I'd like to be there with you."

They both turned when they heard steps coming down the dock. It was George Hansen. He seemed a bit surprised to see Emily. Immediately, he both could see he had been crying and was very upset.

"Jonathan, I've been looking all over for you since last night when I heard about your dad, then this morning…" He couldn't continue.

"George, this is Emily Compton. I don't think you two ever met."

He just nodded at her. "Jonathan, I'm real sorry about your Pop, but something else... something terrible's happened."

"What's going on?" Jonathan asked.

"It's Catherine ...Catherine's dead!" He sat on the edge of the dock by the boat.

Jonathan felt like he'd been hit by a sledgehammer, and he was too stunned to even reply. He came up out of the boat and went over to his friend, sitting next to him. "Catherine? What in hell happened?"

Emily kneeled next to the two men.

"An old man and a boy walking on the shore found her this morning. She was washed up on the beach, out near North Point. She's dead, Jonathan. Godammit, she's dead!"

"But what happened?" Jonathan asked again.

"The sheriff came by the house about an hour ago to talk to my parents and to have someone come down to identify the body," George said. "I went with him. My folks were just too shook up. God, Jonathan, I've never had to do anything harder in my life. The war was a goddamn piece of cake compared to going into that room with my sister's body."

"Did she drown?" Emily asked in a quiet voice.

George tried to control himself. "She was pretty badly beaten, and they think she was..." he had to pause. "They think she was raped."

"Oh no..." Jonathan replied, still stunned. "Do they know who did this?"

George looked up at his friend with a frightened look. "They're looking for Luke... and..."

"For Luke!" Jonathan interrupted. "No way he could do something like that!"

"Jonathan, you know they've been having a bad time," George said. "The thing is, she was pregnant."

"Pregnant?" Emily said.

"Jonathan, there's something else. The sheriff also wants to talk to you."

"I don't know where Luke is," Jonathan said, "unless he's down at *The Helm* already."

"No, they want to talk to you about where you were last night after you left the hospital," George said.

Jonathan looked at his friend with a dazed expression, then he looked over to Emily. Her face was immediately a comfort to him.

"Jonathan," she said, "there must be some mistake."

His mind raced in a panic. After dropping his mother at the house last night, sometime around 1:00 a.m., and after all the drinks, he had no recollection of anything until he woke up on the boat this morning. A sick feeling churned in his stomach and a new terror he could never possibly have imagined surged through his brain.

He sat at an old wooden table with six chairs around it. The walls were a dull gray and there were two narrow horizontal windows that reached up high toward the ceiling. Jonathan sat facing the County Sheriff, Willy Potts. The air smelled old and stale. Sheriff Potts' coffee cup and a pad of paper were the only things on the table.

The sheriff had come by the house at around nine that morning and asked if Jonathan could come with him to answer some questions. He had been sitting alone in this room for over an hour before the sheriff had finally come back.

"Jonathan, we found Luke this morning over at Darlene Wilson's place. He spent the night there. Guess he's been seeing her on the side, along with Catherine Hansen," the Sheriff said in a slow steady voice.

"So, Luke had nothing to do with Catherine's..."

"Appears so," the Sheriff answered. "He claims he saw you down at *The Helm* last night around midnight."

Jonathan leaned forward with his arms crossed in front of him on the table. "That's right. I went down to find Luke to tell him about our dad. He wouldn't come back to the hospital with me. Pop was already gone when I got back."

"Yes, I know. I'm real sorry about that, Jonny." The sheriff looked through some notes on the pad in front of him. "Old Bud down at *The Helm* says you came back to the bar around 1:30. That sound right?"

Jonathan squirmed in his seat and sat back, desperately trying to put the pieces of the night back together. He couldn't remember ever going back to the bar. "Sheriff Potts, I must have had too much to drink last night, after my dad and everything. I remember taking my mother home, then... and then I woke up this morning sitting in a boat down at our docks with a bunch of empty beers all around me."

"You don't remember going back to Bud's?"

"No."

"You don't remember sitting there with Catherine Hansen and drinking till Bud threw you out about 2:30?"

Jonathan couldn't hide the expression of shock on his face. At first, he just shook his head slowly, trying to remember. "I haven't seen Catherine since I got back to town."

"Well, I got three witnesses say you saw her real good last night down at *The Helm*. You sat drinking shots and beers with her for some time. Then, about 2:30 or so, you walked out with her. No one saw her again till she was found this morning, naked and dead out on the beach."

"That can't be," Jonathan said. "Why would I hurt Catherine?"

"I know you two were close back in school before the war."

Jonathan nodded.

"So, I hear she turned to Luke while you were gone. You come back from the war all torn up and pieced back together and find your brother's been shacking up with your girl, turned her into a drunk and knocked her up. You think that might have something to do with your feelings about the girl?"

"No... no, Catherine and I were through a long time ago." He couldn't hide the panic he felt. "Ohmigod... you can't think I'd do this?"

"Son, all I think is you better call a good lawyer. I'm gonna have to hold you 'til we get this sorted out. We got the medical examiner coming down from Petoskey this afternoon to start their work on the body. You better start thinking real hard about where in the hell you were after walking out of that bar last night."

An hour later, Jonathan was back in the room, this time facing George and Emily. He was struggling hard to keep his composure.

"I keep going back through the night and what I can remember," he said. "There's this big black hole. I just can't remember."

Emily started, "Jonathan, we spoke to your mom. She said you brought her home sometime between 12:30 and 1:00. She said you grabbed some beers out of the refrigerator and walked out the door. She didn't see you again. Did you just go down to the boat?"

"You really can't remember going back to *The Helm* and seeing Catherine?" George asked.

Jonathan shook his head no.

"I called a friend of our family, a lawyer back in Detroit," Emily offered. "I'd like to help you. He's going to come up later this afternoon."

Jonathan looked across at his friend George and the woman who kept coming back into his life. His world was spinning out of control, but they were still here to help. He just couldn't get the doubt out of his mind.

"Has it occurred to either of you I might have done this?" Just saying it out loud made him nauseous.

"I've known you all my life, McKendry," George said. "I've seen you drink a few too many beers on occasion. I've never seen you anywhere near where you could do something like this."

"The sheriff says that war can do some strange things to a man's brain," Jonathan said in a low, pained voice.

The door opened, and Sheriff Willy Potts came back into the room. "We'll have to wrap it up here folks. The people from the medical examiner's office are here and they want to talk to Jonathan."

George and Emily stood. Emily reached out and took Jonathan's hand. "There's just no way," she said. "There's got to be another explanation."

Later the next day, Emily was coming out of her house walking toward the car parked in the driveway. She noticed another car pulling up. It was a black convertible with the top down. Connor Harris was sitting alone in the driver's seat. He waved, and Emily walked down to the curb.

"Connor, how are you? You're up for the summer, too?" she asked.

"Yeah, I just came up a couple of days ago. My dad wanted me to work in his office this summer, but I convinced him I needed a little R&R before getting back to school."

"How have you been?" she asked. "I haven't seen you since the Christmas party up here at your parents."

"Just trying to keep the grades up so I can get into law school next year. Can I give you a ride somewhere?"

"I was going into town," Emily said. "You've heard about the Hansen girl's death? They think one of the McKendry brothers did it."

"Yeah, so I hear," he answered. "I also hear you're helping with his defense. What's that all about?"

"Jonathan was a patient down at the V.A. where I've been working," she said. "I spent a lot of time with him during his rehabilitation. There's just no way he could have been involved in this."

"Emily, I can speak from experience. These McKendry boys are trouble. You know the older one damn near killed me that summer. I've still got headaches from that sonofabitch," Connor spat.

Emily stepped back. "That was a long time ago and Jonathan is nothing like his brother, Luke."

"You seem to be an awfully good judge of his character. How well did you two get to know each other?" Connor asked in a sarcastic tone.

"We became good friends," she said defiantly, "and frankly, it's none of your business."

"I really can't believe you're getting your family into the middle of this thing. Do you have any idea what people are saying?"

"I don't give a damn what people are saying. It's the right thing to do!"

"I'm sorry. Sure I can't give you a ride?" Connor offered.

Emily just turned and walked away.

Chapter Twenty-one

She felt weightless, floating effortlessly in a gauzy light haze. There was no sound and nothing touching her body but the air and a warm sense of peace. Her mind wandered through fragments of memories and glimpses of lost moments.

A soft pull on her arm seemed out of place and a hard focus began forcing its way back into her brain. She thought she was hearing a small voice but couldn't make out the words. It seemed just a whisper.

Sally opened her eyes and saw a low ceiling of wood paneling. Something pulled at her arm again and she turned to see Megan Clark smiling down at her.

"Good morning, Sally. Are you awake?" the little girl asked in a quiet voice.

Sally took her hand and smiled back. She remembered now she was aboard the *EmmaLee,* and they were cruising south along the shore of Lake Michigan. They had been in Traverse City the past evening and were heading down to Leland for their next stop.

"Good morning, Megan."

"Sally, I just had to wake you. Bobby the chef is making the most wonderful pancakes, and I don't want you to miss them."

"What time is it, dear?"

"Oh, I don't know. It has to be time to get up, don't you think? The pancakes will be ready any minute."

"I'll tell you what," Sally said, sitting up and looking out the small round window, "you tell Bobby to save some pancakes for me, and I'll be down as soon as I can splash some water on my face and wake up."

"Do you like real maple syrup?" the little girl asked.

"You know, I love maple syrup, so make sure you save some for me."

Megan giggled. "I'll try, but you better hurry." Then she was out the door and gone.

Sally looked out at the morning again and could see the far shore of Grand Traverse Bay off across the lake, calm and shining a bright blue in the early morning sun. The big boat rode smoothly over the surface of the lake and she could hear only a soft hum of the big engines far to the rear of the boat.

The events of last evening began to come back to her, being served dinner on deck with Ben and Megan, anchored offshore from the resort town of Traverse City. It had been a beautiful warm and clear night and as the evening went on the stars slowly made their way out from the day's fading brightness.

She and Ben had moved to soft lounge chairs on the foredeck as darkness fell and Megan went off to bed. With a bottle of wine between them on the boat deck, they had talked until well after midnight. Every few minutes a shooting star would divert their attention and they would both point at the same time.

They talked about their childhoods and their marriages. Ben shared the story of his business and the incredible good fortune he happened into during the internet boom. As the evening continued, it was inevitable they would talk again about the losses in their lives, Ben's wife dying much too young from cancer and Sally's daughter and parents and their accident.

As Sally thought back now on the evening, she felt some comfort in the sharing. It had been easier to talk about those difficult times. When the wine was gone, they walked to the rail of the boat and stood together looking at the lights from the town, holding hands. Ben took her into his arms and held her closely. He whispered in her ear, "I love you." They had stood looking into each other's eyes, and she remembered seeing the soft light from the stars shining back at her. She kissed him softly and put her head on his shoulder. She could still feel the warm comfort of him in her arms.

"I love you too, Ben Clark," she said, looking out across the lake. She had kissed him again, then said good night, leaving him there at the rail.

She got out of the bed and went into her bathroom to wash up. She looked at herself in the mirror and saw the familiar morning face of tousled hair and slightly puffy eyes stare back at her. She ran cold water and leaned down to splash it across her face several times. The cool shock helped clear the last cobwebs of the night's sleep.

She dressed and got ready for breakfast quickly. Opening the door to her cabin, she walked out into the narrow hallway, lit in the early morning light by small wall lamps along both sides. There were a series of closed doors to the many sleeping berths up in the front of the ship. She made her way back toward the galley and dining hall. She heard Megan's delightful laugh and then Ben laughing with her.

Later that morning, they were all up on the foredeck, sitting in lounge chairs reading and enjoying the comfortable weather. A cooling breeze swept over the rail from the west and took the edge off the hot summer sun. The *EmmaLee* cut through the smooth even swells of the lake, barely lifting into the coming push of the waves. High dunes of white sand pushed up from the beach cutting into high rounded hills along the uninhabited lakeshore. Sally looked up from her book and off to the west she could see the low shadows of the Manitou Islands coming into view.

North and South Manitou Island rested over ten miles out from the small towns of Leland and Glen Arbor. Nearly uninhabited in modern times, they had once teemed with loggers, cutting and removing the valuable tall cedars. Now, hikers and campers trekked over the island trails, ferried out daily from the docks in Leland.

The calm waters around the islands on this morning were deceiving. Over the years of shipping history in this area many ships had been blown off course in heavy weather and perished on the treacherous waters surrounding the islands.

Sally felt a hollow ache in the pit of her stomach. She could only think of her parents with her young daughter out on this water when the weather came up and her father no longer able to control the boat. She couldn't stop the tears from welling in her eyes and she tried to put the images of her family who had perished off those islands on that dark night out of her thoughts.

She rose to go below and be away from everyone. Ben reached out and grabbed her arm.

"Please don't go. I know…" he paused.

"Why did you bring me here?" she asked, trying to hold back the sobs building in her chest.

He stood and walked with her to the rail of the *EmmaLee*. They looked out across the barren stretch of water to the Manitous.

"I had hoped we could help you bring some small bit of closure to this," he said, as he held her hand.

"You don't expect me to just forget?" she said, pulling away.

"No, of course not," Ben said. "I struggled with this, Sally, but in the end, I thought it would help you to confront this."

"No, this is…"

"Sally, the morning my wife died she had been unconscious for several days, heavily medicated for pain. I always thought she would come back, even for just a short while so we could say goodbye. But she never came back. That morning, I watched her breathing grow slower and slower. I held her hand all morning as the family came to see her for maybe the last time. Megan came again with our nanny and I watched her hug her mother as she had done for so many months. I prayed she would actually get to talk to her mother, too."

"Oh, Ben..." she turned to him and went into his arms, putting her face against his.

"Later that morning, I was alone with her. I may have been dozing, but I suddenly sensed she had squeezed my hand, ever so lightly. When I looked up, I saw her take one long slow breath... then she didn't breathe again. She never came back."

Sally was unable to hold back her tears and now cried unashamed. When she looked up again, she saw Ben's face also streaked with tears.

"For months, I was haunted by the fact we had never talked really at the end about her leaving. I always thought there would be more time."

"How could you have known?"

"I don't know. I really don't know." He looked over the water toward the islands. "She had asked to be cremated and she wanted her ashes to be released in the wind off a high cliff in the Blue Ridge Mountains where we used to camp. It was three months after she passed before I was able to get myself together and go up there and honor her request. As I opened the canister that morning and watched her ashes blow out over the valley, I was finally able to say goodbye in a way that gave me some sense of peace. As I walked back down the mountain trail that morning, I felt such a huge burden begin to lift."

Sally pulled away and placed both hands on the rail of the ship, looking again at the Manitous, growing closer on the horizon. She didn't notice, but Ben had signaled the Captain of the *EmmaLee*. After a few minutes, she turned and saw the man walking up to them across the deck. He had a large bouquet of flowers under one arm and a book in his other hand. One of the crew was coming behind him with Megan holding his hand.

"Sally, forgive me, but I thought if we could have some kind of final service for your family out here, it might help you."

Her first emotions touched on anger and then a deep sadness again as she resigned herself to the terrible loss she had carried on her heart all these years. She looked into the kind face of the ship's captain and then down to little Megan with tears she couldn't wipe away fast enough. She reached out and took the flowers in her arms. They were yellow and red roses with stems held together by a silk bow. She looked at Ben, then just nodded without speaking.

The Captain moved with everyone to the rail of the *EmmaLee*. The Manitous loomed even larger now. He opened the Bible in his hand and as he read a passage about life and death and resurrection, she opened her heart to his words. She closed her eyes and tried to remember the faces of her parents and her young daughter, Ellen. She tried to remember the many times they had shared laughter and love together. She felt Ben's arm around her shoulders. Megan came up beside her and took her hand, looking out at the lake.

When the Captain finished, she opened her eyes and threw the flowers out into the air and watched them float down gently and land on the blue waters of Lake Michigan.

"I love you all so much," she said softly, looking down at the water and the flowers moving off now, as the ship slowly passed on. Sally knew in her heart she would never truly overcome her grief and sense of loss, but she began to feel there was some hope of controlling the darkness that had overwhelmed her for so many years.

They all stood together on the deck of the *EmmaLee* for some time until the flowers could no longer be seen in the swells of the big lake.

Chapter Twenty-two

It was a week before charges came down. The sheriff and the county district attorney felt they had enough evidence against Jonathan to proceed. I remember how hard those days were as I struggled to believe my best friend could have been involved in the terrible fate of my sister, Catherine. I was not only overwhelmed with the grief of our loss, but also wracked by the guilt of allowing myself to think Jonathan may well have been her killer. The more it ate into me and the longer I stayed away, the more the guilt consumed me.

Emily followed the deputy back through the dingy hallway. The cold gray walls closed in around her. Their footsteps echoed loudly as they approached a large steel door with a small window the size of a shoe box at eye level. The deputy peered through and then pulled the large set of keys on the chain at his side. After sorting through half the keys, he found the right one and unlocked the door. He continued on ahead of Emily. There were three cells down the left side of the hallway with two bare bulbs for light. Another light was on in the far cell.

As she got closer, she felt a dread that frightened her. All she could think of was how could anyone stand to be locked away in a place like this.

The deputy stopped at the side of the last cell. Emily moved past him and turned to her left, looking through the bars. The scene before her caused her to let out an involuntary low moan, "Oh, Jonathan...?"

He was sitting on the edge of the lower bunk, alone in the cell. He was dressed in a dirty white sleeveless t-shirt and gray jailhouse pants with a black stripe down the outside of both legs. His feet were bare. As he looked up at Emily, she saw the strain all of this had put on his face. He was nearly pale white, making the deep circles under his eyes and his unshaven beard even more pronounced. His hair obviously hadn't been washed in days and it stuck out in clumps in all directions.

He just looked at her with a blank expression.

"Jonathan," Emily said. "I wanted to come down and see if you needed someone to talk to or if you needed anything."

"You've done plenty," he said in a low voice. "Thank you for having your lawyer friend come up to help, but you better go now. I don't feel right about seeing you in this place." He looked down at his feet again, slumped over with his elbows resting on his knees.

She looked over to the guard who was facing the far wall, pretending not to be paying any attention.

"Could we have a few moments please?" she asked.

He shook his head no. "No one can be left alone with him." He looked at his watch. "You have two more minutes."

She sighed and shook her head. "Jonathan, have you been able to remember anything else?"

"No, it's like eight hours of my life never happened, lost in the bottom of a boat filled with empty beer bottles." He stood up and walked over to the cell door, grabbing the bars on each side of her.

She could smell his stale body odor and breath and she winced for a moment, and then tried to will herself to be strong.

He leaned close to her face through the bars and whispered, "I think I may have done this." He stopped, trying to keep from crying. "I think I could have killed her. What else could have happened?"

"Jonathan, please no!"

"I think you need to go away. Thank you for what you're trying to do, but it's not good for you be around me anymore."

Emily stood straighter and looked him in the eye. "I didn't walk away from you when you needed help before, and I'm not going to walk away now."

"You know I can't pay this lawyer," he said.

"You don't have to worry about the money. I have my own money."

"I can't let you do that."

"Jonathan, I'm not going to walk away."

He reached through the bars and grabbed her arms. "Aren't you afraid of me? Why don't you think I'm the monster they're calling me!"

The deputy moved over quickly to pull his arms away.

Emily jumped back. She had asked herself those same questions over and over in the past few days, and yet, in her heart she knew it wasn't so. Her parents were furious with her for getting involved, but she knew she was right in not walking away, of not abandoning him.

As the deputy reached out to lead her out of the cell area, she looked back and said, "We're going to make this right. I'll be back tomorrow with David again." She only wished her friend, the lawyer who had agreed to help with the case, was as confident as she was.

Jonathan's mother sat in the small lobby of the jail. The four wooden seats across the front wall were not shaped for comfort. She looked down at her hands clenched in her lap. She jumped when the bell hanging on the door started to clang. She turned to see a young woman walking in with a tall man in a dark gray suit. They both saw her and came over.

"Mrs. McKendry?" said the woman.

She just nodded.

"My name is Emily Compton. I'm a friend of Jonathan's."

"Yes, I know who you are."

The man moved closer and held out his hand.

She took it and held on weakly as he shook it.

"My name is David Krupp. I'm an attorney. Emily has asked me to work with Jonathan."

"Thank you...thank you both for being here." She looked down again at her hands. "Jonathan is so confused and afraid about all of this. He still can't remember and he's starting to believe he really did do this awful thing." She took a handkerchief from her purse to dab the moisture welling in her eyes.

They both sat down on either side of her.

Krupp began, "Mrs. McKendry, first of all, I want to say I was sorry to hear about the passing of your husband."

She nodded without looking up.

"I can't imagine how hard this is for you," Emily offered.

She looked up into Emily's eyes, "Dear, this is a nightmare beyond anything..." She couldn't finish the thought.

Emily thought it strange she would be here all alone at a time like this, then she realized the McKendry family was not going to get a lot of sympathy from the rest of the town.

The bell on the door rang again and George Hansen came in with another man who looked to be an older gray-haired Indian with a black felt hat on and dingy work clothes.

Mrs. McKendry looked up, surprised to see her son's friend.

George didn't make any introductions. "Are you the lawyer for Jonathan?"

The lawyer stood and introduced himself. "David Krupp."

George didn't bother with formalities. "This man is Albert Truegood."

The old man came forward and faced the lawyer.

"He has some information I think you need to hear," George said.

Krupp hesitated. "Jonathan is waiting to see me."

"I think you need to hear this now, then we're going to see the sheriff."

The lawyer pulled two chairs around and offered the man a seat. "So, what do you have to say, Mr. Truegood?"

The old man took the offer and sat down slowly, sighing as he did so. His face was lined with deep creases and weathered a deep brown color.

George broke in, "Albert lives out north of town near McSauba. He was in town the night Catherine died."

The lawyer seemed impatient. "Yes, please go on," he asked hurriedly. "Mr. Truegood?"

The man looked slowly at the faces surrounding him, then he spoke slowly and very softly. Everyone had to lean in to hear. "I was down on Bridge Street that night. I saw her."

"You saw Catherine Hansen?" Krupp asked.

Truegood nodded.

"We know she was in town," the lawyer said.

"Tell her who you saw her with," George interrupted.

"I saw her with young Jonny."

Krupp looked away in disgust.

"No, after that Albert!" said George.

"I saw Jonny and George's sister walking down the street from *The Helm*." His voice cracked, and he stopped for a moment to calm himself. "Jonny was pretty drunk, I think. He couldn't walk too straight. The girl wasn't doin' much better. They stopped and talked a minute. I couldn't hear what they were saying."

Krupp jumped in. "What were you doing down there at two in the morning?"

"I'd been havin' a few beers around the corner. I was on my way home. I was walking. I don't have a car and I don't like to ride my bike home late at night."

"Okay," said Krupp.

"What happened then, Mr. Truegood?" asked Emily, sitting forward in her seat, listening intently to every word.

"Well, she was talking to him, then she pushed him away and started walking down the sidewalk toward me."

"Did he go after her?" Emily asked.

The old man looked at Emily with eyes that shined bright and moist, "No, he went the other way. He went down into the park like he was going home."

"Oh my God!" whispered Mrs. McKendry.

"You saw him walk away and he didn't come back to get her?" asked the lawyer.

"No, Jonny didn't come back."

"Oh, thank God," Emily said, and then wiped at tears welling in her eyes.

"Let him finish everyone, please," George said.

The old man swallowed deliberately, then continued. "She walked past me like I wasn't even there on the sidewalk. She was staggering and had this blank look in her eyes."

"Why didn't you come to the sheriff with this earlier?" Krupp asked angrily.

"He was afraid they would accuse him," George said. "Now listen to the rest."

"When I heard the next day the girl was dead, I got real scared. I thought they'd come lookin' for me, but nobody came."

George grabbed his arm. "Tell them the rest."

Truegood continued. "A car pulled up to the curb and followed her as she walked. Someone rolled down the window and when the car stopped, she went over to talk to the person. I saw her lean into the car, and she was talking to this person. It was a man."

"You don't know who it was?" asked Jonathan's mother.

"No, I couldn't see his face in the light. It was a big car. She got in and they drove away."

Krupp stood up. "Somebody go get the sheriff!"

Chapter Twenty-three

The *EmmaLee* cruised slowly into the waters off Leland harbor, a small man-made inlet protected by rock jetties that pushed abruptly out into Lake Michigan. The ship was too large to dock inside the inlet. The captain and crew were readying anchors to bring her to rest just offshore. The winds were light from the east and the lake was a blue silky calm. Curious boaters maneuvered carefully at a safe distance to get a closer look at the big ship. Most had cameras out to capture the unusual sight.

Daylight was slipping away as a bright orange sun fell relentlessly to the far horizon off towards Wisconsin. A layer of clouds was scattered across the sun's path, painted soft grays and reds.

Leland, Michigan was a small resort town tucked in the wooded hills above the lake. Its early roots were tied to the fishing and lumber trades. In recent times, restaurants, bed & breakfast homes and an eclectic array of shops provided for the local economy.

A launch from the *EmmaLee* had been lowered over the side and Sally sat in the center seat with Ben as one of the crew steered them through the narrow inlet into the harbor. Megan had been on her computer exchanging messages with her friends at home and decided to stay on the boat for the evening. They came alongside one of the docks. Ben jumped out to hold the line as Sally followed.

"Give us two hours, Robby. We're going to do a little shopping and get some dinner," Ben said to the crewman. He looked at his watch. "We'll be back around ten." The crewman just nodded and jumped back down into the launch, pushing away and powering up to head back to the ship.

A crowd of people had gathered on the docks and up on the lawn of the small park above the harbor, looking out at the *EmmaLee*. Ben and Sally stopped and talked with some of the other boat owners who were tied up in the little harbor. All were curious about the owner of the great ship resting offshore. Ben was cordial and answered all their questions about the boat and her return to the Great Lakes.

Sally led him away from the group of boaters to show him the old historic Fisherman's Village that had been restored along the river that flowed down from the hills. They wandered through the shops together, holding hands. In the small fish market they bought smoked salmon and whitefish, caught fresh from the lake by Native American fisherman, to take back to the *EmmaLee*.

With bags in hand they walked up the hill into the village of Leland. It was a typical summer evening in the small town with visitors far outnumbering the local merchants and residents. They found a restaurant with a deck that looked down on the waterfall from the river flowing down into the lake. They were taken to a table next to the rail. The sun was just beginning to fall behind the horizon. A cool chill eased over the hills with the shadows.

Ben talked to the server about a bottle of wine from one of the local vineyards he had heard about. They agreed on a bottle of red. As the server walked away, Ben took Sally's hands in his. They hadn't spoken about the impromptu memorial service out on the lake since they had boarded the launch to come ashore. Ben started to speak and then hesitated. He looked out over the vast lake and then turned to look back at Sally.Before he could say anything, Sally squeezed his hands, "Ben, what you did today..."

"If I overstepped..."

"No, what you did was so special for me... and for my family." She could still see the flowers floating off away from the boat. She could also hear the laughter of her daughter's voice echoing in the back of her mind, but it was no longer a haunting sound. She had been feeling a growing sense of peace seep through her these past hours. She had also felt an even closer bond growing with the man sitting across from her. "This day has been so special," she repeated. "Thank you."

The server arrived with the wine and placed two glasses down in front of them. Ben looked at the label and nodded. They watched as the young girl opened the wine and poured a small amount for Ben to taste. Without pretense, he swirled the wine and watched it wash up against the sides of the glass, leaving a shimmering residue that reflected the colors of the late evening sky. He held the glass to his nose and sniffed deeply, then took a small taste, savoring the flavor. He smiled at Sally who had been watching the ceremony intently, knowing Ben had a fine taste for good wines. He nodded approvingly to the server who proceeded to fill their glasses. After hearing the special for the evening was planked whitefish, they both nodded and handed unopened menus back to the girl.

Sally picked up her wine glass. "Thank you again." She reached over and touched his glass lightly with hers. They both took long sips from the wine and let the cool flavor work its way over their tongues. They looked out across the harbor and the boat masts to see the last of the sun disappear behind the far horizon. They could also see the *EmmaLee* resting comfortably on the calm bay. Others on the deck and down on the docks cheered at the spectacle of the sun as it made its last sliver of an appearance for the day.

"Sally, we're going to start heading back to Charlevoix tomorrow," Ben said.

She nodded, coming back to the moment.

"One of my old business partners is flying in. He says he just has to see me about investing in some new business he's come across. I hope you don't mind having to head back a bit early?"

"No, not at all," she said. "I'm feeling guilty about leaving the shop for as long as I have."

Ben fussed with his napkin, seeming preoccupied with some thought.

"What is it?" Sally asked.

He placed the napkin in his lap and looked up. "We need to start back soon. I mean back home to Newport."

"Yes, I knew you didn't have much more time," she answered with an empty feeling growing inside her.

"Sally, I know we've spent such a short time together, but..." he hesitated. "I feel like you and I are just getting started and we can't just leave it at this and say goodbye in a couple of days."

Sally's mind was racing with thoughts of her home and business in Charlevoix and how deeply set she was in her life there. She smiled at him and said, "Why don't you just leave the *EmmaLee* permanently at dock in Charlevoix, then you'll have an excuse to come back and visit every summer. You'll certainly make George happy. He'll keep an eye on her for you." As she said it, she knew how silly it sounded.

Ben laughed. "It might be a bit cold for the old lady up here in January," he said, looking out at the *EmmaLee*. Her running lights were on now. The ship looked like a small floating island in the growing darkness. "She has her mind set on a nice warm winter harborage down in St. John in the Virgin Islands this winter."

"Don't we all," Sally replied. "The winters get awfully tough up here, even for us locals."

The server brought their salads and placed them down on the table. She refilled their wine glasses and placed the bottle back down on the table.

Sally looked at the face of Ben Clark. She could see the conflict of his emotions written clearly on his face. She was feeling the same things. They were coming to know each other so well and the connection seemed to be growing stronger each day. And yet, they both had such different lives.

Ben broke the long silence. "Have you spoken with Gwen since she left town?"

The question caught her by surprise. "No, we haven't spoken. I thought about trying to reach her in New York. She usually stays with a friend of ours when she goes back to the city to visit. I just felt we both needed some time."

He rubbed his eyes and the bridge of his nose, seeming to contemplate what to say next. "Sally, I'm going to be selfish here. I want you to have as much time as you need to work through all this with Gwen, but I also don't want to walk away from what we have here."

She knew the question was unfair before she even started, but she couldn't think of any other response. "And what do you think we have, Ben?"

He smiled widely, almost in embarrassment. She could see the color rising in his cheeks. His white teeth shone brightly in the candlelight from the table.

"I hope you agree we have something starting here," he said.

"Something?"

"Sally, let me be honest with you. I have such strong feelings for you. I get so much joy being with you." He reached for her hand again. "But there is this divide lurking out there between us. It's both our pasts and it's your roots here in Michigan. How will we know if we can ever get beyond all that? How do I know you even want to consider it?"

She felt her breath grow short. She had no idea how to respond. She had been struggling with the same feelings. When she was truly honest with herself, she knew she had never felt more drawn to anyone in her life than Ben Clark, and yet the reality of her current life with Gwen and with her gallery and the ties she had to Charlevoix, it all seemed to throw up such immovable obstacles. She sensed a growing anger, not at Ben, but at the inevitable decisions that faced her. She looked up and saw Ben had been watching her face intently.

"I feel so badly about putting you in this position, about forcing my way into your life," he said. "But on the other hand, I'm so grateful we've had this chance to come together and to get to know each other. I just want to take the time we both need to work through all this."

She felt overwhelmed by all the conflicts racing through her mind. It was too much to sort through. She thought about Gwen and where she might be tonight and what she must be thinking. She felt an incredible guilt for what she was doing to this woman who she had loved for so many years. She found herself trembling a bit. "I just don't know, Ben. There are no easy answers here."

"I know."

"You're being terrific about everything and it would be so easy to just keep flying down this roller coaster ride together with you, but—"

"I'll tell you what," he interrupted. "Let's try to leave the 'buts' behind us for a few more days."

Sally noticed someone approaching. She turned to see two women making their way around the tables toward them. She recognized them and waved as they came closer. They were two friends she and Gwen had met years ago in the gallery. Friendships had developed and they had remained close for many years. Fran and Susan lived together and owned a sportswear shop here in Leland. Sally knew at once how awkward this was going to be.

"I thought that was you, Sally," said the tall brunette woman. She was dressed casually in tan linen shorts and a peach polo shirt with a white sweater around her neck.

"Fran, how are you?" said Sally, standing to greet her friends. "Hi Susan." She gave them both a hug and kiss on the cheek. Susan was taller with reddish brown hair. She wore a navy workout suit with a golf hat that said 'Arcadia Bluffs'. "Ladies, this is my friend, Ben Clark."

Ben was also standing as they came up and he reached out his hand to both of them. "Very nice to meet you," he said.

Susan let her hand linger in his. "Would you be the owner of that fabulous boat offshore there?"

"Yes, that's the *EmmaLee*. We've been out on the big lake cruising for a few days."

"Sally, we heard your grandfather's boat was up in Charlevoix for the festival," said Fran. "She's magnificent, Ben. How long have you owned her?"

"I've just recently had her restored, and this is her first trip out from the East Coast. Can you two join us for a glass of wine?" he offered, motioning to the two empty chairs at their table.

Fran and Susan shared glances at each other, then Fran said, "Only if we won't be intruding too much."

"Not at all," Ben replied. "Please," he said pulling out a chair for her. They all sat down, and Ben motioned for the server to bring another bottle of the wine and two more glasses.

Sally was trying to make herself comfortable with this gathering of old and new friends. *How long now until they ask about Gwen?*

"So, Ben, tell us how you've come to meet our Sally here?" asked Susan.

"We were introduced when we arrived in Charlevoix last week. Sally's been nice enough to share some of her family's history with the ship with my daughter Megan and me while we've been up here. I asked Sally to join us for this little cruise down the lake this week so she could spend some more time on her grandfather's old ship."

Fran had a devilish look in her eye that Sally recognized. "And where is your daughter... and Mrs. Clark?" she asked.

"Fran, please," injected Sally. "What's with the inquisition of the poor man?"

"It's fine, Sally," he said, reaching across the table to take her hand and reassure her. The two new guests couldn't help but stare at their intimacy. "Megan decided to stay onboard tonight. I think she's getting homesick. I couldn't pry her away from the internet and her friends back home. And my wife... my wife passed away a few years back."

Fran was obviously terribly embarrassed. "Ben, I'm so sorry..." she offered.

"No really, you couldn't have known."

The wine arrived, and Ben supervised the tasting and offered to pour for everyone. "So, you are all old friends?" he asked.

Susan answered after tasting her wine. "Fran and I were up in Charlevoix shopping years ago and we stopped into Sally and Gwen's gallery. We were so taken with their collection we ended up talking for hours and having dinner later that night. We've all been friends ever since."

At the mention of Gwen's name, Sally looked over at Ben to see his reaction, but she detected no change in expression as he listened intently to Susan's story. Sally wondered suddenly how coincidental this meeting seemed to be, or was it? Leland was a small enough town it was very likely for them all to run into each other. She couldn't help but wonder though whether this had all been somehow orchestrated.

"Speaking of Gwen," Fran said, "we just heard from her the other day. She was back in New York visiting, as you know. She called to see if we might be able to sneak away to the city for a few days. You know how the summer season is though, don't you Sally?"

Clearly, they knew everything that was going on, Sally thought to herself.

"How is your summer going?" Sally said, trying to change the subject. "How is the shop doing?"

"Probably our best season ever," Fran answered. "This town just seems to attract more and more people every year."

"Are you open year-round up here?" Ben asked.

"Yes, but we have another shop down in Sarasota and we head south in the fall," answered Fran. "Winter is dreadful here. We have a local girl who runs the shop for us while we're away."

"What a nice arrangement," he said. "The Gulf Coast of Florida is beautiful."

"Yes," said Susan, "we're already looking forward to getting down there."

There was a momentary lull in the conversation, and they all tasted their wine.

"I see you're sampling some of our local vintage," said Susan.

"Yes, it's quite nice and I understand you have several good vineyards up this way."

"If you could stay over tomorrow, we'd love to take you on a wine tour. It's beautiful country and the wine's not bad either," offered Fran.

"No, Ben needs to get back to Charlevoix," said Sally, almost too quickly. "He has someone coming in for a meeting."

"Oh, that is too bad." said Fran. "Maybe on your next cruise through the area?"

"Thank you," he said. "Hopefully, we'll be back again next summer." He looked over at Sally with a grin. He looked at his watch. "You know, it's not too late. Would you two like to come out to the ship for a tour and maybe another glass of wine?" he offered.

Sally felt like kicking him under the table, but she knew he was just being polite.

Fran and Susan looked at each other and without hesitation, nodded enthusiastically.

After they finished their dinner, the launch was waiting for them at the docks. Ben helped the three women onboard. As they approached the *EmmaLee,* her lights and profile shined brilliantly on the still water. Flags were still flying, and soft music could be heard coming from the bridge. Sally listened to her friends converse with Ben as he described the work that had to be done on the ship. They both seemed to be handling all of this quite well considering they had probably gotten an earful from Gwen about her partner's infatuation with the handsome rich guy. She just hoped to herself they would continue to behave themselves. She knew they both had a devious sense of humor.

The stairs were lowered alongside the hull of the ship and they all made their way up to the deck. Ben sent one of the crew off to fetch a bottle of champagne to be taken to the rear deck. He was told that Megan had turned in for the evening.

With glasses full of sparkling wine, Ben led the three ladies throughout the ship on an extensive tour, relating more history of the vessel and weaving in stories of the Compton family he had learned since arriving in Charlevoix. He was taking so much time that Sally was beginning to get the idea he was trying to avoid being alone with her again tonight. *He probably needs as much time as I do to sort all of this out.*

When the tour was finally complete, they returned to the deck of the *EmmaLee* and a carafe of coffee was waiting for them on the serving table. They each helped themselves and sat down in a semi-circle in the large cushioned deck chairs. The sky was clear and even with the ambient light of the ship, they could see stars shining brightly overhead and a thin slice of a crescent moon coming up over the hills onshore, reflecting back to them on the water.

They all sat in silence for a few moments enjoying the quiet and the spectacular view. Fran broke the stillness, "You are a wonderful host, Mr. Clark."

"Thank you. It's been a pleasure getting to know you and Susan tonight."

"Sally, did you tell Ben about the tradition we have up here in the North Country on clear starlit nights?" Fran continued.

"Tradition?" Sally asked, thinking this could only be trouble.

"Well, I've already survived the Venetian Festival. What else can you locals throw at me?" Ben asked.

Susan picked up the conversation. "Ben, we believe that on a night like this, swimming in the nude has marvelous medicinal powers."

"You mean skinny-dipping?" he answered.

"You two clearly need more wine," Sally said.

"Come on, Sally," said Fran, "you know how good it is for the mind and body."

"So, this is a regular event for you all up here?" he asked Sally, laughing.

"I wouldn't describe it as a regular ritual, but it's safe to say we've taken a dip or two, purely for medicinal value," she said, unable to hold back a smile.

"Well, I'm certainly game," Ben said. "We've been known to take a dip or two out east you know. The good thing is, we don't have to worry about sharks here in the fresh water." He got up and brought the coffee pot around to fill everyone's cups.

"Now I'm not a particularly shy person, but I really don't know you all that well, yet. How would you propose that we all, ah... get wet?"

Susan jumped in with her best southern drawl, "We assume you're a gentleman, Ben, and will give us ladies a headstart while you avert your eyes."

"And what about you when it's my turn?" he said.

"You can count on us to do the right thing," Susan answered.

Ben put the coffee pot down and went over to an intercom system on the wall. He ordered a supply of towels, robes and float cushions be brought up on deck.

"You all are absolutely crazy," Sally finally said in disbelief. "Do you know how cold that water is going to be tonight?"

"It will feel wonderful, Sal," Fran answered. "Warmer than the air. You'll see."

The towels and such arrived, and the crewman disappeared down below again. Ben turned his deck chair around to face the rear of the ship. "Ladies first. I won't look until I hear three splashes."

Sally watched as her friends picked up a towel and float and began walking up along the side rail. She shook her head and followed along. *Why the hell not!*

The three women found a darker shadowy spot along the cabin wall and all disrobed quickly, wrapping themselves in the big white towels before moving over to an open section of the rail near the stairs. Fran went first, throwing her towel down on the stairs and her cushion well out into the dark black of the water, then jumping with a wild scream out into the air, naked arms and legs flying in all directions. Sally and Susan couldn't help but laugh and had to hold their sides as they watched their friend splash down into the chilly dark abyss.

"That's one!" they heard Ben yell from the back of the ship.

Fran popped up to the surface. Sally could just make out her form in the dim lights from the ship.

"Oh, it's marvelous, hurry up you two."

Sally looked at Susan, reached for her hand and they both ran together jumping out into the night, their towels dropping behind them on the stairway. Their screams and splashes echoed out through the darkness.

Sally came back up to the surface and was amazed at the comfortable temperature of the water. She heard Ben calling out, "I'm not sure if that was two or three, but here I come." She saw him walk to the open rail with a towel around his waist. "Well, I don't hear any screams of pain, so I assume it's not absolutely ice cold."

"It's wonderful! Hurry up and get in here," Sally coaxed. She let the cool of the water and the giddiness of the night wash over her. "Come on!"

"I can see three pairs of eyes staring up out of the darkness. You all do the right thing and turn toward shore," he admonished.

Sally found her float and rested her arms across it. She paddled over next to Fran and Susan, and they all laughed and turned away at the same time. Sally heard Ben's scream and then moments later felt his splash as he landed just a few feet away. He came up with his hair swept back and a huge grin across his face.

"Yeeow!" he yelled. "Now I'm awake! Wow, does that feel good!"

"Didn't we tell you?" Fran said.

"Ben, you're going to wake up the whole ship and the town," Sally scolded.

They all formed a circle, resting their arms on their cushions and kicking their legs softly. "What time does the coast guard run their patrol?" Ben pondered with a smile. "I can see the headlines...Ship's Skipper Arrested with Three Naked Women."

"You could do worse things to your reputation," Sally said and laughed. She realized she hadn't felt this crazy and unburdened in years. She threw her head back and washed the hair away from her face and looked through the darkness at this man named Ben Clark.

Chapter Twenty-four

Albert Truegood was an eighty-two-year-old Native American who had lived in Charlevoix his whole life. I'd been told his ancestors had been in the area for hundreds of years. He lived out north of town in the woods in a small shack in behind the dunes.

He had worked odd jobs most of his life, sometimes more steady over at the lumberyard down in Boyne. He kept mostly to himself, even on the nights he walked down to Lee's Bar to have some beers. No one could ever remember him causing any trouble, but in those days, well, he was just different, and most people gave him a wide berth.

When he came forward and told what he'd seen that night on Bridge Street with my sister, people at first weren't inclined to believe him. Sheriff Potts himself told me the man might just be making up a story to cover his own crime. I reminded the sheriff there was no good reason for him to come forward if Jonathan was already going to take the blame, unless he was just damn crazy.

For a while, that's what most people thought.

Sheriff Potts had completed his second long interview in two days with Albert Truegood and had just let him leave. Emily Compton and the lawyer, David Krupp, now sat with the portly sheriff in his office along with the county prosecutor. The sheriff's cigar sat half gone and smoldering in a dirty ashtray. The single window in the office had an old blind with layers of dust letting very little light through.

"Did you learn anything more about the car, or who may have been inside?" Krupp asked.

He shook his head, "No, and there's a lot of big black cars in this town."

The prosecutor, Andy Neeland, leaned forward, "Sheriff, what makes you think this old man is even telling the truth?"

"Well, I've known Albert since I was just a kid around town here and I've never known him to be anything but an honorable man... poor, mind you, but honest."

"You don't think he's trying to cover his own guilt?" the prosecutor continued.

"Hell no! Catherine Hansen could run away from the old man, even as drunk as she apparently was that night. Albert don't move much past a snail's pace these days."

Krupp broke in, "Sheriff, I know you don't have another suspect identified yet, but I'm going to ask you again why you can't release Jonathan. It's perfectly clear to see he had nothing to do with this."

Neeland pounced, "It certainly is not! We've got an old man who's been drinking all night, sees a car pull up and take the girl away. He can't identify the car or the driver. We also have the bartender down at *The Helm* who's told us McKendry and the girl argued at the bar that night when she told him she was pregnant with his brother's baby. That spells motive. He had opportunity and we sure as hell don't have anything else solid to consider."

"So, you think Truegood's lying?" asked Emily.

"I think there's just as good a chance he was too drunk to remember what he saw. The bartender over at *Lee's* said he had at least six beers and probably a few before he got there," answered Neeland.

"I'm afraid the boy stays locked up until the preliminary hearing next Monday," Sheriff Potts said with finality.

Emily walked through the side door into the kitchen of their house. She saw see her parents out front on the porch drinking some tea. She thought about heading straight to her room to avoid another confrontation, but her mother saw her through the window and waved for her to come out.

When she got out on the porch, she noticed Connor Harris was sitting there with her parents sharing some iced tea.

"Hello dear," her mother said. "I thought you'd like to say hello to Connor."

Connor jumped right in, "Hey, I wanted to stop over and see how you were holding up through all of this McKendry mess."

Emily bristled. "This is not a McKendry mess at all, and you know that," she said, not trying to hide the irritation she felt.

Her father put a hand up to signal he was taking control of the situation. "Emily, there is no need to get all worked up about this again. We've been talking to Connor. We think you need a break. Why don't you head back down to Ann Arbor in the morning and get away from all this for a while."

"Honey, it's such nasty business," her mother said, and then took a long sip from her iced tea.

Emily didn't even bother to answer. She just wasn't in a mood to fight about the situation again.

"Think about it tonight, honey," her father suggested. "You can catch the early train tomorrow morning. In the meantime, we've got some folks coming over for cocktails on the porch at five, then we're all going down to the hotel for dinner. Why don't you and Connor join us?"

She had finally had enough. "None of you seem to care there's an innocent man being held down at the jail for murder, one who also happens to be a friend of mine."

"Don't tell me you're buying that old Indian's story?" Connor chided.

"Mr. Truegood has no reason to lie or make up such a story. He clearly saw Jonathan walking away towards home where I found him the next morning. And he saw Catherine get into a car and drive away, and that's the last time anyone saw her."

"Come on Em', the Indian was staggering drunk. He's just trying to get some attention. I'm sure they haven't been able to get any more real detail out of him, have they?"

"Connor, you have no idea what you're talking about," Emily said.

"Okay, let's not spoil this nice afternoon," her father interrupted.

The screen door opened, and the cook brought out another pitcher of tea and a glass for Emily. She sat them down on the table in front of Emily's parents.

"Come on dear, sit down and relax with us for a minute," her mother asked.

Emily was still standing facing everyone else. "I don't mean to be rude, but I need to go up and get some rest. I'm exhausted."

"Let me come by around six and I'll take you to dinner," Connor said.

She shook her head in exasperation. "Fine," she said. "Let's just try not to talk about this case anymore tonight. Deal?"

"Deal," Connor agreed.

Luke McKendry walked into *The Helm*. The clock behind the bar showed 5:30. There was a couple in a back booth and no one else except Bud behind the bar. He sat down on his usual stool and lit a cigarette.

"Well, well," said Bud, walking up. "Haven't seen your hide since the night.... well, you know."

"You mean the night that sonofabitch killed my girl and my baby!" he spat. "Give me a goddamn shot and a draft."

Bud served up the drinks and watched Luke throw them both back and push the glasses forward for more. "Is it gonna be one of those nights, son?"

"Shut up, Bud and pour. That's your job, isn't it?"

"So, you're still blaming your brother?"

"Nobody believes that damn Indian, Bud. He's certified crazy and you know it as well as I do. Besides, Catherine wouldn't just jump in some strange car passing by at two in the morning."

"Luke, you know how she'd get when she was in here. She was even worse that night. She was barely walkin' when they left here that night at closing."

"Yeah, I heard."

"You goin' to the funeral tomorrow?" Bud asked.

"Her brother and her parents don't want me anywhere near that place."

"Hey kid. I'm really sorry about Catherine and the baby and all. I know you two was havin' some trouble, but there just ain't no sense in any of this. These first two are on me, how 'bout that?"

Luke was staring at the bubbles in his beer and just grunted.

"You know, it's a damn good thing you was shacked up that night, or they'd be chillin' your ass down at that jail," Bud said. "I never seen two people fight as much as you and the Hansen girl. Why the hell'd she ever stay with you?"

"My sunny disposition," Luke answered gruffly. He finished the second beer in one swallow and let the burn reach all the way down into his gut. "I'm no fool, Bud. Catherine only came to me after Jonathan got hot after that Compton broad and then up and left for the war. She's left here all alone wondering if he's coming back in one piece, and if he does come back, it'll be with the Compton girl hanging on his arm." He stopped for a moment, thinking. "Maybe she thought she was punishing him, but the only one she ever hurt was her own damn self."

Bud poured two more beers from the tap and held his up to Luke's. "God rest her soul," the old man said.

Connor walked out to the car with Emily dressed in a white dinner jacket and black bow tie. He opened the passenger door for her and helped her in. She hadn't said a word since she met him at the door. When he got in on the other side, she was looking out the passenger window.

"Come on, Emily. You need a night out to relax and forget about this for a while."

"Let's just go. I'll be okay," she said quietly, finally looking over to see him. She noticed a cut, or scratch along the line of his jaw. "What happened to your face? You need to be more careful shaving."

As he was backing the car out of the drive, he reached up with his free hand and touched the area. "Yeah, I was out on the sailboat yesterday and caught a weird gust of wind. Damn mainsail jibed and the boom about took my head off."

"You should have that looked at," she said.

They drove up the long, curved driveway in front of the Belvedere Hotel. It was a grand old structure built at the turn of the century. The lawns and gardens were immaculately cared for. The view down the hill and across the lake was spectacular. Several other large cars were parked in the drive. A uniformed valet attendant came out to open the door for Emily, then ran around to take the keys from Connor.

"Thank you, sir," the attendant said, as Connor placed a tip in his hand.

Connor started around the car to help Emily out. She reached down for her purse on the floor. Something bright caught her attention, wedged under the side of the seat. She squeezed her hand down into the narrow opening and was able to get a grip. It felt hard and sharp in her fingers. As she managed to pull it free, she could finally see what it was. A sinking nausea raced through her body as events and facts all came together in an instant of sudden clarity.

She tried to catch her breath. Connor reached her open door and offered his hand to help her out. She closed her hand and slid it into the pocket of her jacket.

"Connor..." she hesitated and couldn't continue for a moment.

"What is it?"

"Connor, I'm suddenly not feeling very well. Something's coming over me. Can you please take me back home?"

An hour later, Emily walked up the stone walk to the home of George Hansen and his parents. She stood on the porch for a moment continuing to question her judgment in what she was about to do. She reached out and pushed the doorbell. Almost immediately she heard movement inside, then the door opened and George was standing there with a surprised look on his face.

"Emily... ?"

When she saw George's face, she could still see the pain of the family's grief wearing on him.

"George, can we go for a walk?"

"Sure," he said, looking behind him and then coming out and closing the door. They walked out to the sidewalk and then turned east, back towards town. They walked in silence for a while, then Emily finally got up her nerve.

She reached into her jacket and pulled out a closed fist. She stopped, and George turned to face her.

"What is it?" he asked, a bit impatient.

She opened her hand and held it palm up in front of him. A silver pendant earring lay in her hand and shined brightly, even in the late evening sun.

"I found this," she said hesitantly as she looked up at him.

George looked at the earring for a moment and then reached out and took it from her. He held it dangling in the air between them with a puzzled look on his face.

"Where did you get this?"

"Do you think this..."

George quickly interrupted her. "Where did you get this?"

"Is it Catherine's?"

"My parents gave these to her last Christmas." He closed the earring tightly in his hand and looked directly into her eyes. "You need to tell me now where you found this."

"Oh George!" she gasped.

He reached out and took her arm as if she might run away before she told everything she knew. "When they returned my sister's effects there was only one earring. We figured it had been lost out at the beach."

"George, we need to go to the sheriff."

A half block away, parked between two other cars, Connor Harris sat in his car watching Emily Compton talking face-to-face with George Hansen, examining some item, too small for him to make out. He suspected something else was wrong with Emily than a sudden illness. He had followed her discreetly to the Hansen house.

He watched as they turned together and began walking quickly toward town.

Chapter Twenty-five

It took most of the next day for the *EmmaLee* to make her way back up the coast from Leland to Round Lake in Charlevoix. The wind had picked up and blew at ten to fifteen knots from the south, giving the big ship a smooth ride on a following sea. Sally had been sitting with Ben up on the deck above the bridge for much of the afternoon, reading and occasionally laughing again about the night before.

They had finally herded Fran and Susan back into their clothes and the launch for one of the crew to get them back to shore sometime after midnight. She and Ben had sat for at least another hour in the warmth of the big cotton robes, sipping brandy, laughing and talking about her two crazy friends from the shores of Leland harbor. As the ship now slowed to head into the channel to Charlevoix, she was thinking about her feelings the night before, sitting there with Ben Clark, naked under her robe. She couldn't remember ever feeling a stronger physical attraction to anyone. It was all she could do to remind herself that sex was a further complication she certainly didn't need at the moment. She wasn't sure how Ben was feeling, but he behaved like a gentleman and they both retired to their own cabins after a long kiss goodnight.

Megan came up on deck to join Sally and her father, and they returned waves from the many people along the pier as they headed into the inlet of Round Lake. Sally couldn't help feel just a bit guilty riding along on the top of such an outrageous display of wealth. She wondered how her mother had felt about it. She had never seemed pretentious about the family's money, at least in Sally's memories of her.

As they came alongside the dock in town, the crew jumped down to secure the lines and lower the stairs. Sally came up on deck with her travel bag and Ben was waiting for her at the stairs. She noticed a middle-aged man standing on the dock at the bottom of the stairs, dressed in a tan designer jacket and slacks with a black silk shirt open at the neck. His hair was dark brown and shiny and brushed straight back. He had a sharp, handsome face with a deep tan, his eyes hidden behind slim black sunglasses. He seemed quite anxious.

"My former partner in crime, Louis Kramer," Ben said, taking her hand and looking down at the man. "I mentioned we had a meeting today. He just had to be here in person to tell me about this new business opportunity. He had his jet fly him into the Charlevoix airport this afternoon." Ben waved. "Lou, come on aboard."

Kramer ran up the steps with athletic grace and shook his former partner's hand and then gave him a big hug, lifting Ben off the ground. "Hey, old man," he said. "This northern climate seems to be suiting you just fine! Who's the pretty lady?"

"Lou, meet my friend, Sally Thomason."

He came over and planted a wet kiss on her cheek and gave her a big bear hug. "My pleasure, Sally! Damn nice to meet you."

"It's nice to meet you, Louis," Sally said. Welcome to Charlevoix."

"Sally's family owned the *EmmaLee* years ago here in Michigan. Actually, her mother was Emily, the ship's namesake."

"Well, you're even prettier than this big old boat!" Louis gushed.

"I guess that's a compliment," Sally said with a grin on her face.

"Whew, Ben, they grow 'em pretty up here in the North."

Sally sensed his Texas accent was just a little affected. "Well, Louis, you're going to get a permanent invitation from the Chamber of Commerce if you keep talking like that," Sally teased. "I'm going to let you two take care of business. I need to get up to the shop and check on some business of my own."

"Sally's a painter and has a gallery up on the main drag there," Ben explained.

"Well, wouldn't you know, I've been looking for someone to paint my portrait for all history to remember me," Louis said in a self-deprecating tone.

Sally laughed, "Your friend certainly has a way with women, Ben."

"Oh yeah, he's a real charmer,' said Ben. "And speaking of charmers, look who's coming down the hill."

Sally looked and saw Mary Alice Gregory walking with determination down through the crowds of people in the park. She had her hair pulled back as usual with a scarf and her long tan legs were displayed nicely beneath a short white sundress and white heeled sandals.

Ben poked his friend in the side as they all watched Mary Alice approach the ship. "Louis, you may have well just met your match."

Mary Alice spotted them standing at the rail and waved. Ben waved back.

Louis whistled quietly. "Damn!" was all he could manage to say.

"Let me clear some space for all of you," Sally said as she leaned over to kiss Ben on the cheek. "Thanks again. You know I will never be able to thank you enough."

Megan Clark ran up and hugged Sally around the waist. "Bye Sally. When are we going to see you again?"

Ben answered for her, "We'll call Sally later, after she's had a chance to unpack. Maybe she can join us all for dinner."

"That would be nice, thanks," Sally said. "And Louis, it has been a real pleasure," she said with a genuine smile. "Maybe we can get better acquainted over dinner tonight."

"Absolutely," he answered, looking back to see Mary Alice Gregory coming up the stairs. Sally passed her going down. "Hello, Mary Alice."

"Why Sally, I was just up at the shop," Mary Alice said. "They said you'd been away for a few days. I had no idea..."

Sally couldn't resist a little dig to get under her skin, "We had a wonderful cruise down to Leland, but I really have to get up to the gallery now. Bye!"

"Oh, bye."

As Sally walked away along the docks, she could hear the fuss Ben's friend was making over Mary Alice Gregory. Good luck Louis. You're going to need it!

Sally walked along the shops and restaurants on Bridge Street on the way down to her gallery. The sidewalks were full of summer visitors and kids on the lookout for kids of the opposite sex. The *Sale* signs were already going up in the windows of the merchants, a clear signal the season was beginning to wind down. The drawbridge was up over the channel and traffic was backed up as far you could see up the hills in both directions. Never try to get through Charlevoix on the half hours this time of year, she thought. Up ahead through the mass of people she saw the familiar face of George Hansen. They sidestepped a few more people and then came together in a hug.

"Welcome home young lady."

"Thank you, George. It was quite a trip." She told him about the service out near the Manitous.

"Well, that Mr. Clark is quite a special fellow now, isn't he?"

"George, it was so hard saying goodbye to Mom and Daddy... and Ellen, again out there. But, when it was done, I have to admit I felt much better."

"I'm glad for you, honey."

"And if you promise not to tell...," she smiled with a wicked grin.

"Of course, I promise..."

"We ran into Fran and Susan down in Leland."

"Oh, God! I can only imagine what those two were up to," he said.

Sally took him by the arm and led him down the sidewalk. "Well, after a few too many bottles of wine last night we managed to all find ourselves bone naked out in the middle of Lake Michigan."

"Girl, you shock me!" he said and laughed. "Why am I not surprised with those two. So, has Ben decided on a departure date?"

"In a day or two. He's got a business partner in town tonight to discuss some new deal."

"Mind if I get a little nosey?"

"Yes, I do mind!" she said punching him playfully in his round belly.

"Well, I'll ask anyway. What's next for the two of you?"

She pushed him away as they got to the door of her gallery. "You'll be the second person to know, I promise."

The gallery had been busy when she walked in and her assistant waved and raised her eyebrows in a sign of relief as she continued to help a customer. Sally went around and talked with the other shoppers and spent the rest of the afternoon catching up on calls and the growing piles of paperwork.

At a little after seven, the phone rang again, and she was surprised to hear Ben's voice. She had forgotten about the dinner discussions since she had gotten so busy back at the shop.

"Can you stand a few more hours with the Clark clan?" Ben asked.

"I don't know, sir. You run with a pretty wild crowd. Can I keep my clothes on tonight?"

"Those were your friends, lady!"

"Something tells me Mr. Kramer is going to be even more to handle," Sally said.

"Oh, I think Mary Alice has got him all wrapped up and ready to deliver."

"Already!" Sally gasped. "That girl works fast."

"Look, the chef was able to run out and pick up some nice steaks for our Texas friend, a little fresh sweet corn and some charcoal for a good old-fashioned barbecue. Thought we might cruise out into Lake Charlevoix and light up the grill."

"Sounds great!"

"It's you and me and the new happy couple."

"Oh boy, a night out with Mary Alice."

"Megan met a new friend in the park this afternoon and the family invited her up for dinner at their house over near where you live. Seemed like nice people, the Baileys."

"Old Charlevoix summer family. Very nice folks. No relation to Mary Alice Gregory."

"Be kind," Ben said. "She may be just what the doctor ordered for the wild child, Kramer. How about eight o'clock?"

"I'll be there."

Sally had time to get home for a quick shower and change of clothes. She found a summer skirt and blouse, and a sweater for later if a chill came in off the big lake. There had been no messages from Gwen back at the shop or on her phone.

She was thinking of Gwen as she walked over the drawbridge and looked out at the parade of boats making their way in and out of Charlevoix's little harbor. What if Ben had never come back to Charlevoix? Was she destined to spend the rest of her life here with Gwen? They had never discussed much beyond the coming season, she thought. One season, then one year had led to the next and suddenly many years had passed. She knew she already missed her friend and partner... and lover. It pained her to think about what hurt she may be causing.

She stopped midway across the bridge, looking out toward Lake Michigan and another beautiful sunset in full bloom. Her thoughts wandered to new possibilities and new sunsets on new horizons.

The *EmmaLee* rested calmly about a mile offshore from the old train depot in Charlevoix. Years earlier, a great hotel had spread across the high bank above the depot and had attracted people from around the world to enjoy its elegance and magnificent views of Lake Charlevoix. As with many of the great resort hotels in the north, it had passed its prime and been demolished many years ago. Private homes now lined the hillside.

The crew of the *EmmaLee* had set a beautiful table for four on the rear deck. They put torches of citronella candles all along the rails to light the dining area and keep away the bugs. A *James Taylor* album played softly over the ship's sound system. The four diners had been enjoying a new wine from Australia Ben had suggested with their first course of salads. The men were dressed in sport coats and white shirts with no tie. Mary Alice had surprised no one by wearing an outrageously low-cut dress that exposed much of her surgically enhanced assets.

"Damn if those steaks don't smell like down home in Austin," Louis said.

"You haven't been to Austin in twenty years, Louis," Ben teased.

"Them's my roots, son."

Mary Alice squirmed a bit to adjust her short skirt. "Sally, did you know Louie's family was actually in the oil business back in Texas?"

"No, Louie, I didn't know that about you. Were you a wildcatter?" Sally asked, grinning.

"Didn't cotton much to the ol' bidness. Went east, met this young fella at school and damned if we didn't figure out another way to make a buck in all this internet nonsense."

"Let's not get bogged down in business tonight," Ben said, "but old Louie here has put together quite a proposal for a new venture. We're going to meet some folks back in New York next week to discuss putting money into this new deal. You never cease to amaze me, Louie!"

"You can call me Louis, sir. Only my closest friends, like Ms. Gregory here are allowed such intimacies." He leaned over and gave her a kiss on the cheek. She giggled her big girl giggle and beamed with pride at her latest catch.

"Mary Alice and I are flying out tomorrow to Miami," Louis said. "I was telling her about my place down in Ocean Reef and damned if her folks don't have a place down there, too. Thought we might take a little cruise down through the Keys before I have to get back up to New York next week. Ben has seen my boat. Nothin' like the *EmmaLee* here, but plenty comfortable for two."

Sally noticed his hand slide over onto Mary Alice's bare thigh. She felt tempted to inform Mr. Kramer that Mary Alice had two ex-husbands with places down in Florida but decided he probably wouldn't care anyway.

Mary Alice slid over closer to Louis. Sally saw that look in her eye she knew meant trouble.

"Ben, a few days ago you were talking about *your* place down in Florida," Mary Alice began with a wicked grin. "Where did you say, Boca Raton?"

"That's right," Ben answered, almost under his breath.

"Didn't you say one of your old assistants was living down there now, kind of taking care of the place? What was her name... Sylvia?"

Sally felt like an ice pick was stuck straight into her heart. She swallowed hard and tried not to show any emotion. Mary Alice just smiled at her, waiting for a response from Ben.

She looked over at him for some sign of reassurance or explanation, but he wouldn't make eye contact. He continued to look down into the wine he was swirling in his glass. She was amazed he wouldn't just come out and be honest with her about the situation. *What else will I learn about Ben Clark tonight?*

Louis obviously sensed the tension of the situation and went into diffusion mode. "Yeah, Sylvia used to work for us. She ran one of our companies down in Miami."

Sally was trying with all her will to remain calm. She knew Ben certainly had a life before they had met, just as she had, but why couldn't he be honest with her about it? Finally, she couldn't stand to sit silently any longer. "Yes, Ben, tell us about your place in Boca Raton."

He looked up slowly from his wine and exchanged an odd look with his friend, Louis. He took a long drink, then turned to Sally. "Yes, I've had a house down there for years. I keep a boat there and go back and forth in the winter." He paused, taking another sip of wine. "When Louis and I sold our business in Miami a year or so ago, Sylvia Lasser was looking for a place to stay and I asked her to house-sit for me."

Sally had to bite her tongue and she wanted to reach out and strangle Mary Alice, who was watching Ben squirm and obviously enjoying every minute of it. She refused to let her emotions show. "That's very generous of you," was all she could manage in response.

The rest of the evening had been strained at best for Sally, but Mary Alice and Louis continued their new obsession with each other as if nothing had happened. The *EmmaLee* was tied up again at the dock by midnight. Sally quickly made her way to leave. Ben walked with her, the first time they had been able to be alone since dinner. He reached for her arm as they walked along the rail, but she pulled away.

He finally stopped her by saying, "Sally, I need to apologize for what happened earlier. There is some history down in Florida that frankly, I was just embarrassed I hadn't told you about earlier."

Sally just nodded, trying to collect her thoughts.

"Our 'friend,' Mary Alice, made it seem like some clandestine kind of thing," he said, holding both of her arms gently.

"You don't need to apologize for her rude behavior or your life before we met," she said, trying her best to keep her anger at bay. "Thank you for dinner. I'm exhausted and really need to get home." She turned and pulled away.

Ben didn't try to stop her.

Chapter Twenty-six

Connor Harris was brought in for questioning later that night. We were told he came quietly. I waited in the lobby of the sheriff's office with Emily Compton and the attorney, David Krupp. I can remember the emotions racing through my mind that night. The rage in my heart was tempered by the reassuring possibility that my friend Jonathan could possibly be freed by the end of the night.

Sheriff Potts came out at a little past eleven.

"We're driving Harris home now," he said, as he sat with George, Emily and Krupp.

"You're letting him go!" said George, jumping up from his chair.

The sheriff motioned for him to sit back down. "George, we've got all the information we need from him tonight. We're keeping his car so we can take a closer look at it in the morning."

"What did he have to say, Sheriff?" Krupp asked.

"You know I can't share the specifics, but he's got a pretty damn good story and alibi for that night. We'll be checking it out tomorrow."

"How did he explain my sister's earring in his car?" George asked.

"Let's just say he claims Catherine was in his car on several occasions recently, including earlier the night she was attacked.

He dropped her at *The Helm* when she went in and met up with Jonathan."

Emily was shaking her head. "What was she doing riding around with Connor? I didn't think they even knew each other."

A deputy came out and signaled for Potts. As he turned to leave, he said, "You all get home now and check back with me midday tomorrow. You let us worry about Harris. We'll have someone watching him tonight." He walked out of the room with the deputy.

Krupp gave Emily a ride back to her house. It was close to midnight. The streetlights had a soft halo showing through a light fog drifting in from Lake Michigan. She got out by the curb and thanked him for the ride. He offered to pick her up at nine in the morning to head back down to the jail.

She watched as the lights from his car faded into the haze of the evening. She turned and looked up at the big house. Lights were out in most of the windows. Only the crickets chirping broke the quiet of the night.

Her mind was racing in so many directions. *Could Connor really be involved with this? What will he think when he finds out I went to the police? What will my family think?*

So much pointed to Connor... the big black car picking Catherine up on the street that night, the scratch and bruise on his face... and the earring.

She walked across the lawn toward the house. Out of the dark shadows of the bushes around the porch she sensed motion and turned quickly as the prickly sensations of fear knifed through her veins.

Connor's face came into the light. He grabbed her by the arm and pulled her away into the shadows before she could do or say anything. She wanted to scream, but fear had taken her voice.

"Emily, relax, I'm not going to hurt you," he whispered, holding both of her arms.

She was trembling and still couldn't find words.

"Emily, please, I just needed you to know I didn't have anything to do with this. I couldn't have you thinking I could do something like this."

"Connor, I..." she stammered.

"Listen," he said with more urgency. "I understand why you felt you had to go to the police. I know it doesn't look good."

"How long have you known the Hansen girl?" she finally asked.

"We've kind of been seeing each other, off and on, for the past couple of summers."

She felt anger replacing her fear. "In other words, you've been sleeping with her just to get back at Luke McKendry?"

He didn't answer.

"My God, Connor, what were you thinking?"

"Look, you just need to know I had nothing to do with her death. I dropped her at *The Helm* earlier that night. We had been together in my car out north of town at the beach. She said she had to meet someone at the bar, and I dropped her there. I never saw her again. I swear to you, Emily!"

"Sheriff Potts said they'd be watching you tonight."

"I slipped out the back. I think the deputy was asleep anyway, but I need to get back."

"Connor, I don't know what to say."

"You don't need to say anything. I just couldn't stand having you think the wrong thing here."

She looked at his face and could just make out his features in the dark shadows. "You need to go."

He nodded, then reluctantly backed away and disappeared around the side of the house.

She walked through the house and back to the kitchen. Her father was sitting at the counter in his pajamas and a robe with a cup of coffee cradled in both hands. He looked up when he heard her enter. She could see the anger in his face immediately.

"Emily, have you lost your mind!"

"Daddy..."

"I was on the phone earlier with Connor's father. They told me you and that Hansen boy turned Connor in to the police for that girl's murder."

"Her name is Catherine Hansen!" she said, losing her temper as well.

"I know you have these crazy feelings for this McKendry boy, but turning in one of your best friends?"

"Daddy, there were just so many things coming together that pointed to Connor. I found one of Catherine's earrings in his car..."

"Emily, stop! None of that had anything to do with this murder, and I think you know that now. Do you realize what people are saying around here? You wouldn't believe the looks and comments we got down at the club after dinner tonight. First, you're helping this local boy who's probably a murderer and a rapist, and now you turn in one of our family's best friends based on some wild notions you've cooked up with this other local kid."

"Daddy..." she tried to interrupt.

"This has got to stop now!" he almost shouted he was so angry.

Emily looked away. The clock over the sink said 12:30. She was exhausted. Her emotions were flying in all directions. She didn't know who to believe or what to do anymore. Impulsively, she headed back toward the door. "I need to go see someone." She was out the door and into the car before her father could stop her.

George was still up, sitting on the front porch when she pulled over to the curb. He looked up, wondering who it was.

Emily got out of the car and walked up to the porch. George looked back down at the ground, his arms locked around his knees. She sat down next to him. The evening was still warm and comfortable. The haze from the lake had progressed to a deepening fog.

"George, I had to see you. I just saw Connor."

He looked at her with a puzzled expression. "I thought the police were watching..."

"He slipped away from his house to come and see me." She told him the story Connor shared with her earlier.

"Harris had been seeing my sister?"

She nodded.

"I had no idea, and I'm not sure I believe it."

Emily put her head in her hands. "George, I'm not sure who, or what to believe anymore either. Do you think Luke had any idea about Catherine and Connor?"

"I really don't know. I didn't know any of this was going on."

She stood and walked around for a moment, trying to collect her thoughts. "If we go and talk to Luke about this and he didn't know, it will only re-ignite the feud those two have had."

George finished her thought. "But, if he knew about Catherine and Harris, he may know a lot more about this whole situation than anyone thought."

They looked at each other for a while, considering the possibilities.

George finally broke the silence. "I'm pretty sure I know where we can find him."

Emily and George walked into *The Helm* at a little after 1:00 a.m. As George had suspected, Luke was sitting at his regular spot at the bar. Smoke lay heavy across the air in a thick gray cloud. The music was turned up loud and two couples were dancing in the back. Bud the bartender stood across the bar from Luke, doing most of the talking.

George led the way and sat down between Luke and Emily. Luke kept looking down into his beer.

"Luke, hey it's George." No response. He pulled on Luke's arm and spoke again, "Hey, it's me!"

Luke pulled his arm away suddenly and then slurred, "Wha' the hell you want?" He turned to look at George and saw Emily was with him. "Who's the bitch?"

"All right Luke, bad timing here," said George. "You sober up tomorrow, you call me. We need to talk to you about Catherine."

"I ain't got nothin' else to say." His head was weaving back and forth, and his eyes were trying to focus on something to gain purchase. He seemed to gather some clarity for a moment and looked directly into George's eyes. "George, I didn' wanna tell ya this... but your sister was really messed up. She was gettin' ta be a bigger drunk than me, and with the baby and all..."

"You knew about the baby?" Emily asked.

Luke turned his gaze over to her. "Yeah... I knew about that. She told me. She also tol' me it wasn't mine!" He turned and took a drink from his beer.

"Did she say who the father was?" Emily asked.

Bud tried to interrupt. "Can I get you two anything to drink?"

They both said *no*.

George turned Luke toward him again. "Luke, who was the father?"

Luke looked at him for a moment and then shook his head, "How in hell would I know?"

Emily sensed Luke knew far more than he was sharing. "Luke, this must be so hard for you. When was the last time you saw Catherine?"

"George, who is this bitch?"

"Luke, you know Emily, Emily Compton," George said.

"Yeah... right."

"When was the last time you saw her?" she asked again.

He hesitated, took another drink and scratched his head looking across the bar at Bud. "We weren't seein' each other no more."

"That's not what I asked you," she persisted.

"She told me the baby wasn't mine and I told her we were done!"

Emily got up from her chair and walked around George to stand next to Luke. She leaned down near his face. "Did you see her that last day?"

He shook his head no, looking straight forward.

Bud chimed in. "Luke, you too drunk to remember coming in that night when she was here with Jonny? I never seen you come in here and leave so fast."

Luke looked up at Bud with contempt. "Yeah... I saw her here with him. I asked her if she was gonna do my brother now, too... the stupid bitch."

"And you just left?" George asked.

"Yeah, he was outta here in no time," Bud said again.

"I said the hell withum' and got my ass outta here and over ta Shirley's for the night."

Emily pulled on his arm to turn him to face her. "But you didn't stay there all night, did you?"

"Wha' the hell are you talkin' about? I told Potts where I was and Shirley, she vouched for me."

Emily pressed on. "But you came back here later looking for Catherine, didn't you?"

"George, you better get this bitch outta my face, now!" he said, red veins beginning to bulge along the side of his neck and across his forehead. "Do you hear me, George?"

"Luke, whose car did you drive back in?" Emily asked, pressing closer to him.

He didn't answer and instead reached for his beer.

Emily felt fear surging through her but kept pushing him. "You must have been pretty upset to find out your girlfriend was having a baby with another man, then see her with her old boyfriend again... your own brother."

Luke's expression turned from rage to confusion as he seemed to be considering her question. Then, very softly he started to speak, looking blankly at the wall behind the bar. "I tol' her I'd forgive 'er. I tol' her we'd get over all this." He paused, continuing to look on with a blank stare. "She was so damn drunk. She just kept tellin' me to go to hell!"

Neither George nor Emily dared speak. They let him continue to rattle on. Bud seemed nearly as drunk as Luke and just listened.

"The bitch is tellin' me to go to hell...she's the one droppin' her pants all over town. That asshole, Harris..."

"She told you about Connor?" Emily asked, breathlessly.

"Damn right she tol' me. She tol' me she did him that same day... in the car out at the Point."

"So, you took her back out there that night," Emily said. It wasn't a question.

Luke slowly seemed to focus as he considered what she'd said and obviously realized he'd said enough.

He stood suddenly and pushed her away. She caught her leg on George's bar stool and fell to the floor, sliding on the slippery beer-soaked tile.

"Get out of my face!" He reached for his glass, took a last swallow, then threw it at Emily's head. In his drunkenness, he threw it wide and it crashed on the floor beside her.

George jumped from his chair, stunned by Luke's sudden attack. He knelt quickly to see to Emily. "Are you okay?"

She nodded, trying to overcome the shock of Luke's outburst and all he had just shared.

Bud had come around from behind the bar and hovered over them, not offering to help, but staring helplessly.

267

George stood up slowly and turned to face Luke. "You sonofabitch! My sister! How could you..."

Before he could finish, Luke lashed out with a whiskey bottle he had been holding at his side and caught George across the temple. The bottle shattered with a sickening explosion against his skull. Blood squirted from a gash that opened across his forehead.

Emily watched in horror as George's knees wobbled, then collapsed and he fell to the floor next to her. Luke kneeled down at her side, the jagged edges of the broken bottle still in his hand.

"You stupid bitch...," he snarled and held the sharp glass inches from her face.

Emily's emotions were shattered and she lost all sense of composure, screaming out, "No, please... Luke!"

The old bartender threw his body at Luke and knocked him away, "No son, you gotta stop this!"

Emily watched as Luke struggled to his feet. He looked down at her again for a moment with a crazed look on his face, tears running down his cheeks. Then he ran with his ragged limp out the door and was gone.

Sheriff Potts and two of his deputies met Emily at the emergency room at the hospital. The doctors had checked her out even though she told them she only had a few bruises. One of the bar patrons drove her and George to the hospital. George had regained consciousness on the way, but he was bleeding badly. They had taken him back for stitches and further examination.

Emily took the Sheriff and his men through everything that had happened since she had seen Connor at her house and what she and George had learned when they confronted Luke at the bar.

"I'll be goddamned!" was all the sheriff could say, at first. "I never would have thought Shirley would lie for that boy."

"She may not have known Luke ever left," Emily said. "She could have been asleep or passed out drunk."

"You have any idea where he might have been headed?" Potts asked.

She shook her head *no*. "If George is up to talking, he may have some idea."

"Okay, we'll get a bulletin out around the area towns. We'll find him. I'm leaving one of my deputies with you tonight. I don't want that crazy ass coming back after you two."

"Sheriff, what about Jonathan?" she asked.

"One step at a time, Miss Compton."

Chapter Twenty-seven

Sally sat alone in the office of her gallery early the next morning after the dinner with Ben, Louis and the *lovely* Mary Alice Gregory. She had endured a long, mostly sleepless night trying to sort through her emotions and the various paths she now faced. She stared at the steam from her coffee, watching it drift off up into the quiet spaces of her office, its aroma the only sensation that seemed to make its way into her brain.

She was concerned about overreacting to the revelations about Ben's previous life, as if she had any right to do so in the first place. She had reacted just as Mary Alice had hoped, and she was furious with herself for taking the bait. Then, there was Ben and the realization she was about to jump into a whole new relationship with this man, abandoning so much of what she knew and felt comfortable in.

She now realized how little she actually knew about Ben. She certainly couldn't condemn him for having previous relationships. She kept trying to come up with reasons to rationalize his behavior the night before. She kept trying to convince herself it wasn't that important. *He did apologize, after all.*

Every time she was close to putting it all aside, a lingering doubt found its way back in. She wanted so badly to pick up the phone and call him, to talk it all through, but there were just so many questions.

An hour later she opened the gallery for business and almost immediately had a shop full of people that kept her busy most of the morning. Her assistant came in at eleven and gave her a chance to go back to her office for a break. She sat at her desk sipping on a bottled water, a dozen thoughts and emotions racing through her mind. She happened to glance over at the paintings stacked in the far corner. Suddenly, she had a very clear sense of something she did have to deal with.

Walking over, she began sorting through the canvases. She stopped when she reached the last one resting against the wall. The unfinished painting of her daughter, Ellen, stared back at her. She pulled it out and held it in front of her. The face was almost complete. The clothing and background still needed considerable work. She looked into the eyes of her daughter and for the first time was able to smile and find joy in the beauty of her little girl. She hugged the canvas to her chest and let out a soft moan. "Oh Ellen," she whispered.

She took the canvas over to an easel in the middle of her studio and placed it carefully down. Standing back, she examined it again. She hadn't painted in weeks and now, suddenly, it seemed the most important thing in her life.

She grabbed a palette and brushes from her work bench and began sorting paint tubes looking for the right colors, loading her palette and mixing colors to get just the right hues. Pulling a stool over, she began to work. Her hand flowed easily and with purpose.

She hadn't thought about how much time had passed when she heard the bell hanging on her office door ring. Looking down at her watch, she realized she had been painting for over two hours. She turned to see who had come in.

Gwen stood there in the doorway.

They both just looked at each other for a moment.

Gwen broke the awkward silence. "Hello stranger," she said. "I flew in yesterday afternoon to Traverse City. When I got to the shop, I found out you were out on the ship with Ben, so I decided to go spend the night at a motel."

Sally got up from the stool and walked over to the doorway. She reached out her arms and they came together in a long embrace, resting their faces on each other's shoulders.

"I've missed you," Sally said. "I'm so glad you've come back. We really need to talk this through."

Gwen noticed the painting of young Ellen Thomason. "I see we've made a breakthrough on your painting."

Sally turned and looked at her work. "For all of the insanity of this past week, at least I've been able to start coming to grips with this part of my life."

They sat down together on a couch over against the far wall. Sally told Gwen all about the memorial that Ben had arranged for her family out on Lake Michigan.

When she was finished, Gwen said, "He must be quite a special person?"

Sally reached out for Gwen's hand. "I just don't know what to do."

"We need to be absolutely honest with each other, honey. What do you feel for this man?" Gwen asked.

Sally looked into the eyes she had found such comfort and peace. She couldn't bring herself to cause her any pain. "Gwen, I just don't know how I feel."

"No, I think you know very well, you're just not being honest with yourself, or with me," Gwen said calmly, with no hint of anger. "I've been able to get a lot of thinking done this past week. What it all seems to come back to is you and I have become so accustomed to this life we've built here and so dependent on each other and yet, when it comes down to it, neither of us has been able to give the other the kind of life that can make us truly happy."

Sally let the words sink in for a moment. "You don't think we can be happy? What the hell is that anyway? Life is what it is.

We get by and if we have someone to share it with, shouldn't we feel blessed?"

"But we all have choices, Sal," Gwen said. "We all have to make choices. Sometimes you just can't let life keep running along on autopilot."

"So, you think we should just walk away from all these years together because something new comes along?"

Gwen got up and walked over to the painting of Sally's daughter. "This was your life before. You were a great mother. You loved this little girl more than anything." Gwen tried to wipe away tears building in her eyes. "You were meant to be a mother, to have a family. How could we have both left our lives behind us all these years? What have we been hiding from?"

"Gwen, don't say that!" Sally said and now was wiping at her own tears. "You did more than just come along! You saved my life."

"I think we saved each other, and I wouldn't give back any of what we've had together. But, does everything have to last forever? Can anything last forever?"

Sally got up from the couch and went over to Gwen and put her arms around her shoulders and pulled her tight against her. "I love you so much," she said softly.

"And I love you, honey and I will keep on loving you," Gwen whispered back. They kept holding each other, letting the tears come, unashamed. "I just have to hope we can find a new way together."

Sally felt Gwen pull back suddenly. She turned and saw that Ben was standing in the doorway.

"I'm sorry, the door was open," he said apologetically. "Obviously, this is really bad timing."

"Yes, I'm afraid it is," Sally said.

"No," Gwen interrupted. "I think it's probably perfect timing. You two need to be as honest with each other as we've just been, Sal."

"No, please don't leave again," Sally said.

"I've told the Hansens I'd like to stay for a few days," Gwen said. "They're going to put me up. I'll be around. I need to run up to the house and pick up a few more of my things. I think you two need some time now." She kissed Sally on the cheek and then walked over to the door. When she came up to Ben, she stopped for a moment. "All I ask is you make damn sure you know what you want."

Ben didn't respond. He just turned and let her pass.

Ben and Sally stood looking at each other. She tried to wipe the tears away from her cheeks. Ben noticed the painting behind her. "She was a beautiful little girl, Sally."

She walked over to get some tissues from her desk and tried her best to wipe all the moisture from her face.

"I didn't know Gwen had come back," Ben said, walking over to look at the painting more closely. "I'm sorry I walked in like that."

"Maybe it was best you did. We really do need to talk. Can we get out of here? Let's go for a walk."

They left the shop in silence, walking down the sidewalk without speaking, doing nothing more than trying to avoid the heavy foot traffic. Sally just kept replaying Gwen's words in her head. *I hope we can find a new way together.*

They continued on for several blocks with no particular destination in mind. Then, Sally knew exactly where she wanted to go.

A few minutes later they were standing in front of the big Victorian house up on the hill, her grandparent's old house. She reached for Ben's hand and led him up the walk to the front porch. They sat down together on the front steps. Sally felt the familiar comfort she always got when she came to this place. She could feel her family all around her. The images from the old photo albums made it all the more real to her.

Ben spoke first. "Sally, I don't know where you and Gwen are, I probably don't even deserve to ask." He leaned forward with his elbows on his knees. "I need to tell you about Sylvia and anything else you want to know about my life, about my past. I want you to know everything."

"You really don't have to do this," she answered.

"Well, yes I do. It was so stupid of me last night to not just come right out and acknowledge I had met someone since my wife died who had been special to me and I had been together with. It just seemed so awkward with Lou and Mary Alice there, and I didn't want to hurt you. I was just embarrassed I hadn't told you about it earlier."

"We shouldn't have to apologize for our past lives," Sally said, turning to face him. "I've certainly had a history... with my marriage and everything that's happened since."

"But you have always been totally honest about it," he said. "I need to tell you this woman and I did have a relationship for about a year. At first, it was professional, and then we became very good friends. When my wife died, we just slowly came together, and she helped me get through those times."

"I'm glad you had someone," Sally said.

"It's been over for more than a year now. I think we both knew from the beginning it wasn't going to last. We're still friends. She's taking care of my house down in Florida and she may even buy it from me. It's a closed chapter on anything personal. I'm being totally straight with you on this."

"I know you are," Sally said.

An older couple walked slowly by on the sidewalk holding hands. Two young children on tricycles followed them closely, probably their grandchildren, Sally thought. She watched them pass. She thought about the days when her own family had walked these streets together, when they had played and laughed on this porch and this lawn. Now they were all gone, just images in her mind and in her old scrapbooks. Her family had been gone for so many years.

Ben's words brought her back to the present.

"Sally, there's more. I loved my wife very much and I remember those feelings." He hesitated, then, "Those feelings are back." He reached over to hold her hand.

Sally heard the words and let them linger for a while between the two of them. Again, she thought of Gwen, *I hope we can find a new way together.*

She closed her eyes and laid her head down on his shoulder. "Ben, you are truly the fortunate one... to know what you feel. I've had so many conflicting emotions and feelings and then the shambles of my marriage. I'm not sure anymore what was love, what was loneliness, what was necessity."

"Sally..."

She stood up and reached for his hand. "Come on, I want to show you something."

They walked down the hill towards Round Lake without speaking, holding hands. She led him down a narrow alley between two buildings that came out to a dock along the lake. They could see the *EmmaLee* off to their left tied up at the city docks.

"Come on, over this way," she said, leading him to the right, down along the docks. She stopped in front of a small boathouse painted brown with white trim and a white door that opened onto the lake. There was a small side door to the boathouse, and she reached up along the sill of the door and found a key. She noticed her hand was trembling as she tried to fit the key in the lock. Using both hands, she finally got the key to slide in and turn, and she pushed the door into the darkness.

Ben followed her in. She found the light switch on the wall and three overhead lights flashed on.

"I'll be damned!" Ben said, truly stunned.

The boathouse had dark walls painted brown with a high peaked roof and exposed beams. A few small windows high on each wall allowed in a little more light. A narrow dock ran down each side and the water from the lake came under the building and all the way to the back wall. Resting in the water was a small wooden runabout tied with ropes hanging loosely to both docks. While the boat was clearly of an old design and vintage, it looked brand new in the lights of the boathouse, its varnish shining brightly, the frame of the windshield and the stainless fittings polished to a brilliant shine. The leather seats front and back were a rich brown color and looked almost new as well.

The name of the small boat was clearly visible in crisp gold letters with black trim across the transom of the boat. Ben read the name out loud, *"EmmaLee II."*

"My father restored this boat for my mother when they first met as kids up here at the lake. His father owned a boatyard that used to sit on this property. When I turned sixteen, they gave the boat to me as a birthday present."

"It's absolutely beautiful, Sally," Ben said, mesmerized by the boat. "You've taken such good care of it. It looks brand new."

"It's my most prized possession. We all loved this boat and spent so much time together with her. I always suspected my parents lost their virginity on the backseat there," she said, and laughed. "My father loved boats and learned to build them. He had a very successful small company building custom boats. The building is still over on the way out of town to East Jordan. It's used for boat storage now."

"How does she run after all these years?" he asked.

"Oh, I'm sure she still runs just fine. The marina puts her in the water for me every year and give her the best care. I just haven't been able to bring myself down here since I lost... since they've been gone."

"You haven't taken her out in all those years?"

"No, I'm sure the folks over at the marina think I've lost my mind. Every year they come to me with offers from someone who wants to buy the boat. How could I possibly sell her?"

"No, I can see why she would mean so much to you."

"I've felt terribly guilty letting her sit here all these summers, without even a chance to let her run around the lake and have everyone admire her. I think it's about time though, don't you?"

"Absolutely."

She pushed another switch on the wall and the motor for the door buzzed on and began lifting the big heavy wooden door up over the boat. "The key is down in the glove box. Start her up!" Sally said. She climbed in and untied the lines, then jumped into the rear seating area. Ben found the key and after they aired out the engine compartment, he pulled out the choke and pumped the throttle a few times before turning the key. The engine fired immediately, and the low rumble echoed off the walls of the boathouse.

"Oh, what a beautiful sound!" yelled Sally. She freed the ropes to the other dock. Ben let the engine idle for another minute and then threw the shift into reverse and began backing the *EmmaLee II* out into Round Lake. Sally jumped up in the front seat next to him.

"Here, you should drive," he offered.

"No, go ahead. I want you to."

The smell of old leather and varnish and gasoline fumes closed in around her and she thought it was just wonderful. The old inboard engine ran like it had just been delivered from the factory, and it kicked up a low bubbling wake behind the boat as Ben turned her out into the channel towards Lake Charlevoix. He steered the boat slowly out into the main lake, and they cruised along the west shore. He put his arm around Sally and held her close. She leaned in, feeling her emotions swirl, trying to grab on to some thread of common sense and direction.

She pulled back again and pushed her hair away from her face. "For so many years I was surrounded by my family, my grandparents, my parents, my husband and our daughter. My uncles are both gone now, and I never see them. We were all together and shared so much. Then, so quickly, they were all gone, and it's been just me. You get to feeling you are meant to be on your own. I've honestly never even thought about having a family again. It just didn't seem to be an option. I think that's why Gwen and I have been together for so long, we're both so damned independent."

He put the boat in neutral and turned off the key. The boat continued to drift on silently. He turned her face gently to him and kissed her and then pulled her face close into his chest, resting his lips in her hair.

Chapter Twenty-eight

Luke McKendry put quite a dent in my face that night. When I came to and realized what had happened, my first thought was of Emily and whether the bastard had hurt her. She was there with me in the back of the car holding a towel to my head to try to stop the bleeding. She told me she was fine, just a little shaken up.

The doctor stitched me back together and took an x-ray to see if there was a skull fracture. My head must have been as hard as my father always said it was. They told me it was a mild concussion, in addition to the surface wound.

The sheriff came into the emergency room. I told him what I could remember. He asked if I had any idea where Luke might go. We talked about the obvious choices like Shirley's and his own place, maybe even back to his mom's house. They had already sent people to check them out. It occurred to me that Luke was drunk and would probably keep drinking, and he wouldn't make the smartest decisions about trying to avoid being caught.

Jonathan sat in the holding cell with his lawyer, David Krupp and Emily Compton. It was early morning and the sun was starting to brighten the room through the small window high on the wall. Emily had just finished sharing the events of the previous night.

Jonathan sat in silence listening to the story of his brother's murderous act and his attack and flight from Bud's bar. He found no joy in the news of his exoneration. He could only think of his brother, the good times they had shared as kids, and the tough times as they grew older. *How many times have I tried to help Luke and reach out to him? Some people just don't want to be helped.*

"We stopped by to see your mother this morning before we came over," Emily said. She reached out and took Jonathan's hand in hers.

He felt her warmth spread up through him like a gust of summer wind. He tried to smile as he looked into her eyes, but he couldn't find the will.

"The police had already been by looking for Luke. She's really upset, as you can imagine. She wants to know when they're going to let you out."

He just nodded. He thought about his mother and how she was going to be able to cope with all of this. What would the two of them do about the boat business now that his father was gone? His mind was swirling. When only minutes ago his future seemed doomed to gray walls and iron bars, now he searched for the relief his impending freedom would bring and the new possibilities. He still couldn't lift the heavy sadness and uncertainly that bore down on him.

"I spoke with the prosecutor this morning just before we came over," Krupp said. "He explained they will need to confirm the information they've received from Emily and George, and from old Bud over at the bar. They need to make sure they have a real case against him, and then he'll need to see the judge later this morning to discuss dropping the charges against you."

Jonathan felt Emily's hand squeeze tighter. "How can I ever thank you for what you've done?" he asked.

She moved over and sat beside him on the cot. She reached out and put her arms around him and he returned her embrace.

The comfort of her body against his felt soothing and protective. He could feel the tears welling up in his eyes and he made no attempt to stop them from dripping down his cheeks.

It was early afternoon when Jonathan walked out into the sunshine from the jail with his mother holding his arm. Emily and Krupp followed a short distance behind. A reporter from the Charlevoix paper came up to them. He had tried to interview Jonathan a couple of times during his stay in jail, but he had always refused.

"Jonathan, we hear they're looking for your brother for the murder of Catherine Hansen. Is that correct?" the reporter asked.

Jonathan pushed by without even acknowledging the question. They all got into Krupp's car. He got in the back with his mother and Emily sat up front with the lawyer. A few people stopped on the sidewalk and watched, whispering to each other. Krupp drove them toward his mother's house. He looked out the window, beginning to feel a sense of relief seep through him as he watched the people of his hometown move around as if it was just another ordinary day.

They drove by the park downtown and he looked down across the green lawn and city docks and Round Lake. Boats were cruising in all directions at low speed, some heading under the drawbridge to make their way out to Lake Michigan, some cruising in single file the opposite direction out to Lake Charlevoix. He looked across and was surprised to see the *EmmaLee* docked in front of her boathouse along the south shore of the small inland harbor. Her white hull shone bright in the afternoon sun and dwarfed the other boats that came alongside her. Crew members were scurrying around on deck attending to cleaning and maintenance.

He broke the silence and asked her about the ship. Emily turned to look at him. "The Navy had the *EmmaLee* brought back home. She just got in yesterday."

When they arrived at the McKendry house, a small group of family friends had come by to welcome Jonathan home and to help his mother deal with the uncertainty of another son being sought after for a horrible crime. Everyone got out of the car except David Krupp. Jonathan went around to his window and leaned in, shaking his hand.

"Thank you," was all he could manage to say.

"I'm going back over to see the prosecutor to get all of this finalized. Good luck to you, Jonathan," the lawyer said, as he turned to back the car out of the long gravel drive.

Several of their friends came over and hugged him or shook his hand. He couldn't help thinking there was so little reason to celebrate. He saw Emily standing, talking with his mother. The two came together and held each other for a long time. The sight of them sharing such deep emotion was overwhelming to him. He turned and walked down toward the lake.

He made his way past the old boathouse he and his father had put so many hours of hard work in. He walked out onto the dock, his shoes echoing softly and causing the boards to creak under his weight. Out at the end of the dock he stood leaning against a tall cedar piling. Boats of all sizes cruised past, a few people waving at him as they passed.

He looked down and saw Emily's runabout tied up in the last slip. Her father had paid them to dock the boat there for her each summer since they had sold it to her. He thought back to that summer working on her boat, the first times they had met. His awkwardness and awe around her in those early days finally brought a narrow smile across his face. How could he have ever known how many times she would come back into his life and pull him up out of the depths, from those first days when he would see her go past on the deck of the *EmmaLee*, oblivious to his stares and attentions, to their time together that first summer when they shared the joy of her new boat. The thoughts of Emily Compton ever present in his mind all those years away at war and during his recovery, and then her comfort and help during his time at the V.A. hospital down in Ann Arbor.

Once again, Emily had been there for him now when his life was on a ledge that could have fallen away at any moment. She had never doubted his innocence when so many others had condemned him.

He was deep in thought and didn't notice her coming up behind him on the dock. He was startled when she came beside him and put an arm around his waist, standing silently with him watching the boats. He looked down and saw the soft freckled beauty of her face. The wind blew gently on her hair and he reached out to push it away from her face. He turned and pulled her close.

"You saved my life... again."

She lifted her mouth to his and kissed him, gently at first, then leaning back to look into his eyes. Then she kissed him again, long and slow.

An hour later he had showered and cleaned up with fresh clothes, a pair of jeans with a swimsuit underneath and a white short sleeved shirt. She was waiting for him in her boat down at the docks. He pulled the lines free and threw them into the boat. She started the engine and he sat on the dock holding the boat with his bare feet while the engine warmed up.

Emily had gone home and returned with her swimming suit on under a pair of shorts and a denim shirt. She had asked their cook to prepare some food for a picnic and the basket sat on the seat in the back.

The engine evened out into a slow steady rumble and he pushed the boat back out of the slip, jumping in beside her in the front. The sun still shone brightly in the late afternoon. and only a few billowy white clouds floated against the deep blue of the Michigan summer sky.

She guided the boat out east through the channel into Lake Charlevoix, the boat gently swaying on the smooth swells coming in from the lake. They cruised under the railroad trestle bridge, watching two young boys fishing on the rocky shore.

Jonathan thought back to the many times he and George had fished in that exact spot. He had talked to George briefly on the phone. He was still being held at the hospital to rest overnight. He told him he would stop by later after he was able to get some more rest.

Through the channel and easing past the big red channel buoy, Emily edged the throttle down and the boat roared up and into the white capped waves coming at them all the way down from Boyne City on the other end of the lake. He could see the white triangles of large sailboats tacking across to make way up into the wind. He looked back and saw children splashing in the shallow water along the beach, their parents watching comfortably from shore.

He felt her hand on his knee and looked over.

"I was thinking about Horton Bay for a little picnic," she said loudly over the roar of the engine.

He just nodded and smiled.

With the anchor secure in the calm waters of the bay, they stripped down to their bathing suits and both dove into the water together. Jonathan felt the icy shock wash away the heavy weight of his ordeal these past days. He stayed under as long as he could, savoring the sensation of floating in the green silence of the lake.

When he came up, Emily had just surfaced and was pushing the hair back from her face. She swam over to him and put her arms around his neck, wrapping her legs around his waist. He laughed as they slipped below the surface of the lake. He could see the blur of her face close to him under the water. He pulled her closer and they kissed, slowly sinking deeper. When his lungs were about to burst, he let her free and they both swam back to the surface. They came up and he saw she was shivering, and he pulled her close again, paddling hard with his legs to keep them afloat.

They kissed again, then she pulled free and swam back over to the boat. He helped her climb up onboard, then followed her. She threw a towel at him that had been warmed by the sun and he quickly wrapped up in it as she did the same.

"It feels like that first summer, again," she said. "You could almost forget about the War and..." she hesitated, "and all that's happened these past weeks."

"There have been so many times when I wondered if I would ever be in this place again," he said, almost to himself. "Even yesterday, locked in that cell, I was thinking about the lake and fresh air... and about those trout over there coming up from the creek."

"You have a whole new life out ahead of you now."

"Because of you."

Later, they had finished the sandwiches and Cokes packed in the basket. They sat together quietly in the long leather seat at the back of the boat and watched the sun disappear over the trees surrounding the bay. Darkness came quickly and soon the brighter stars began to show. Behind them a half moon rose. Two other boats anchored in the bay had left earlier and they were now alone in the quiet of the bay, surrounded by darkness and only the sounds of tree frogs screeching from the woods and big bullfrogs croaking near shore. They clung together, looking up into the sky, each silent with their own thoughts.

He felt Emily move next to him and she sat up facing him and kissed him again. "You've probably figured this out McKendry, but I may be falling for you."

He had never heard sweeter words and he felt a peace come over him. He kissed her again. "I thought you were just after my money," he said, and laughed.

She punched him softly in the stomach. "Of course."

"I just never thought this could happen."

She fell into him and held him tight and as he looked up into the stars, he found himself silently thanking a God he thought had abandoned him so many times before.

It was close to midnight when he eased the boat back into the slip at the boatyard. He drove her home and they kissed in the front seat of his father's truck before she left and walked up to the big house and disappeared inside.

He turned in at the drive to his mother's house and heard the loose gravel crumble under the big tires of the truck as he pulled down slowly and parked. The lights were out inside. His mother typically fell asleep early. He thought he should go down and check that the boats were all tied securely before going to bed.

One large light on the top of the boathouse illuminated his way through the dry-docked boats and empty boat cradles in the yard. A thousand bugs swarmed around the bright light and he saw bats darting in and out of the light picking up an easy meal in the swarm. The large doors of the boathouse were still open and in the darkness, he was startled to see the glow of a cigarette. He stopped for a moment to try to make out who was inside. He walked toward the door and as he came inside out of the glare of the light, his eyes quickly adjusted. He saw his brother sitting against the far wall, his knees up to his chest and his head down. Luke took another pull from his cigarette and let the smoke out slowly.

"Hello, little brother," he said with a slow, muffled voice.

Jonathan saw an empty pint of whiskey at his brother's side and another in his free hand. He didn't know what to say or what to do, then a growing anger came over him. "Luke, you need to tell me how you could have done this?"

Luke put the bottle to his mouth and threw his head back, taking a long drink. He grimaced as the whiskey burned. "Some things are just meant to happen, little brother."

"You killed her, Luke!"

"From the day I was born, I've been headed t'wards this, Jonny."

"That's bullshit, Luke. We all have choices."

Luke struggled to his feet, stuffing the bottle in the front of his pants. He staggered over and leaned against a bench filled with tools. "You gotta help me get outta here, Jonny."

He felt a pain rip through his gut. How many times had he wished his brother would have asked for his help or accepted his help? "I can't do anything about this, Luke. It's gone too far."

Luke grabbed the bottle and held it out for Jonathan, an offering across the wide divide of two brothers torn apart. Jonathan shook his head *no* and watched as his brother took another drink.

"You know Pop and me could just never see eye-to-eye," Luke said slowly, as if he was only half-awake. "I never could measure up for that old sonofabitch!"

Jonathan just stood and listened, his thoughts racing, thinking about what he could do for his brother.

"So now the old bastard's gone, and you and Mom are stuck with this piece a shit boatyard. So, big war hero, you ever think you'd be varnishin' boats here for the rest of your life?"

"Luke, why don't we go in and get some coffee and we'll talk to Mom, and then you and me can go downtown."

"I'm not goin' ta jail, Jonny..." he mumbled. "I'm not gonna rot in any damned jail!" He took another drink. "You and that

Compton girl... she's quite a piece of ass, Jonny. Too bad you're gonna be stuck here in this boathouse and she'll be off to the big city. You know, I coulda killed her too, last night."

"Luke, put the bottle down. I'm gonna drive you down to the sheriff's office." Jonathan moved closer to take the bottle away.

Luke placed the bottle down on the tool bench and staggered a bit to keep his balance. He reached out for something that lay on the bench.

Jonathan saw him turn and stood frozen as his brother lashed out, a big pipe wrench in his hand. He put his arms up to block the blow, but he was too late and felt the sharp pain shoot through his shoulder and heard the sound of cracking bone. He staggered back holding his shoulder, trying to keep his head up. The second blow seemed to come from nowhere and caught him across the side of the head. He staggered as his consciousness clouded over and he felt himself falling.

Random images crept back into his brain. A crushing pain ached in his head and his arm as he opened his eyes. He saw stars above him and realized he was lying in the dirt outside the boathouse. He tried to sit up, but the pain pushed him back down into the dirt. He sensed a strange smell and then realized it was smoke. He lifted himself up on his good arm enough to look over at the boathouse. Through the open doors he saw the light of flames flickering against the inside walls. Smoke was just beginning to seep out through the top of the door, wafting up into the night sky.

Then, there was a small explosion inside and the flames burst out across the floor of the big building and quickly spread to the far wall. In the light of the flames and the big light overhead, Jonathan saw the tracks from his legs being dragged through the dirt out from the boathouse. He tried to get to his feet again but couldn't stand the pain shooting through his body.

The flames were now rolling out the top of the open doorway and up the face of the building. The door was almost totally engulfed.

"Luke!" he yelled out helplessly. "Luke, where are you!"

A window on the side of boathouse exploded loudly from the heat of the flames.

He heard his mother's voice off in the distance. "Jonathan, Jonathan... oh my God!" she yelled, and he saw her running down the path from the house. Then, he sensed movement and turned to see Luke standing in the doorway of the big boathouse. His face was illuminated from the flames. He stood there with the whiskey bottle in his hand.

His mother came up beside him and knelt down, horror on her face from the shock of the fire and the blood all over her son's face. She saw her oldest son in the doorway and yelled, "No... Luke!"

Jonathan watched as a strange smile came across his brother's face. He looked on helplessly as Luke took another drink from the whiskey bottle and then he turned and threw it into the burning building. He started walking through the door, slowly at first, dragging his bad leg along. He was just a few feet into the building when there was another loud explosion from inside. Luke looked up as a large piece of the rafters, roaring in flames, crashed down on his head. He crumbled under its weight and lay trapped, motionless beneath it.

Jonathan's mother screamed a sickening wail and he watched as his brother's clothes caught fire. Within moments, another large piece of the roof came crashing down in flames and sparks, and Luke was lost in the growing inferno.

Chapter Twenty-nine

Gwen came up the walk to Sally's house. It was just past eight in the morning and the sun was coming up through the trees across the street. The porch light had been left on from the night before. The door was unlocked, and she walked in.

She stood for a moment, taking in the familiar feel of her friend's home. Listening for sounds of Sally, in the kitchen, or maybe upstairs; she heard only a few birds squawking out on the back patio through an open window. Walking back to the sun porch, she looked out over the early morning calm of Lake Michigan. A half empty glass of wine rested on a table next to the couch. A lamp was still turned on.

Then, she heard a floorboard creak from upstairs. She turned and walked down the hall and up the steps. Looking into the bedroom, she saw the bed had not been slept in. She noticed the door in the back to Sally's studio was open and a light was on.

As she walked through the door, she saw Sally standing in front of a painting resting on an easel. Her back was to Gwen and she hadn't noticed her walking in.

"Good morning," she said quietly, trying not to startle her.

Sally turned and simply said, "Hi."

As Sally moved away from the easel, Gwen saw she was working on the portrait of her daughter, Ellen. The soft smile of the young girl looked back from the canvas. "She's so beautiful," Gwen said.

Sally looked back at the painting. "I had to finish this," she said simply.

Gwen walked over and stood by the canvas, looking at Sally. "I heard Ben and Megan are leaving this afternoon."

Sally nodded, still staring at the painting.

Chapter Thirty

News traveled fast through our small town that my sister and her unborn child's killer was also dead. Luke McKendry had taken his own life in his final act.

The fire in the boathouse spread to two outbuildings and destroyed them all, sparing only the small apartment residence that was the McKendry's home. Several large boats were also lost before the firefighters could arrive and bring the blaze under control.

As the sun came up that next morning, a large black cloud of smoke still hung low over the waters of Round Lake and up into the town. Many walked from town to view the destruction or passed by the docks in their boats. The charred rubble stood in stark contrast against the hillside thick with trees and adjoining houses and boathouses.

Jonathan had been brought into the hospital shortly after the fire department arrived. His arm was badly broken, and he had a serious head wound across the back of his skull. They rolled him into my room at about six that morning. He was still unconscious from the anesthetic. Emily had arrived earlier and told me about the night's horrible series of events while Jonathan was in surgery to repair his arm.

Luke McKendry had taken so much from all of us. In the end, perhaps not without purpose, he also gave new hope.

A week after the fire, Jonathan stood in the small bathroom of the McKendry home and looked at himself in the mirror. His mother tied his tie for him since his left arm was immobile in a large cast up to his shoulder, resting in a sling around his neck. The stitches in the back of his head were mostly covered now by his hair. He was wearing the pants and sports jacket he had worn back in Ann Arbor when he went out to dinner with Emily Compton. With the cast, he was only able to wear one sleeve and he had draped the coat over his other shoulder.

He still felt a little unsteady on his feet. He had been in bed almost the entire week since the fire trying to regain his strength and allow his body to heal. He woke in the hospital to find both George and Emily there waiting for him. George had been released later that day and had come by the house each day since Jonathan had been home to check in on his friend. Emily had also been by his side and had been helping his mother care for him.

He felt a nervous hollow feeling as he thought about the coming evening. Emily had invited him to attend a party with her family on the *EmmaLee*. The thought of facing her parents and their friends was not something he had been looking forward to. She had insisted he needed to get out and move beyond the events of the past weeks. He also knew her father had been furious with Emily for hiring a lawyer and going so far to help him. He worried he would be on display all night, standing out as some poor freak.

Emily told him she would pick him up at six. He still wasn't able to drive. He heard her car coming down the drive and he went out into the kitchen and hugged his mother with his one free arm. She smiled back at him.

"You have a nice time with all those fancy people tonight," she said. "Watch your manners."

"I just hope I don't fall overboard. I'm still a bit tipsy."

"You'll do just fine," she encouraged.

He kissed her on the cheek and went out the back door.

Emily was waiting by the car, holding the passenger door open. She was dressed in a beautiful light blue summer dress. He walked up to her and tried his best to return her warm hug.

"Are you sure this is what you want tonight?" he asked.

"Yes, absolutely."

Her smiled warmed him and reassured him, just a little.

As they made their way slowly down the walk to the ship, Jonathan leaned heavily on Emily for support, both physically and emotionally. The great ship lay ahead, resting calming in the harbor waters of Round Lake, tied securely to the pier alongside the Compton's boathouse. Lights had been strung high above the deck in the riggings and she seemed lit up like a Christmas tree in all her glory.

Two crew members met them at the gangway along with other guests who were arriving. Jonathan thought back to the day when he had been doused by the swab bucket of two of *EmmaLee's* crew as he walked by. It seemed a thousand years ago now after all that had happened.

Looking up at the top of the ramp, Jonathan saw Emily's parents meeting guests as they came aboard the ship. All he could think was to try to remain calm and not do anything to embarrass Emily. Mr. Compton saw them coming up the ramp. His glare was less than welcoming.

"Father, I know you've met Jonathan when we got my boat a few summers ago," Emily began.

Jonathan reached out his hand and the elder Compton slowly put his hand out. He looked directly into Jonathan's eyes with a piercing gaze. His grip was crushing. Jonathan returned the favor.

"Yes, McKendry. Sorry to hear about your father. Our deepest sympathies."

"Thank you, sir, I..."

Compton turned to his side, "I'd like you to meet my wife. Honey, Emily's friend, Mr. McKendry."

She turned from the couple she had just been talking to. "Well, Jonathan, you've had quite a summer," she said. "I must say we were quite relieved to hear you had been exonerated in that horrible case."

"Thank you, Mrs. Compton. It was awful for everyone involved. I'm just glad it's behind us now. Your daughter has been a tremendous help for me and for my family."

"Yes, she certainly has," Stewart Compton said sternly.

"Daddy, please..." Emily scolded.

"You both have a good time tonight," her mother said. "We'll see you a bit later for dinner."

Emily guided him past and they made their way over to a bar set up on the foredeck. She picked up a glass of wine and a beer for Jonathan. They walked across the smooth teak deck of the ship to the far rail, looking out over Round Lake and the many boats at anchor, or tied up at the docks around the lake.

She raised her wine glass in a toast, "To freedom and new beginnings."

"Amen." They touched glasses and took a drink.

"Have you talked to your mother about the business, after the fire and all?"

Jonathan looked down the lake to the charred remains of his family's business.

"I'm afraid we're not going to be in business anymore," he said, turning back to her.

"What are you talking about?"

Jonathan raised his glass again, "Like you said, to new beginnings."

"Jonathan?"

"My father had a good insurance policy on the business. We've decided to sell the property and what's left of the business. My mother is going to move down to Detroit to live with her sister and help take care of her kids. There will be enough money for her to live comfortably for a very long time."

"Oh, that's wonderful," she said, then paused letting her smile slip away. "And what will you be doing?"

"There will be enough for me to go to school along with money from the Navy. I'm going to enroll in the engineering program down at Michigan this fall."

She kissed him on the cheek. "I am so excited for you and your mother. And how did you happen to decide on the University of Michigan?" She smiled.

"You see, I have this guardian angel who lives most of the year down in Ann Arbor. I thought I would make it more convenient for her to take care of me."

They both laughed and brought their glasses up again in another toast.

"I can't tell you how excited I am about this," she said.

"Yeah, well wait until your parents hear about it."

"I'll take care of my parents."

Music started playing from the rear of the ship. They turned and saw a small band set up along the stern rail. They also saw Connor Harris making his way across the deck towards them.

"Oh great," Jonathan whispered.

Conner was dressed in dark slacks and a white dinner jacket. His hair was combed wet straight back. He had a drink in his left hand. He still walked with a slight limp from the head injury he received from Luke McKendry those many summers ago.

"Ah, the guest of honor. McKendry, you clean up pretty good," Connor said. "I must say you look a lot better than in those prison stripes."

"Connor, let's not start," said Emily, moving between the two of them.

"So, it was your brother all along," he said. "That boy just had a mean streak. Damn near killed me, too."

"Connor, that's enough!" Emily shouted.

Jonathan moved around Emily to face Harris. "You think running around with his girlfriend helped the situation?"

"I thought she was your girl," Connor said, laughing.

"Connor!" Emily jumped between them again.

Jonathan felt his anger burn hot. He tried to keep calm. He had promised himself he wouldn't embarrass Emily. "Harris, if you have anything else to say about this to me personally, I would be glad to get together later tonight to... discuss things." His tone was perfectly clear.

"Oh, I'm through discussing things with you McKendry boys. A person could get himself killed." He laughed and walked away.

Jonathan stood there shaking his head, letting his anger settle. He noticed several of the guests on deck were staring at him and then whispering to each other. He thought about all the times he had wished he could be up on this ship with Emily Compton. Now, here he was, and everything seemed to be heading towards trouble.

Emily interrupted his thoughts, "I've been friends with Connor since I was a little girl coming up here to Charlevoix. Our parents are best friends. I just keep asking myself how I ever saw him for anything other than a total asshole!"

Jonathan turned in shock, "Emily, what kind of talk is that for a lady?" He started laughing out loud and she joined him.

Later at dinner, twenty guests were seated around the long mahogany table in the dining cabin. Servants hovered, bringing in the many courses of food, keeping wine glasses full. Stuart Compton sat at the head of the table with his wife to his left. Emily was at his other side with Jonathan sitting next to her. He had met many of the other guests as they were all asked to come below for dinner. Most had been polite, but clearly uncomfortable meeting the young man who only a few days before had been in jail on charges of rape and murder. They also weren't used to a "local" being on the guest list for any of their parties.

Emily kept her smile and good spirits up, despite the behavior of other guests. She was doing all she could to make Jonathan comfortable and allow him to try to enjoy himself. She had showed him around the ship earlier. He had been fascinated by the bridge and all of the controls and mechanisms. The captain had taken him through, explaining the ship's workings.

Her father tapped a spoon on his wine glass to get everyone's attention. "Thank you all for being here with us tonight. It's another wonderful summer evening in Charlevoix, and we are so pleased you could be here to share it with us." He raised his glass, and everyone toasted those around them.

When the toasts were finished and the conversation began to quiet again, Connor Harris raised his glass again. "I think it's appropriate for us to also toast our special guest here tonight." He looked down the table at Jonathan. "Our local war hero returns and promptly finds himself behind bars..."

"Connor!" Emily interrupted.

Stewart Compton and the rest of the table remained silent.

Connor continued, "But fortunately for our war hero, it was actually the evil brother who was the murderer."

Jonathan jumped to his feet.

Connor's father also stood across the table from him. "Connor, that is enough!"

Jonathan reached down for his glass, struggling to remain calm. His voice hesitated slightly as he began speaking, "I think we should all say a prayer for a young woman and her family who have suffered so much... for a young woman and her unborn child who were treated so poorly by so many." He looked directly at Harris. "May she rest in peace."

There was quiet around the table. Everyone was looking at Connor. News of his affair with the Hansen girl had spread quickly. His face was turning red and he began shaking he was so angry. He threw his napkin down on the table and walked out of the room.

Emily's father broke the silence. He stood, picking up his wine glass. "May she rest in peace. Thank you for reminding us, Jonathan."

All of the guests raised their glasses in tribute to Catherine Hansen and her family.

After dinner, they were up on deck again. The band was playing, and Jonathan and Emily danced to a slow song.

"You move pretty good for having a broken back, a smashed arm and who knows what shape your head is in," she teased. The song ended, and they walked over to the bar. Emily's father came up.

"Jonathan, I want to apologize for my behavior earlier and for Connor at dinner. I just spoke with his father. They're sending him home to Chicago tomorrow for the rest of the summer. They'll be putting him to work for the first time. Maybe they can work some of the anger out of him."

"Thank you, sir," Jonathan said, shaking his hand.

"You need to call me Stewart, young man. And about my behavior earlier, again I'm sorry. You've been through so much, with the war and now with your family. I'm just awfully glad one of the Compton's had enough damn sense to stick by you." He grabbed his daughter around the waist and kissed the top of her head. "You two have a good time tonight." He walked away.

"Wasn't that interesting?" Emily said. "The old man might just be coming around."

"I wouldn't jump to conclusions just yet," he said with a smile.

"You know, I was thinking this would be a great night for a cruise."

"I don't think the *EmmaLee's* going anywhere tonight.

"I wasn't thinking about this *EmmaLee*," she said and gave him that smile that he couldn't resist.

Jonathan and Emily managed to slip away and leave the ship shortly after nine o'clock. Ten minutes later, they were sitting in the front seat of the *EmmaLee II*, heading out of the channel into Lake Charlevoix. Emily was driving while Jonathan struggled to get comfortable with his cast leaning on the side gunwale. He felt so relieved to be away from the big ship and the party. Despite Stewart Compton's apology, he still felt so out of place with those people. It amazed him he had become so comfortable around Emily. He looked over and watched her hair blow back in the wind and the smile on her face as she steered her boat.

They cleared the last channel buoy as darkness was falling around them. The lights from the dash illuminated the small cockpit. They could still hear the band playing back at her parents' party.

Emily pointed to one of the gauges. "We've got a full tank of gas. Any suggestions on a destination?"

"If we had thrown a fly rod in, we could head down to Horton's Creek and pick up a few trout for dinner tomorrow night," he suggested.

"I don't think you'll have a fly rod in your hand for a while, but I was thinking about Horton Bay again, too," she said, looking over at him. "But I wasn't thinking about fishing." She flashed her white teeth at him in a big glorious smile.

"What are you waiting for?"

She buried the throttle and the *EmmaLee II* roared up and into the night.

When they came around the point and headed into the bay, they were in almost total darkness. They couldn't see any running lights from other boats but proceeded slowly in case there were others anchored off without lights on. By the time they reached the center of the bay their eyes had become better adjusted to the night and they could see they were alone in the seclusion of the quiet harbor. Emily turned the engine key off and the little runabout floated silently across the surface and then came to rest on the calm water.

Emily jumped up in bare feet and stepped over the seat into the back compartment to throw an anchor over the side. "You sit tight, McKendry," she said. "You're in no shape to do anything more than enjoy the ride."

"I'm enjoying every minute of it, especially watching you do all the work."

"I suppose you won't be able to go swimming with me with that big cast on your arm?"

"No, but I can watch."

She stood there in the back of the boat and began unbuttoning the front of her dress.

Jonathan looked on in amazement.

"A gentleman would turn his head," she said quietly.

"You know I'm no gentleman. Do you know how beautiful you are?"

"Only when you keep reminding me." She pulled the dress off her shoulders and let it fall to the floor of the boat. She stepped out of it and threw it across the front seat next to Jonathan, standing there now in a white bra and panties that stood out in contrast with the dark of the night. She made no effort to cover herself, but instead leaned forward and kissed him. "I wish you could join me."

"I'll be waiting for you right here with a warm towel when you come back."

She stepped up on the side deck and teetered there for a moment, trying to keep her balance. Jonathan grabbed a float cushion and threw it overboard in front of her. "I know you can swim, but I don't want to lose you again."

"Don't go away." she said calmly, then dove out into the night. He turned and saw her dive down into the dark water, her splash barely creating a ripple. She came up moments later and he could just see her swimming out away from the boat in a slow, graceful stroke.

"The water is beautiful," she yelled back. "Are you sure that cast isn't waterproof?"

"I could get another cast. It's my arm I'm worried about," he said.

"No, you stay right there. I'm getting a little tired of patching you back together."

He saw her swim over and grab on to the cushion and rest in the calm of the bay. He got up and painfully climbed over the seat into the back and picked up one of the towels.

"Is there a more heavenly place in all the world, Jonathan?" she asked.

"I've seen a lot of the world, mostly from an old Navy ship, or a train and I think I'd just as soon be right here with you."

"Good choice."

In the dim light, he saw her let go of the cushion and slip beneath the surface. When she didn't come back up right away, he started to get concerned and he moved to the side of the boat to get a closer look. Then, she game back to the surface and took a big gasp of air.

"Don't scare me like that. I'm not sure I'd be much good trying to come in after you," he said.

He saw her turn suddenly in the water and throw something and a moment later her wet bra and panties hit him in the face. He pulled them away and tried to wipe the water away with the towel. "You're making it harder and harder for me to stay onboard here, lady."

"You just sit tight," she said.

In the dim reflection from the rising moon he could just make out her form on the water as she pushed away from the cushion, floating on her back. The rise of her belly and breasts pushed up through the surface of the water as she paddled and kicked slowly backwards. Then, she turned over and swam back to the cushion.

"Do you have that towel ready?" she asked.

"Come and get it!"

She swam around to the back of the boat and climbed up on the low deck across the back of the transom. She sat on the back deck and Jonathan threw her the towel. She stood up in the darkness and began drying herself, first her hair, then the rest of her body. Jonathan sat back on the middle deck between the rows of seats. She wrapped the towel around herself and stepped down onto the back seat and then the floor of the boat. She came over to him and put her arms gently around his neck. He stood up and took her around the waist with his one good arm and pulled her to him. He could see her smile and a gleam in her eyes, even in the low light. She lifted up on her tiptoes and kissed him.

"Have I told you I love you?" she said in a low whisper.

He was so overwhelmed, he couldn't speak. Slowly, he shook his head no.

"Is that all you have to say for yourself?" she teased.

He managed to collect himself. "You are the most beautiful woman I have ever seen in my entire life, and you're standing here half naked with me in this boat in my favorite place in the whole world. You've just told me you love me, and you expect me to be able to make a coherent sentence?"

"I think you just did," she said, and kissed him again, this time letting her lips linger.

"I do love you, Jonathan."

Losing his balance, he sat back down on the seat of the boat. She moved with him and stood between his legs, keeping her arms around his neck. He looked up into her eyes and saw the light of the moon shining in them. She leaned down and kissed him again.

An owl swept in low and crossed the reflection of the moon on the water. They turned and watched it fly off into the darkness of the night.

Chapter Thirty-one

The captain of the *EmmaLee* powered the long ship away from the docks in Charlevoix for the last time. He steered her slowly in reverse, back out into Round Lake. It was a cloudy morning and low clouds rushed in over the hills from Lake Michigan. An occasional light mist settled down across the lake. A large crowd had gathered at the docks along the park to see the big ship off.

Ben and Megan Clark stood together at the rail in the bow of the ship, the large bowsprit pointing out ahead of them. They had yellow rain slickers on, and Ben held his daughter with his arm around her shoulder. They had said their goodbyes earlier to the friends they had met during their stay. The Hansens, George and Elizabeth, were both there and had urged Ben to bring the *EmmaLee* back again for next summer's festival. He had thanked them sincerely for all of their hospitality and promised he would do his best to be back.

The Mayor had also come down and held a small ceremony, giving Ben a key to the city. The newspaper had a photographer there to capture the moment.

The night before he had seen Louis Kramer and Mary Alice Gregory off at the municipal airport. The sleek jet had lifted off and banked sharply south, heading for Florida. Ben had wished them well, knowing they would both have their hands full with each other.

Ben looked across the crowd onshore and marveled at the time they had just spent in this small little town. He thought about first finding the *EmmaLee* all those months ago back east. He had no idea then how much this big old boat would change his life, the places he would visit and the people who would come into his life.

He waved again at George and Elizabeth who were waving their hands frantically in farewell. Then, he saw Gwen Roberts push her way through the crowd and stand next to the Hansens. When she spotted him up in the front of the ship, he waved to her. Gwen lifted her arm to wave goodbye and he saw a smile come across her face.

The smile was for Sally, who came up behind Ben now. She placed an arm around his waist and on the shoulder of his daughter.

He pulled her closer, as the ship's horn sounded their farewell.

New Beginnings

I've spent much of my life in this little town, tucked down in the north woods. I've watched my family and those of others grow here and build their lives here. I've had close friends and loved ones as well, who have shared their lives with me here. We all say how quickly the time seems to pass and when so much of your life is already behind you, the years and the memories blur.

The time shared with Jonathan and Emily, and in later years with their daughter Sally, comes back to me so often. Our time together held so much joy and love, and all too frequently, deep pain and sadness.

The day Jonathan and Emily were married is a memory that remains etched so clearly in my mind. I had just started dating Elizabeth, and I can remember standing with her on the deck of the EmmaLee with our friends and the families of the Comptons and the McKendrys. Emily had such a special glow in her face that day. Her love for Jonathan brought him back from the damages of war and our families' tragedies. She helped him put so much of that behind him, and on that day of their wedding on the big ship, surrounded by the love of so many, I saw Emily's light wash over him and renew him, and I know he lived a truly happy life with her and their beautiful Sally.

On the night I received the call we had lost them both and their little granddaughter, Ellen, in the storm off the Manitous, I remember going to Sally's house and holding her and crying out our loss together. I know we both felt then there could never be happiness in this place again. It took many years and the pain never truly goes away, but we turned to those we were still blessed to have in our lives, and we found our way. We stayed here, and we continued to live out our lives the best we could. New people came into our lives who helped us fill the spaces in our hearts and the love that had been taken away.

I watched Sally leave today, again up on the deck of the big ship. I saw the joy and light in her face I had seen so many years earlier with her mother. As she stood there at the rail with Ben and his daughter, Megan, I felt such joy for her. Her family had been taken from her so long ago. Here was a new beginning and a new family who loved her as much as we all do.

We know they'll be back often, and we will continue to share their lives. Those of us who remain behind will carry on with the routines that have kept us going and perhaps, find new paths as well.

I often find myself sitting out on the calm waters of the lake in my little fishing boat. I go there mostly alone these days. The trout are nearly gone now. The little creek still flows, but progress and development have slowed her waters. Late in the evenings when the sun has passed below the tall trees onshore and the cool of the night spreads out across the bay, I listen to the sounds of the past in my mind, a fish rising, a friend laughing. I see the faces of those I've loved and shared this place with, reflect back at me in the smooth surface of the lake. So many of us have moved on now. All of us will forever have this place together in our hearts.

THE END

A NOTE FROM AUTHOR MICHAEL LINDLEY

I hope you enjoyed this first book in the *"Troubled Waters"* historical mystery and suspense thriller series. Next up is the sequel, *THE SUMMER TOWN.*

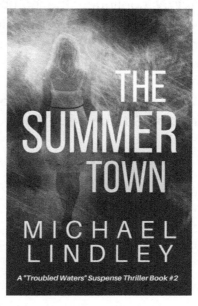

It's 1951, and Jonathan McKendry's best friend and small-town lawyer, George Hansen, has found himself on the wrong end of bad situations in the past, but never one so unpopular as when he steps up to defend a local Native American man accused of a shocking crime. Jonathan, now married to Dr. Emily Compton McKendry, desperately tries to help his friend save the life of an innocent man as well as save his wife and a young family who are threatened by an abusive and murderous father who Emily is trying to help.

In the parallel present-day story, George Hansen looks down from his passing into the next world to see the events that develop in the search for his killer, as well as the challenges faced by the Clark family as Sally Thomason Clark's husband Ben tries to save his business empire and his marriage from a ruthless partner and daughter Megan lets her infatuation for a young local boy alienate the summer families who she thought were her friends.

THE SUMMER TOWN continues the compelling love stories and challenges of Jonathan and Emily, and Ben and Sally in the idyllic resort town of Charlevoix, Michigan.

To keep reading *THE SUMMER TOWN*, you can place your order online at Amazon. Thank you! ML

If you don't want to miss the release of my next new book...

We all know that Amazon lists literally millions of new novels each year. I'm so glad you found your way to mine! If you would like to know when I release my next new book, rather than leave it to chance, sign up here for my *Behind the Scenes* author newsletter and I'll email you an early alert with a special launch price.

I'll also send you a free copy of the prequel novella to my Amazon #1 bestselling "Hanna and Alex" Low Country mystery and suspense series.

Just drop an email to michael@michaellindleynovels.com and you'll be signed up and the link to your free eBook will be on its way.

About the Author

Hello, Michael Lindley here!

Rather than a long career summary and a boring list of accomplishments, I thought you might like to know a little about why I write the books I write and how my life experiences have influenced the stories I tell.

From an early age, I found myself drawn to heroic and emotional stories played out on my family's little black & white television set, the movie screen down at the town theatre and on the pages of the countless books I read throughout my early years.

I often find that writers are compelled to write what they love to read. I've always been drawn to stories that are built around an idyllic time and place as much as the characters who grace these locations. As the heroes and villains come to life in my favorite stories, facing life's challenges of love and betrayal and great danger, I also enjoy coming to deeply understand the setting for the story and how it shapes the characters and the conflicts they face.

I've also love books built around a mix of past and present, allowing me to know a place and the people who live there in both a compelling historical context, as well as in present-day. I try to capture all of this in the books I write and the stories I bring to life.

I spent much of my early life in a small northern Michigan lake resort town. I have wonderful memories of my time spent out at my great grandfather's marina and boatyard on the lake. I remember the many wealthy *"summer people"* who came north each year for a few short months and their grand boats and homes that graced the lake. All of this was inspiration for my first two novels, *THE EMMALEE AFFAIRS* and *THE SUMMER TOWN*, set in this marvelous little town of Charlevoix and the stories of two ill-fated love affairs, generations apart, and the tragic and life-changing events they endured.

Later in life, I worked and traveled and lived across our southern states and grew fond of the northern Gulf Coast of Florida, as well as the Low Country of South Carolina along the Atlantic coast, all blessed with magnificent beauty and fascinating history and culture.

My third novel, *BEND TO THE TEMPEST*, is set in 1920's era Atlanta and the remote village of Grayton Beach along the Gulf of Mexico near Destin. It tells the story of the fictional Coulter family who control the liquor trade in the South during this turbulent time, and their son, Mathew, who tries to escape the corruption of his family and finds himself caught up in the lives of a young mother and her daughter who face incredible challenges and who will change the course of his life forever.

My time along the Carolina coast led me to write what is now an Amazon #1 bestselling mystery series. The *"Hanna and Alex"* Low Country mysteries feature attorney Hanna Walsh who runs a free legal clinic in Charleston, and Detective Alex Frank who comes to Hanna's aid when she faces a grave family tragedy and great danger in the first book, *LIES WE NEVER SEE*. Their often tenuous relationship continues in the subsequent books in the series as they find themselves in the cross-hairs of the dangerous forces of crime and corruption in the Low Country of South Carolina.

After a long career in marketing, I am blessed now to be able to write full-time from my home in southern Florida, returning still in the summer months to the beautiful shores of Lake Charlevoix in northern Michigan. The sunrises and sunsets are still glorious and the lake as cold as ever!

Thank you for your interest in my stories!

Michael

Follow Michael Lindley on Facebook at Michael Lindley Novels. If you would like to join his mailing list to receive his *Behind the Scenes* updates and news of new releases and special offers, and get a free copy of the into novella to the "Hanna and Alex" Low Country mystery and suspense series, send a note to michael@michaellindleynovels.com.

Made in the USA
Middletown, DE
01 August 2023

36094365R00179